Snakes in the Grass

Icy fingers clutched at Boone's chest as he realized what he had done. He had taken his eyes off the grass. He remedied that just as the ground in front of the palomino erupted and out of it reared an Apache. Boone glimpsed a stocky, swarthy body clothed in a long-sleeved brown shirt and a breechclout and leggings. He saw steel flash, and he fired from the hip, two swift shots that slammed the Apache back and down.

Boone used his spurs. To his right and left more figures reared, and they had rifles. He fired at a warrior on the left, swiveled, and fired at a warrior on the right just as the warrior's rifle banged. Pain seared his side but he didn't stop.

Ahead rose two more, with bows this time. Strings twanged and arrows took flight. Boone fanned a shot, but the Apaches went to the ground. He reined to the left just as a feathered shaft whizzed past his neck. He was not as lucky with the second. It sheared into his left shoulder, and the shock nearly unhorsed him.

The palomino was at a gallop. Soon the Apaches fell behind; they never kept coming once it was pointless. They would follow, track him at their own pace, and if his wounds brought him down, they would finish what they had started. . . .

Ralph Compton

Bullet for a Bad Man

A Ralph Compton Novel

by David Robbins

SIGNET
Published by New American Library, a division of
Penguin Group (USA) Inc., 375 Hudson Street,
New York, New York 10014, USA
Penguin Group (Canada), 90 Eglinton Avenue East, Suite 700, Toronto,
Ontario M4P 2Y3, Canada (a division of Pearson Penguin Canada Inc.)
Penguin Books Ltd., 80 Strand, London WC2R 0RL, England
Penguin Ireland, 25 St. Stephen's Green, Dublin 2,
Ireland (a division of Penguin Books Ltd.)
Penguin Group (Australia), 250 Camberwell Road, Camberwell, Victoria 3124,
Australia (a division of Pearson Australia Group Pty. Ltd.)
Penguin Books India Pvt. Ltd., 11 Community Centre, Panchsheel Park,
New Delhi - 110 017, India
Penguin Group (NZ), 67 Apollo Drive, Rosedale, North Shore 0632,
New Zealand (a division of Pearson New Zealand Ltd.)
Penguin Books (South Africa) (Pty.) Ltd., 24 Sturdee Avenue,
Rosebank, Johannesburg 2196, South Africa

Penguin Books Ltd, Registered Offices:
80 Strand, London WC2R 0RL, England

First published by Signet, an imprint of New American Library,
a division of Penguin Group (USA) Inc.

First Printing, October 2008
10 9 8 7 6 5 4 3 2 1

PUBLISHER'S NOTE

This is a work of fiction. Names, characters, places, and incidents either are the product of the author's imagination or are used fictitiously, and any resemblance to actual persons, living or dead, business establishments, events, or locales is entirely coincidental.

The publisher does not have any control over and does not assume any responsibility for author or third-party Web sites or their content.

The Immortal Cowboy

This is respectfully dedicated to the "American Cowboy." His was the saga sparked by the turmoil that followed the Civil War, and the passing of more than a century has by no means diminished the flame.

True, the old days and the old ways are but treasured memories, and the old trails have grown dim with the ravages of time, but the spirit of the cowboy lives on.

In my travels—to Texas, Oklahoma, Kansas, Nebraska, Colorado, Wyoming, New Mexico, and Arizona—I always find something that reminds me of the Old West. While I am walking these plains and mountains for the first time, there is this feeling that a part of me is eternal, that I have known these old trails before. I believe it is the undying spirit of the frontier calling, allowing me, through the mind's eye, to step back into time. What is the appeal of the Old West of the American frontier?

It has been epitomized by some as the dark and bloody period in American history. Its heroes—Crockett, Bowie, Hickok, Earp—have been reviled and criticized. Yet the Old West lives on, larger than life.

It has become a symbol of freedom, when there was always another mountain to climb and another river to cross; when a dispute between two men was settled not with expensive lawyers, but with fists, knives, or guns. Barbaric? Maybe. But some things never change. When the cowboy rode into the pages of American history, he left behind a legacy that lives within the hearts of us all.

—Ralph Compton

Brothers Born

The Civil War was over.

The horror of citizen brother pitted against citizen brother ended with the brothers from the North killing more of their brothers from the South than the brothers from the South could kill of their brothers from the North. The South surrendered while they still had brothers left.

The brothers from the South went back to a land blighted by the brutal slaughter.

Many of the brothers from the North went back to their old lives too. But some wanted something new.

Ned Scott was from the North. He was born and raised in the same state as the president, who had decided that spilling blood was the only way for brothers to settle a dispute.

Ned enlisted early in the war and went off to fight his brothers in gray. He enlisted not because he thought slavery was the greatest evil ever known, although he did believe no man had the right to lord it over another because his skin color happened to be different. He enlisted not to preserve the glory of the Union, although he did believe in the Constitution of the United States of America and felt the states should stay united and not break apart.

Ned enlisted because he wanted excitement in his life. At the start of the war he worked as a clerk and made enough money for him and his wife, Lillian, and their young son, Epp, to get by. During the war he was granted leave to go home for a week, with the result being that after the war he had another mouth to feed in the form of his second son, Boone.

Ned knew he had been fortunate. Many thousands killed, many thousands maimed, and he had gotten through the war without a scratch. It helped that he was assigned to the artillery and not the regular infantry or the cavalry. He got to lob cannonballs at the enemy and blow them apart from a distance rather than rush up to them and bayonet them in the guts.

With the war at an end, Ned needed to keep feeding the mouths of his family. He could not go back to being a clerk. The very notion made him cringe. Clerk work was boring, the same dull routine day in and day out. The prospect of spending the rest of his days in a cage made of stocked shelves scared him more than the cannonballs his brothers from the South had lobbed at him during the war.

Ned did what many young veterans were doing. He decided to head west. Land was to be had for the taking and a man could make something of himself if he was willing to take a few risks. Hostiles were one of those risks. Renegade whites were another. Wild beasts, floods, starvation and dying of thirst were also on the list, but Ned considered them minor nuisances compared to the boredom of clerk work.

So it was that in 1866 Ned packed his family onto a Conestoga and lumbered west at the vanguard of the restless tide seeking more out of life than was offered east of the Mississippi River.

Ned and Lillian had talked it over. Ned did most of the talking and Lillian did most of the listening. First Ned wanted to head for Texas, but Lillian said there were Comanches in Texas, and of all the red devils ever born, Comanches were the worst. She refused to live in Texas no matter what. Next Ned proposed they go to Oregon country, but Lillian said that meant they would live at the far end of the continent and she would hardly ever get to see her parents. She refused to live in Oregon no matter what.

"How about Arizona Territory?" Ned asked. He did not know much about it other than that Congress had created the territory a few years ago and there was supposed to be a lot of land for the taking. There were also supposed to be Apaches, but he did not know much about them either, and he decided not to mention them after Lillian's tiff over Comanches.

Arizona Territory it was.

The hand of Providence had kept Ned safe during the war, and the hand of Providence was at work again as Ned crossed the mile-wide Mississippi and ventured where few white men had ventured before him. He and his family made it across the vast prairie to Bent's Fort and joined a freight train to Santa Fe. From there they rattled and clattered to the southwest until they came to Phoenix, and from there drifted to Tucson.

Lillian was tired of traveling and tired of living out of a wagon and just plain tired. She told Ned he had better find a place for them to live and he had better find it quick, and Ned, startled by her rare burst of temper, then and there made up his mind.

Ned had heard about a valley. An old man with a beard down to his waist and a bottle of whiskey in his hand had been leaning on a post outside a Tucson saloon when Ned brought his wagon to a stop in the dusty street. The man asked Ned where he was from, one thing led to another and the old man told Ned about the valley.

It was between the San Pedro and the San Simon rivers, and south of the Galiuro and Pinaleno mountains. It had that rarity of rarities in Arizona, a year-round stream. The grass grew green and there was plenty of it, the old man assured Ned. The old man had stumbled across it during his trapping days, and he would live there himself except that it was too far to Tucson, and whiskey.

Ned asked the old man to write directions on how to get there, but the old man could neither read nor write so he sketched a map. The map was not much of one, but Providence once again showed it was fond of Ned and he found the valley without much difficulty.

And what a wonderful valley it was. Everything the old man, whose name Ned never asked, had said it would be. A great circle of green with a single red butte at its center. Ned named the valley Circle Valley and the butte Red Butte and claimed them for his own.

Naming the stream proved harder. Ned wanted to call it Lillian, as a gesture to his wife, but she said she did not want animals drinking out of her and people washing their unmentionables in her and she would rather not have a stream named after her, thank you very much. Ned thought that was just about the silliest thing he ever heard, but he honored her request. From then on, it was just "the stream."

Ned hauled timber from the mountains and built a house and a barn and a corral. His idea was to take up farming. But then he was in Tucson one day buying supplies and he struck up another fateful conversation. This time it was with a drummer who was selling everything under the sun, and then some.

The drummer asked Ned what he did for a living and Ned proudly mentioned he was going to raise wheat and corn.

"And do what with it, Mr. Scott?"

"Why, sell the surplus, of course," Ned informed him.

"Who to?" The drummer pointed out that Arizona did not have enough hungry bellies for Ned to make much money. "What you need to do," the drummer then said with the air of a man who knew all there was to know about the business of business, "is to go into cattle."

"Cattle?" Ned said dubiously. "Do you mean raise cows?" He made it sound about as smart as raising chickens for a living, and no one in their right mind did that.

"Not the kind of cows you are thinking of," the drummer said. "The kind you find in Mexico and can bring north."

The drummer had traveled all over, and he had talked to a lot of people and everyone swore that the demand for beef would soar now that the war was over. All those people in the East liked to eat meat and there just wasn't enough of it.

"Those same people will need wheat and corn too," Ned pointed out.

"Yes," the drummer conceded. "But you don't have to plant cows. You don't have to fertilize cows and keep them free of weeds and worry they will be destroyed by high wind or hail. Cows take care of themselves. All you need is grass and water, and to round the cows up now and again. Cattle are a lot less work than crops."

Ned liked the idea of not having to work as hard to get his due. He liked it a lot. A month later he hired two local men to help and they drifted into Mexico and helped themselves to some cattle they came across. It was that easy. Ned had the start of his herd.

The years passed and Ned prospered. His herd grew. The Circle Valley Ranch became known far and wide for its fine beef.

By 1880 Ned had twenty hands minding his thousands of head of cattle. He smoked five-dollar cigars. He wore the best of clothes. His boots were polished daily by his servants. When he went into Tucson he did so in a carriage, not a buckboard.

Ned liked having money. He liked the trappings that went with having money. He liked it so much, he did not think of much besides money.

Lillian didn't mind. She liked money too.

As for their sons, each had a different opinion.

Eppley was twenty-two. He was fond of good clothes and good food and he grew fond of Tucson's sporting houses, as well. He often complained of the days he wasted getting there and back. As for the ranch, he did the work his father asked of him, but he did not like doing it. He did not like to work at all.

Boone was sixteen. He did not mind work. He went in for plain work garb, and his mother's cooking was enough to suit him. And he liked the ranching life a lot.

Everything revolved around their cattle. Each year the cows had to be rounded up, the calves had to be branded and hundreds of head had to be driven to market.

Cows, cows, cows—that is all Epp's life was, and he hankered after something more. Like his father, he liked excitement. He liked it more than anything.

Boone was content with ranching. Still, his brother's constant talk about how wonderful the rest of the world was stirred him. One day he mentioned to Epp that he was thinking of going off and seeing some of what it had to offer.

Epp smiled. He was bigger and heavier than Boone. He had his father's hooked nose and brown eyes, but his bushy eyebrows were his own. Those eyebrows were always pinched together, as if in disapproval of the world around them. His mouth was thin and nearly always curled down. Epp looked, as one of their punchers once put it, like an overfed wolf hungry for more.

Boone was lean and muscled and had hair the color of corn. His eyes were blue, like his mother's, and his small ears and oval chin were hers too. His hands came from his father. They were strong, swift hands, so swift that he could draw and fire a revolver three times in the time it took most men to do it once.

Boone spent almost all his spare time practicing. He

was partial to a black leather rig decorated with silver conchas. His revolver came direct from the Colt factory, a special order he placed for a nickel-plated beauty with ivory handles and a four-inch barrel. The grips were etched with eagle heads, and the cylinder and barrel engraved.

As one of their hands remarked, "That there is the prettiest six-shooter I ever did see."

Ned Scott was proud of his son's ability with a pistol, but Lillian said time and time again that no good would come of it.

Then came the day she was proven right.

It started as most days did, with an early breakfast. Boone had a healthy appetite, but Epp picked at his eggs and took only a few bites of toast and was done.

Since the Circle V was a ranch and not a farm, the barn had become a stable, and a corral had been built at the back. Boone and Epp saddled their horses and headed out across the Circle V range just as a golden crown poked above the rim of the world.

"Another roundup," Epp complained. "Why Pa insists we help I will never know. Dan Morgan can take care of things."

A Texan by birth, Morgan was the Circle V foreman, and as cow savvy a man as ever lived. Ned had heard about him from a fellow rancher and induced Morgan to come work for the Circle V by offering him twice as much money as he was making in Texas.

"We are Pa's sons." Boone's horse was a buttermilk he had raised from a colt, and he loved it almost as much as he did his ivory-handled Colt.

"So what?" Epp said irritably. He always rode whatever horse happened to be handy. Horses meant as little to him as cows.

"So Pa expects us to follow in his footsteps and take over the ranch someday."

"That does not explain why we have to attend every damn roundup."

"A boss should show he does not mind getting his hands dirty."

"Dirtying hands is what we pay the punchers to do," Epp persisted. "When I am in charge I will be damned if I dirty mine."

"When *we* are in charge," Boone amended.

Epp looked at him. "I thought you were hankering to go see some of the world."

"I am. I just can't find the gumption to say so to Ma and Pa."

"What you need is to get away from the Circle V for a while," Epp proposed. "Come with me to Ranson after the roundup is over."

"I don't like that place."

"You have never been there. I have, and I like it a lot."

Ranson was a wart that liked to call itself a town. It got its start as a trading post and grew to include a dozen buildings. That four of those buildings were saloons and three were houses of ill repute was the reason it had grown so fast. Cards, whiskey and women were to be had any hour of the day or night.

Cowhands from every ranch in the territory came to Ranson for entertainment. There was no law. There was no church. Shootings were common. Hardly a month passed that the cemetery did not sprout a new tombstone. Or at least a square of wood with the name of the deceased.

Ned Scott had told his sons to stay away from Ranson. "It is a nest of killers and gamblers and women of loose morals. If you go there you are asking for trouble."

Lillian had agreed. "Ranson is Sodom and Gomorrah rolled into one. Sin is its trade, and hell is its reward."

Boone had listened, and stayed away.

Epp went there every chance he got.

Now, as the brothers crossed the rich grassy range that would one day be theirs, Epp again urged, "Come with me after the roundup. You will like it more than you think."

"I reckon it can't hurt to go there just once."

Epp turned his head to hide his vicious grin.

Parting the Tie

The night was warm, the air as still as a held breath.

Boone Scott rose in the stirrups and stared at scores of glittering fireflies that seemed a mile away.

"Nervous, little brother?" Epp Scott teased.

"Got a kink in my back. And I have told you before not to call me that."

"But you *are* my little brother," Epp said. "Remember how when we were small I would pound you if you didn't do as I wanted?"

"You don't pound me these days."

"A man would be a fool to try. You are greased lightning with that smoke wagon of yours."

"No one can accuse you of being puny either."

"I suppose not," Epp allowed. "But unlike you, I do not show off what I can do."

"I am no show-off."

"A poor choice of words," Epp said. "But you must admit you are not timid either. Ma is worried you will come to no good if you keep on as you have been."

Boone pushed his wide-brimmed hat back on his curly corn-colored hair. "I don't savvy why she carries on like she does. I have never killed anyone. I don't even get into fights."

"It is all that practicing you do. For an hour every day, without fail, you bang away."

"I like to shoot."

"You do not just like it. You live and breathe it."

Boone nodded at the glittering fireflies. "Given how often you come here, is that what you live and breathe?"

"I love Ranson," Epp admitted. "God help me, but I love the sights and the sounds and the feel. I love to play poker. I love the burning feel of whiskey in my throat. I love to have a warm dove in my lap with her fingers in my hair."

"Lordy," Boone said.

Epp laughed. "Ma would blister my ears for being a sinner if she heard me talk like that. But I am how I am and I will not change for her or anyone else."

"Be nice, as Ma would say."

Epp shot him a sharp glance. "That was fine when we were little. It was important to her that we get along and be nice to everyone. But we are grown men now, and the world is not the nice place Ma would like it to be. If a man wants to make his mark, he must stake out what is his and not be nice about getting it and keeping it."

"I don't know what I want out of life yet," Boone said.

"I do."

"What?"

"To be king of the roost and do as I damn well please. To snap my fingers and have work get done."

"What will you do? Go off to St. Louis or New Orleans or some such and make your mark?"

"I can do all that right here."

"Pa is young yet, only a little over forty, and fit as a fiddle. It could be twenty years or more before he is ready to give up the reins. And then you would have to share them with me."

"You never know," Epp said.

The fireflies had grown to rectangles and Ranson had grown to a bustling beehive. Horses at hitch rails and parked buckboards and wagons lined the main street. People were everywhere, hurrying to and fro, talking and joking and laughing.

"It sure looks friendly," Boone remarked.

Epp laughed. "A rattler looks innocent until you step on it. Make no mistake, little brother. There are nothing but wolves here, and they will eat you alive if you are not careful."

"Bosh. You have been to Ranson many a time and made it home safe and sound."

"I am a wolf my own self," Epp said.

Now it was Boone who laughed. "You forget I know you. You arc hardly a bad man."

"How would you know? I am not the same at the ranch as I am here. For a reason."

Their conversation was interrupted by the pounding of hooves. They reined aside as half a dozen riders swept down on them from out of the night. Whooping and hollering, the six cowhands thundered past, one of them yelling, "Yonder she is, boy! We are going to have ourselves a fine time!"

"You are not the only one who likes to come here," Boone said as he gigged his buttermilk.

"Sin is more popular than being good."

"What a thing to say."

"It's true. Look at all these people. More than you will find in church in Tucson on Easter Sunday. And why? People would rather drink and gamble and bed whores than pray to God."

"Stop," Boone said.

"Stop what?"

"You are just saying that to rile me."

Epp leaned on his saddle horn and regarded his brother with amusement. "Since when did you become a defender of public virtue? I am saying it because it is true."

"Don't ever say it to Ma. She will keel over, and we wouldn't want that to happen."

"Of course we wouldn't."

Around them was bedlam just this side of chaos, men and women hurrying every which way, batwings constantly opening and closing, and the bawdy houses doing a booming business in carnal delights.

"It sure is something," Boone said.

"I keep forgetting you are only sixteen. You are big for your age and look older."

"So?"

"Nothing." Epp reined toward a hitch rail. "This is my home away from home, you might call it."

The saloon was the Acey-Deucey. It was the largest and most popular. It was also the noisiest, thanks to a singing troupe of four ladies who performed on a stage with considerable enthusiasm, if not much talent. As skimpy as their outfits were, no one cared whether they sang off-key. Every table was filled, the floor crammed, the bar lined end to end. When the songs ended and the ladies left the stage, the babble of voices rose to the ceiling.

The Acey-Deucey was a giant heart pulsing to the throb of Ranson's wild nightlife.

Boone gazed about him in wonderment. "You have told me what it is like, but I never imagined it was like this."

"Stick close." Epp shouldered into the crowd.

Hooking his thumbs in his gun belt, Boone trailed in his brother's wake. Curious glances were thrown his way. A dove in a tight red dress brushed against him and asked him to buy her a drink. "Maybe later."

There was no space at the bar. Epp motioned to get the nearest bartender's attention, and the bartender immediately came over and pointed at a long hall at the rear, saying, "Your room is reserved as always. I will bring a bottle of your favorite and the glasses."

After the glare and blare out in front, the small empty room they entered was a haven of quiet.

Epp closed the door and took a seat at a table. He patted the chair next to him, saying, "You are welcome to sit in if you want."

"Sit in on what?"

"What else? Poker." Epp patted the table. "Condit will be here soon and bring other players."

"Who?"

"Charley Condit. He doesn't own the Acey-Deucey, but he runs it. You would be smart to make his acquaintance. He is a big man here in Ranson. Give him a few years and he will be one of the biggest in the territory. Almost as big as me."

"You must have plans."

"Grin if you want. But yes, I have made plans. Plans that might surprise you."

The door opened and in whisked a portly volcano

in an expensive suit and bowler. "Epp!" he exclaimed, his moon of a face alight with delight. "I wasn't expecting you until next week." He stopped and glanced quizzically at Boone. "Who is this?"

"My kid brother. I told you about him." Epp motioned. "Boone, I would like you to meet Charley Condit. Anything you need, you ask him."

"Indeed," Condit said, offering a pudgy hand. "Any kin of Epp's is a friend of mine."

Boone shook. "I had no idea my brother is so well liked."

Condit went on shaking long after he should have stopped. "Your pa owns one of the richest spreads around, and rich makes a fellow popular."

Epp patted the chair on his right. "How about it, little brother? Do you want to play some cards?"

"Not at the moment," Boone said. "I want to take a stroll and see what Ranson has to offer."

"You do that. It is your first time here." Epp smiled but his smile faded as soon as the door closed. He glared at Condit. "What the hell were you thinking? Rich makes me popular?"

Condit blanched. "The Circle V *is* one of the largest spreads in the territory."

"I don't care. Watch what you say. For this to work he must not suspect." Epp scowled. "Do you know where Jarrott is?"

"Over to Maddy's. She has a new girl."

"Fetch him. Tell him to come in the back way. If he doesn't want to leave the girl, remind him of what it means to make me mad."

Charley Condit turned to go. "Why Jarrott anyhow? I can think of four or five I would pick over him."

"Some others might be faster, but he is always careful and that counts for more."

"You are not letting any grass grow under you."

"Why should I? I finally talked the kid into coming. I want this over with so I can get on with the rest." Epp paused. "Why are you still here?"

"On my way."

Epp sat back and drummed his fingers on the table. He took his watch from his vest pocket, opened it and noted the time. He removed his hat and placed it beside him, then put it back on again and pulled the brim over his eyes.

The bartender brought the best whiskey the saloon offered, glasses and an unopened deck of cards, all on a wooden tray. Without saying a word he set the tray down and left.

Epp consulted his watch again. He opened the bottle. Forgoing the glass, he tilted the bottle to his mouth. After several swallows he smacked his lips and set the bottle down. For a while he did more finger drumming; then he scowled at the door, opened the cards and began playing solitaire. He stiffened when voices sounded, but no one entered and he put a black jack on a red queen. Catching himself, he swore and picked up the jack.

The door opened. In came Charley Condit, trailed by a short, sallow man in clothes that could stand a washing. So could the man. He had buckteeth and stubble and grime under his chin. Shifty eyes and full cheeks lent him the look of a ferret. His hat needed stitching and his boots were badly scuffed. Wedged under his belt was a Smith & Wesson that looked to have seen as much use as his clothes.

"Here he is," Condit said.

"Wait out at the bar."

Condit nodded and departed.

Epp pushed out a chair with his foot. "Have a seat, Jarrott."

"I am fine as I am," the ferret man said, sounding as if he had a mouthful of marbles.

"It is time," Epp informed him.

"Condit told me. So you got him here like you wanted. I will take care of him. But you owe me money first."

"Our deal was half in advance, half when the deed is done. That was what we shook on and that is how we will do it."

Jarrott shrugged. "So long as I am paid. The last hombre who cheated me did not live to brag of it."

"Are you threatening me?"

"Not now, not ever. I am only saying." Jarrott came to the chair and placed his left hand on top of it. His right hand was close to the Smith & Wesson. "Let's not have a spitting contest. I will do what you want. You will pay me the rest. And that will be that."

"Remember what I told you. He is a kid but he is god-awful fast. Do not let him touch his hardware."

"Relax. I know my business. I am the killer, not him. His speed does not worry me."

"It should."

"I have done fast gents before. The trick is to take them by surprise."

"Condit will point him out. Do it in the back. Claim he was drawing on you. I will act shocked when they come to tell me. Then I will tend to the body and take it home to my folks."

"Your own brother." Jarrott smirked. "And for what? A few handfuls of dirt."

"The Circle V is more than a few. And as he reminded me a while ago, he is entitled to half. Since I am not inclined to share, I have hired you."

Jarrott grinned. "Your brother is as good as dead."

Den of Chance

Boone Scott looked older than he was. His bronzed skin, from countless hours spent under the burning sun, had a lot to do with it. But it was his ivory-handled Colt, conspicuous on his hip, that drew more than a few glances as he mingled with the saloon's patrons. Fancy Colts like his cost a lot of money, and men who wore them were the kind to watch out for.

The poker games interested Boone for a while. All the players were armed, some with revolvers stuck under their belts, others with their jackets swept back to reveal holsters. They sat like roosting hawks, tense, alert, their movements quick, their faces as inscrutable as they could make them.

The professional gamblers stood out because they were so at ease and relaxed. They also stood out because of their black frock coats and wide-brimmed black hats. They did not flourish weapons but there was no doubt they were heeled.

Boone had played poker before. On occasion he would sneak out of the ranch house and join the Circle V punchers in the bunkhouse for their usual Saturday night game. His mother branded poker—and all gambling—

as the devil's handiwork and urged him to resist temptation. His brother was doomed to perdition, she would say, but he need not be.

Boone's father did not like that perdition talk. No son of his, Ned maintained, was bound for hell, and he would thank his wife to stop saying they were.

Ned went to church with Lillian when she visited Tucson, and he said grace at the supper table, and when the boys were little he had said prayers with them at bedtime. But about a year ago Ned shocked Boone considerably one night by remarking that religion was for those who did not like the way life was so they made up a way to make life tolerable.

"Are you saying you don't believe in God, Pa?" Boone had asked.

Ned scowled and shook his pipe as if about to hurl it at the Almighty. "I am not sure what I believe. I confess it is all too confusing for me and always has been."

"What part confuses you?"

"Every part. But you can start with God is love. The parson says that all the time, and your mother, God bless her, must say it twenty times a week." Ned had gazed out the parlor window. "But if God is love, why does he allow all the horrible things in this world? Why does he let people get sickly, and die? Why does he let our bodies wither and grow feeble to where we can't use a chamber pot without help?"

Boone was sure he did not know and said so.

"The war opened my eyes, son," Ned had told him. "The things I saw, the awful things I never talk about, changed me. Men with their arms and legs blown off, screaming and wailing in pools of blood. Boys no older than you, gutted like fish with their insides hanging out and begging for someone to put them out of their misery. An officer I knew, the nicest, kindest man you'd ever want to meet, took shrapnel in the crotch and would never be a man again." Ned shuddered. "Now I ask you: How can a God of love let awful things like that happen?"

"You would have to ask God."

"I have, son, many a time. I have prayed and prayed for the answer to that and other questions I have. And do you know what the answer to my prayers has been?"

"No, Pa. What?"

"Nothing. Nothing at all. I talk to God like your mother says to do, but God doesn't talk back."

Boone had not known what to say so he had not said anything.

"Maybe it is me," Ned said. "Maybe I lack something. Maybe that is why God does not talk to me."

"Could be," Boone had said since his father was looking at him as if he expected him to say something.

Ned had sighed. "Religion confuses me. I doubt I will make sense of it this side of the grave, and once I am on the other side it will not much matter."

Boone never forgot that talk. It scared the hell out of him.

Now, watching a gambler lay down a full house and rake in a pot, Boone placed his left hand over the poke in his pocket but did not take the poke out. He was thinking of his mother, and perdition.

From the poker tables Boone drifted to the roulette wheel. Like everyone else, he was fascinated by the bright colors, and how the wheel flashed when the dealer gave it a spin. This particular wheel took two bits to bet and paid out as much as ten dollars.

Farther on, a dice dealer placed dice in a metal cage, closed the tiny door and gave the cage a spin. Players waited with bated breath for the cage to stop so they could see if they were winners or losers.

Boone strolled on and was soon confronted by a game he never saw before. The wheel of fortune, it was called. A giant wheel, as high as he was, painted in gaudy colors. Along the rim were small squares with the four suits, diamonds, spades, hearts and clubs, repeated over and over again. The dealer would give the wheel a hard spin and it would whirl around and around, clicking and clacking thanks to a spoke along the outer edge, and finally come to a stop with a pointer over the winning suit.

Boone started to reach for his poke, but once again he stopped himself.

The next table had another game new to Boone. It was called crown and anchor. The dealer set out squares of paper marked with the different suits, and players put their bets on whichever suits they thought would win. Once all the bets were placed, the dealer took a single die that had the suits painted on its sides, put the die into a small basket and shook the basket. Whichever suit ended up faceup was the winner.

Beyond were faro tables. More popular than poker, faro drew scores of players and onlookers. The idea behind it was simple. The dealer had laid out thirteen cards representing the one through the king, and players would place their money on the card they liked. Matching cards were in a small box in front of the dealer. He would slide two cards out and show them.

Whoever had placed a bet on the first card lost. But whoever bet on the second card was a winner. Bets placed on cards that had not been drawn were allowed to ride or were removed.

Someone jostled Boone and he glanced up in annoyance. That was when he noticed that everyone was watching the faro players except a short man with buckteeth on the other side of the table. He was staring at Boone, and when Boone set eyes on him, the man quickly looked away.

Boone moved on to the craps table. He watched a while, and when he saw the bucktoothed man sidle near, he circled around the craps table to a backgammon table. Out of the corner of his eye he saw the bucktoothed man staring at the backgammon players.

Coming to a decision, Boone took several quick steps as if he were about to hurry off. The man gave a start and came in his direction. Suddenly stopping, Boone wheeled. "Why are you following me, mister?"

The man appeared taken aback. "What in hell are you talking about, sonny?"

"You have been following me. I want to know why."

"Are you loco?" the man said more loudly than he needed to. "I don't even know you."

"You were at the faro table and the craps table," Boone persisted.

The man gestured and practically shouted. "Look around you, boy. This place is packed. Is everybody here following you?"

People were staring.

Boone, uncomfortable, shifted his weight from one foot to the other. "I reckon I could be wrong."

"Sounds to me like you are drunk. Do not bother

me with your antics again." So saying, the man barged off.

Boone stared after him, conscious of the glances he was getting. He had pivoted to head for the back and the room his brother was in when a warm hand brushed his and the voice of an angel spoke into his ear.

"You better be careful, whoever you are. That there was Sam Jarrott and he is as mean as they come."

Boone turned. The angel was a girl not much older than he was. She had big hazel eyes, long eyelashes and an oval face. Her dress gave him the impression it would burst at the seams if she exhaled.

"Jarrott has notches on his six-gun. I saw him earn one of those notches with my own eyes." She held out a small hand. "I am Lucy, by the way. What might your handle be?"

"What?" Boone said.

"Your name. You do have one, don't you? Most mothers don't call their children 'it.' "

"What?"

"Are you addlepated?" Lucy asked. "You do not seem to have all your wits about you."

"I have plenty of wits."

"You could not prove it by me. But I will try again. Do you have a name or not?"

Boone forced his tongue to tell her who he was.

"Scott, you say?" Lucy repeated, her brow furrowing. "Land sakes. I suppose it is silly to ask, but are you by any chance kin of Epp Scott?"

"I am his brother."

"You don't say." Lucy was impressed. "He is a big man in these parts. Any bigger and he would be governor."

"You must have him confused with someone else."

"I would not confuse the man I work for."

Boone chuckled. "Now I know you are mistaken. My brother is a rancher. Our stable has horses, not doves."

"Try not to make it sound like the plague if you can help it," Lucy said testily.

"I didn't mean—" Boone began.

"A girl has to eat," Lucy said. "When she is adrift with no family or friends, she cannot be choosy."

"You are all alone?"

"Not all the time. But say. I can't stand here doing nothing but talk or I will get in trouble with Condit."

"Why?"

"Condit doesn't like it when his doves don't earn their keep." Lucy grinned and clutched his arm. "Why don't you buy us both drinks so I can spend more time with you?"

His ears strangely warm, Boone said, "I would like that. But I am not much of a drinker."

"You don't say? Yet here you are in a saloon. When you are on a horse do you say you don't ride?"

"Of course I can ride. And good too. I can also rope and throw a steer when I have to."

"My, oh my," Lucy said while leading him toward the bar. "A man of your abilities is apt to turn my pretty head."

Boone's chest grew tight.

"Are you about to be sick?"

"No. Why?"

"You were green there for a second." Lucy laughed merrily. "I like you, Boone Scott. You are not like most men I meet. A good like, not a bad like."

Boone spoke before he could stop himself. "I am glad it is good. And I like you too."

Smiling sweetly, Lucy brought him to the end of the bar. She bawled for a bottle, and a bartender promptly brought one over, along with two glasses.

"So, what do you say, Mr. Scott?"

"Call me Boone. And what do I say to what?"

"The glass or the bottle. I can stay with you longer if it is the bottle."

Boone nodded at the bartender. "Leave it."

"I have not been this flattered since I can remember." Lucy winked and rubbed her fingers across the back of his hand. "How would you like a nice quiet place where we can talk in peace?"

"I would like that very much." Boone gazed around the crammed saloon. "But where? Outside?"

"Do it in the street?" Lucy said, and was convulsed with merriment. "Goodness. You are more bold than I imagined. But no, thank you, I have my limits and a public street is one of them." She tugged on his wrist. "Come on. There are rooms at the back."

Boone let himself be led past the room his brother was in and on down a narrow hall flanked by door after door. She opened one without knocking and playfully pushed him in ahead of her. A small oak table and a bed were the only furniture. On the table was a lamp, already lit.

"They have beds in a saloon?"

Lucy shut the door and faced him, tilting her head as if she were trying to figure something out. "The floors are too hard. Not that this bed has much to recommend it. I would not use it but I can do without the chafing."

Boone was aghast. "This is where you live?"

"No, silly. I already told you. This is where I work." Lucy pulled him with her and they bumped against the bed. "Have a seat. I will pour."

"I would rather stand."

"Don't be silly. We can be comfortable, at least." Lucy gave him a shove.

Boone tried to catch himself, but there was nothing to hold on to. He fell onto the bed and promptly sat up. "You are a bit bossy."

"Some men like bossy." Lucy opened the bottle and filled first one glass and then the other. "Here you go." She held a glass out to him. "Drink up. You will need it. If you are what I think you are, I am about to give you the treat of your life."

"Excuse me?"

"Must I spell it out for you? The festivities are about to commence."

Shades of Virgin

"This is more festive than I have been in a coon's age," Boone Scott remarked.

"You might as well get your money's worth."

Boone gave a start. "That reminds me. We plumb forgot to pay the bartender."

"You can pay me for all of it when we are done." Lucy tipped her glass to her red lips and downed the contents in a gulp.

"How do you do that?"

"What?"

"Drink like that."

"How else does a person drink? We can't use our ears."

The notion made Boone chuckle. He took a sip and winced as the liquor seared a liquid path from his throat down into the pit of his stomach. Coughing, he said, "Now I know why Indians call it firewater."

"You are comical," Lucy said.

"I told you I do not have much experience at this kind of thing. I have only had liquor a few times, and then only a little."

Lucy gave him another intent study. "This is not an act you are putting on? You are serious?"

"About what? If you want to laugh I could tickle you except it would not be proper."

"My God."

"What? I was only teasing about the tickling."

"Have you ever been with a woman?"

"I am with you," Boone said.

Lucy set her glass down and leaned against the table, her hip thrust provocatively. "No. I mean, have you ever *slept* with a girl?"

"With my cousin once. But we were eight and there were not enough beds or my ma would never have allowed it."

"My God," Lucy said again, and shook her head in bewilderment. "Can it be?" She came over and sat next to him and took his hand in hers. "I am sorry. I thought maybe you were funning me. Some men do that to get me to treat them extra nice."

"You are plenty nice," Boone said.

Lucy gazed deep into his eyes. "How can this be? Do your folks keep you down in the root cellar all day?"

"What kind of question is that? Of course not. I work the range with the punchers."

"I just don't get how you can be so innocent about *this*," Lucy said, and patted the bed.

Boone stared at the bed and then at her and then at the whiskey bottle on the table and then at the closed door and then at the bed again. "We are not here to talk, are we?"

Lucy cupped his cheeks in her hands and pinched

them. "Has anyone ever told you how adorable you are?"

Boone gripped her wrists and removed her hands from his face. "That will be enough."

"Don't be upset. You are a virgin, aren't you?" When Boone did not reply, Lucy merrily exclaimed, "I knew I was right! You have never lain with a female and you are afraid to lie with me."

"Have you lain with a lot of men?"

"Land sakes, yes. Why else would I be here?" Lucy chortled. "It is how I earn my keep. I smile and talk nice and get men to spend money on booze. Then I bring them back here and let them think they are having their way with me."

"How much?" Boone asked.

"How much what? How much money do I earn? That is personal. But I will tell you that in a couple of years I will have enough of a nest egg to move to San Francisco and open my very own sporting house. That is where the big money is. Sporting houses."

"How many?"

"I just told you. I do not talk about my earnings."

"How many men?"

Lucy tilted her head as was her habit. "Whatever would you want to know a thing like that for?"

"How many?"

Something in his tone turned Lucy's smile into a frown. "I don't much like your tone. And I will be hanged if I would say even if I knew. Which I don't, because I have never counted them."

Boone bowed his head and stared at the blanket covering the bed. It was a ratty, moth-eaten thing. He looked at Lucy and saw a mole on her neck he had not seen and lines in her face where he had not seen lines before. He noticed how pale her skin was, as if she had spent most of her life in a cave. He saw that her teeth were not as white as he had thought, and her perfume reminded him of sour grapes. "Well," he said.

"Well what?"

"I reckon I will be going now." Boone went to stand, but she grabbed his wrist.

"Hold on. What is wrong? Now that we are here, why not do it? I promise you a good time." Lucy bent close and pecked him on the neck. "A *very* good time."

"No."

"Give me a reason."

"You are pretty and all, and you are as nice as nice can be, and I am flattered that you brought me back here." Boone gestured at the ratty blanket and the whiskey bottle. "But this is not how I want it to be."

"Want what to be?"

"My first time."

Lucy recoiled as if he had slapped her. Conflicting emotions twisted her face: anger, amazement, sorrow, puzzlement. "So I was right."

Boone nodded.

"But why not? I mean, we all have to go through it. Why not go through it with me? I will please you. I will make it special."

"I would rather not, but thank you."

Anger won out over the other emotions and Lucy snapped, "Why the hell not? What is wrong with me? Or are you a Bible lover, and you think you are too good for me?"

"I am not too good for anyone," Boone said. "And

I have not read much of the Bible so I can't hardly thump it." He stood and put a hand on her shoulder. "Please don't look like that. I would if I could but I can't. It is not in me."

"You are male, aren't you? That is usually enough."

"I am sorry." Boone turned to go, pausing when he heard a slight sound in the hall.

"Hold on, handsome," Lucy said. "I am not giving up that easy." She stood and came around in front of him.

At that exact instant the door burst open. Framed in the doorway was Sam Jarrott, his Smith & Wesson level at his waist. He fired from no more than six feet away. The slug intended for Boone Scott struck Lucy in the back. It shattered her spine, tore through her insides and glanced off her hipbone.

"Oh!" Lucy said.

Sam Jarrott swore and extended the Smith & Wesson, taking deliberate aim.

Boone's Colt leaped from its holster. He was not conscious of drawing. One instant his hand was empty; the next the Colt stabbed flame and lead and Sam Jarrott staggered back against the hallway, shock writ on his features. "Not like this," he said, looking down at himself. "Not a wet-nosed kid."

Boone's blood was roaring through his veins so loudly that he barely heard himself ask, "Why?"

Jarrott looked at him and tried to raise the Smith & Wesson but couldn't.

"He was right about you."

"Who?"

"Damn him and damn you." Jarrott gripped the Smith & Wesson with both hands. It shook as he thumbed back the hammer with an audible *click.* "I can still get it done." The muzzle rose.

Boone fired, not once but three times, fanning the Colt as he had practiced doing day after day for the past two years. Practiced until he could hit five cans placed on the top rail of the corral five times out of five. Practiced until he could not only hit them, but hit them close to dead center.

Jarrott grunted and rose onto the tips of his toes. Then he let out a long breath while slowly sinking to the floor. Spittle dribbled over his lower lip and down his chin even as a bright red ribbon trickled down the front of his shirt. "Hell," he gurgled, and died.

"Boone?" Lucy said softly.

Boone turned, and swayed. A low cry escaped him at the sight of her curled on her side on the floor with wet scarlet spreading from under her. "God!" He dropped to his knees and held her head in his lap.

"Boone?"

"I am here," Boone said softly.

Lucy's eyes were open and staring right at him, but she said, "I can't see you. Why is everything so dark? Is the lamp lit?"

Boone opened his mouth and closed it again.

"How bad am I? Am I dying?" Lucy's right hand groped for his and he grasped it and held it to his chest. "Why won't you say something? Please. I need to hear you."

"I am here," Boone said again.

"That was Sam Jarrott, wasn't it? Why did he shoot me?"

Boone glanced at the heap in the hall and his eyes

became flinty. "I reckon he was after me and you got in the way."

Lucy shivered as if she were cold. "I am growing numb. I can't feel my legs."

Boone had to force his next words from a constricted throat. "Maybe you shouldn't talk."

A fit of coughing made Lucy groan. "Oh God. I don't want to die. Stay with me, please."

Boone had a coughing spell of his own. "I am not going anywhere," he assured her.

"What a stupid thing to happen. I never did anything to Sam Jarrott. Where did he get to?"

"He is dead."

"I didn't hear you."

"He is dead," Boone said louder.

Voices at the saloon end of the hall preceded the patter of running feet that slowed as they neared the body.

"Look here!" a man declared. "It is Sam Jarrott! And watch you don't step in all the blood."

"Someone has bucked him out in gore!" another man cried.

"Find Condit! He will want to know!"

"I am surprised he hasn't shown up," said the first man. "He had to hear the shots. Everyone else did."

Boone felt a slight pull on his hand and looked down. Lucy was strangely peaceful save for a red line from the corner of her mouth to her neck. "I am still here with you."

Lucy swallowed. "Thank you." In a bubbly whisper she said, "I am not long for this world. I can feel myself slipping away."

"God, no."

"I am sorry we did not get to know each other better. I like you, like you a lot." Lucy stopped and coughed. "Pay no mind to what I said about you being a virgin. I wish I still was. I wish I was a girl again and living with my folks in Ohio. I wish we never came west. I wish we never drank that bad water and they never died. Most of all, I wish I never met Charley Condit."

Boone held his tongue. It had dawned on him that talking was all she could do. He did not suggest she stop.

"It was Charley got me started in this work. Him and his sweet talk. He got me to trust him. Treated me like I was his own girl. Then he took me, and I had no choice but to do what he wanted."

"Took you?" Boone said, and did not recognize his own voice.

"You know," Lucy said. "Plied me with wine and had his way." She suffered the most violent attack yet, and when it subsided, she lay spent and exhausted and gasping for breath. "Life ain't fair."

"No, it's not. I never realized how not fair it is."

Heads poked past the jamb and excited babble filled the hall.

"Look! It's Lucy!"

"She's been shot!"

"So what? She is just a whore."

Boone glanced at the man who had spoken. "I will be getting up in a bit and coming out. If you are still there, you are dead."

"What did I do?" the man bleated. He did not wait for an answer but turned and ran.

Lucy plucked at Boone's shirt. "I heard that. You are not to kill anyone on my account."

Boone stroked her forehead, then bent and kissed her on the cheek. "I wish I had taken you up on your offer."

"You sure are sweet, Boone Scott." Suddenly Lucy arched her back. Her mouth opened wide but no sounds came out. Instead, her entire body deflated. She went completely limp as her eyes slowly closed, never to reopen.

"I hardly knew you," Boone said.

"Lucy is dead!" someone yelled.

Boone shook as he carefully lowered Lucy to the floor. Straightening, he clenched his fists so hard, his nails dug into his skin. He took several short, sharp breaths. Then he replaced the spent cartridges in his Colt, slid the six-shooter back into his holster and stalked from the room.

Gun Spree

The hall was empty save for the body.

Boone Scott stopped. He drew back a leg as if to kick it but then lowered his leg, and squatted. He studied Sam Jarrott's pasty face. He went through each of Jarrott's pockets. In one he found a wad of bills. Close to five hundred dollars, by his quick count. He stuffed the wad in his own pocket, rose and made for the saloon.

Faces peered at him from the far end of the hall, but they hastily drew back. None of the doors that lined the hall were open. Boone came to the room where he had left his brother. Again he paused. But he did not open it. He strode on.

A stillness gripped the Acey-Deucey. All eyes were on Boone as he emerged. Frozen figures and fearful expressions showed that word had spread and everyone knew death was abroad.

Two men wearing revolvers barred his way. One was stout, the other skinny. They did not look scared. They looked angry.

"You there!" the stout one said.

Boone stopped.

"That was our pard you just killed. We came here with him, and we do not take kindly to what you've done."

"We do not take it kindly at all," the skinny one said.

"An eye for an eye is how we see it." The stout man's thick fingers dipped toward his revolver.

Boone drew and shot the stout man through the head and swiveled and shot the skinny man in the throat. Both collapsed, the skinny man thrashing and gurgling. Boone calmly replaced the spent cartridges and slid the Colt into his holster. "Where is Condit?"

No one had moved. No one had so much as twitched. Violence was not uncommon in Ranson, but this violence was of such suddenness and purity that it shocked most into a state of stunned amazement.

"Where is Condit?"

A man near the bar stirred and motioned at another man standing amid the poker tables and together they converged. They wore suits, not work clothes, the cheap general store variety that could be ordered through a catalogue and seldom fit as well as advertised. The cheap suits matched the unkempt ugliness of the men. An ugliness of the soul reflected in their dull eyes.

"You son of a bitch," declared the man who had been by the bar. He was taller and wider and his jacket was pulled back to reveal a Remington. "Who the hell are you and what the hell do you think you are doing?"

"I want Condit."

"We work for him," the second man revealed. "It is our job to take care of troublemakers."

The man with the Remington said, "That is three men you have shot. You will not shoot any more."

The second man's fingers were splayed over a Hopkins & Allen army revolver. "We are no bluff."

"I'll ask one last time. Where is Condit?"

"We have not seen him in a while. It could be he left and did not tell us." The man held out the hand that was not poised to draw. "We want your hardware, mister."

"You do not know where he is?"

"I just told you. Now hand that Colt over, nice and slow. You must answer for your killings."

"There's no law in Ranson."

"True. There isn't. You will answer to Condit. He decides what to do with your kind."

"Go home," Boone said.

"What?"

"If you have families, go to them. If you just like breathing, leave while you can."

"Bold talk for a boy."

"We are paid to do this. It is our job. Now give up the Colt. You have our word we will not harm you."

"Did you know her?" Boone asked.

The man with the Remington scrunched up his face in confusion. "Are you drunk? Is that why you are doing this?"

"Did you know Lucy?"

"Lucy Fuller? Of course. She works for Condit too. She is one of his doves." The man stiffened. "Wait. Why did you ask?"

"You don't know?"

"Mister," said the man with the Hopkins & Allen, "all we know is that we heard shots, and then someone came out of that hall saying that Sam Jarrott was dead, and some girl was dead too. Would that be Lucy?"

"It would."

"Who killed the little whore? And why, for God's sake? She was good for nothing except spreading her legs."

Boone drew and sent a slug into the man's forehead. The lead blew out the back of the man's head, showering hair, brains. Half the people in the saloon jumped. Several women screamed. Some were too stunned to move. Others, aghast, wiped at their spattered clothes.

Boone slid the Colt into his holster and faced the man with the Hopkins & Allen. "Your turn."

The man could not take his eyes off his partner. He also could not stop saying, "Jesus! Jesus! Jesus!"

"Where is Condit?"

The man licked his lips and held out his hands. "You just hold on! You just by God hold on!"

"Condit?"

"Honest to heaven, I don't know!" the man said, shaking now, his face twitching as if he were on the verge of a fit. "He does not tell us where he will be every minute of the day."

"Did you like her?"

"Who? Lucy? Sure I liked the little—" The man stopped and glanced at his dead friend, and his Adam's apple bobbed. "Sweet gal. I liked her a lot. Shared drinks with her now and then. She talked about her folks a lot. They live back East somewhere. Have a farm, I think she said."

"They are dead."

"What?"

"You lied."

"Please!" the man screeched, and frantically tore at the buckle to his gun belt. "I don't want to die! I never did anything to Lucy! It was Condit. He sweet-talked her and got her good and drunk and had his way with . . ." The man's words trailed off. He was caked with sweat. "God in heaven, I am stupid."

"Did you try to stop him?"

"What

"Did you try to save Lucy Fuller from Condit?"

"He's my boss. I have no right to tell him what to do. He tells me."

"That is not what I asked you," Boone said quietly. "Did you try to stop him from violating Lucy Fuller?"

"Violating?" the man said, and gave a nervous bark. He looked around at the faces fixed on him and then at Boone. "You are fixing to blow out my wick, aren't you? Oh God, oh God, oh God." His eyes rolled up in his head and his arms fell at his sides and he fainted.

Someone laughed.

Boone surveyed the room. "Anyone else here work for Condit? Don't be bashful. Speak up."

Apparently no one did.

"Leave," Boone Scott said.

A roulette player nervously coughed. "What did you just say, mister? I am not sure I caught it."

"Leave. All of you. Now."

"Who do you think you are?" a dice player asked.

"There is only one of you and fifty to sixty of us," said a man at the craps table.

"You can't shoot all of us," was the opinion of a man at the wheel of fortune. "You are the one who should skedaddle before more of Condit's hired help show up."

Just then one of the bartenders heaved up from behind the bar with a scattergun. "Out of my way!" he bawled at several drinkers who flung themselves at the floor.

Boone's ivory-handled Colt was already up and out. His slug blew apart the bartender's left eye and burst out the rear of his cranium in a shower of grisly bits and pieces. A bottle behind the bartender shattered and a hole appeared in the mirror.

In the stunned silence that followed, a man exclaimed in horror, "The boy is a natural born killer!"

Shock had piled on shock so that now a few people were drifting toward the batwings. Once they moved, others joined them, so that within seconds a mass exodus was under way. An orderly exodus, until some started to shove, and the people they shoved went and shoved back. Soon everyone was pushing and yelling and cursing.

The saloon emptied.

Boone stood all alone in the quiet and listened to the tick of the clock. He surveyed the bodies and then noticed a gray-haired faro dealer who had not left. The man had his hands in the air but appeared otherwise unconcerned. "You were supposed to go."

"I must stay at this table until quitting time. It is my job."

"Is it worth your life?"

"You won't blow out my wick."

"What makes you so sure?"

"I am unarmed. So far you have only shot those

who were out to shoot you. Well, except for the idiot who insulted her. But he should not have talked the way he did."

"I regret him," Boone admitted.

"I knew Lucy," the faro dealer went on. "If her folks hadn't died, she would be living a nice life in a nice house somewhere, maybe with them, or maybe with a husband and kids." He sadly shook his head. "That poor girl did not deserve the hand life dealt her."

"She did not deserve to die either."

"That is how things are. Life beats on you and beats on you. You can only take so much and then you turn hard and wonder where is the sense to it all. Whoever made this world has a heart of darkness."

Boone smiled. "Yesterday I would have thought you were loco." The smile died and Boone turned and went down the hall to the first door. He opened it, found the room empty and went to the next. A naked woman and a half-dressed man were on the bed and drew back against the wall in stark fear.

"Don't shoot us, mister!" the woman bleated.

"We heard what was going on," the man said. "I don't know no Lucy and I am kind to females."

The next room was filled with pungent smoke. A woman, fully clothed, lay on her back on the bed, gazing dreamily at the ceiling. She looked at him and smiled a peculiar smile. "How do you do? I am right tickled to meet you." She giggled and raised a long-stemmed pipe.

The next door was to the room Boone had left his brother in. He pushed it open. Three of the four men at the table playing cards glanced over in alarm. His brother merely nodded and crooked a finger.

"Come on in."

Boone entered but kept his back to the wall and sidled to where he could see the other men clearly. "Condit," he said.

Charley Condit was peppered with drops of sweat and had a handkerchief in his left hand. He was holding it so that it bulged in the middle. "What do you want, boy?"

"Why did Sam Jarrott try to kill me?"

"You would have to ask him."

"I can't. He's dead, but you already know that. So are two of his friends and one of your gunnies and a bartender."

"Hell, boy," Condit said. "Do you have any idea how hard it is to get a good bartender? Mixing drinks is a science."

"Stand up."

Epp sighed and put down his cards. "Enough of this." He pushed out his chair. "What has gotten into you, little brother?"

"You did not come to see if I was all right," Boone said. "You had to hear, yet you did not come."

"All I heard was shouting and shooting," Epp said. "I did not know it was you. Now you say you have shot five men? God in heaven, how will Ma and Pa take it? They didn't raise a son of theirs to be a lead slinger."

Charley Condit's handkerchief started to rise, and just like that Boone drew and shot him in the face. The slug smashed Condit's nose and made a ruin of the rest; he oozed onto the table and from there thudded to the floor. The derringer under the handkerchief slid from his lifeless fingers.

The two other men jumped and gaped in fright at Boone and his smoking Colt.

Epp merely nudged Condit with a toe and said, "Six, now. This will break Ma's heart. It surely will."

Boone walked over and gazed down at his gory handiwork with newborn dismay. "What do I do, Epp?"

"Why are you asking me?"

"You are my brother. You care for Ma and Pa as much as I do." Boone swallowed, hard. "This *will* break her heart, won't it? Pa's too, I reckon." He gripped his brother's arm. "Please. You have to tell me. What do I do?"

"There is only one thing you can do," Epp Scott said.

The Living Dead

The Circle V continued to prosper, but a shroud of sorrow clung to the owner and his wife.

Ned Scott went through the motions of ranching, but his heart was not in it. Lillian Scott went through no motions at all. During the day she sat in a rocking chair on the porch and gazed longingly and forlornly out over the valley. At night she sat in her rocking chair in the parlor, rocking. She never spoke unless spoken to and she answered in as few words as it took to say what she had to say.

The servants whispered among themselves and avoided her as much as they could. Maria, the cook, took to crossing herself every time Lillian walked past.

Before the Ranson shooting affray, the Circle V was a plum ranch to work at. The pay was better than most, the food stuck to the stomach and the boss knew cattle and did not look down his nose at those under him.

After the Ranson affair, the mood changed. Ned Scott was somber and surly. He never visited the bunkhouse, as he did in the old days, never talked to the punchers except to give orders, never joked and laughed with them as he used to do. He let his foreman, old Dan Morgan, pretty much run things. Morgan respected the men and had their respect in return, but he was troubled, deeply troubled, and grew more so as time went on.

Epp Scott, to the considerable surprise of many, was the cheeriest person on the spread. He smiled more than he used to. He laughed more. He was in such good spirits that two months after he came back from Ranson alone, Dan Morgan approached him one evening over near the stable and cleared his throat. With Dan the throat clearing was always a sign he had something to say.

"What is on your mind?" Epp asked.

"You."

"Me?"

"It might not be my place to say, but you have been acting damned peculiar." Dan Morgan had hair that was almost white, a square jaw and hands as calloused as hands could be from decades of honest work.

Epp had been about to light his pipe, but he lowered it and studied the old man. "You will have to explain. I do not own one of those crystal balls."

"Your brother has become a killer and disappeared. Your ma is close to losing her mind. And your pa is not half the man he used to be."

"Thank you for reminding me of all that. What do you do on parade day? Pray for rain?"

Dan snorted. "That there was a perfect example."

"Of what?"

"Of you joking and acting as if you do not have a

care in the world when your world is falling apart around you."

"I see," Epp said, nodding. "You want me to fall apart like my ma or to lose all interest in life like my pa. Would that make you feel better?"

"Damn it, Eppley, that is not what I said," Dan angrily replied. "All I am saying is that your happy face is out of place. And I am not the only one to think so. Some of the punchers have remarked as much."

"Some of the punchers are biddies who love to gossip." Epp sighed and gazed toward the house. "Listen, Dan. I could let it get to me. I could go to pieces and not give a hoot about anything or turn to drink or you name it. But what good would that do anyone?"

Dan Morgan fidgeted.

"Would it help my ma to recover? Would it help my pa to remember how much the Circle V means to him? No, it would not. All it would do is make matters worse. Is that what you want?"

Dan fidgeted again.

"Of course you don't. No one does. I am trying in my small way to shed some of the gloom. To show that, yes, what my brother did was terrible, but we must run this ranch as it should be run and not crawl into shells like my ma and pa have done."

"So all your smiles are for our benefit?"

"Why else? For my parents most of all. I want them to get over their loss and be as they were."

"That is asking a lot," Dan said. "They love that brother of yours. What he did has crushed them. I will never savvy why he didn't come back with you and own up to his mistake. That boy always struck me as levelheaded."

Epp shrugged. "Who can say why people do what they do? Who can say what made Boone snap?"

"Talk is that a girl was to blame. That he was sweet on her, and for some reason she was shot, and that set him off."

"I doubt we will ever put all the pieces together," Epp remarked. "The important thing is for us to get on with our lives."

"I am sorry I brought it up."

"Don't be. You have the hands to think of. Spread the word. Tell them I do not want to see long faces. Make them understand we can't mope around forever."

The old man promised that he would and headed for the bunkhouse. Epp stared after him, then chuckled and bent his own steps toward the house. He climbed to the porch and gazed to the west. The sun was about to disappear over the rim of the world, and the sky was splashed with brilliant streaks of orange, red and yellow. "Do you like the sunset?"

Lillian did not look up from her rocking. Her jaw muscles twitched, but she did not answer.

Epp went over and squatted next to the rocking chair. "You can't keep this up, Ma."

"Go away."

Laughing, Epp clapped her on the shoulder. "That is the spirit. Treat me like cow droppings. I am not the one who gunned those men down. I am not the one who rode off and left you and Pa."

Lillian's head snapped up and her eyes blazed with a fire they had not had in many weeks. "You should have looked after him. You're the oldest. He was your responsibility."

"He's sixteen, Ma," Epp said. "Practically a full-grown man. What was I to do? Hold his hand the entire time we were in Ranson?"

Lillian's fingers gripped the arms of the rocking chair until her knuckles were white. "What was he doing there anyhow? He never went there before. You are the one who likes that den of iniquity."

"Don't blame me. He wanted to see it for himself. I tried to talk him out of it. I told him you would not approve. But he said he would do as he pleased."

Lillian's eyes narrowed. "That does not sound like Boone. That does not sound like him at all."

Epp rose and placed his hands on his hips. "What are you suggesting, Ma? Say it plain."

Lillian looked down.

"You always did like him more than me. You always have treated him special."

"That is not true."

"The hell it isn't. When we were little, I got ten spankings for every one of his."

"You misbehaved ten times as much," Lillian said, defending her punishments. "You sassed me. You threw fits of temper." She smiled wistfully. "Boone never did any of that. He always did his chores and listened to what I told him."

"The perfect angel," Epp said bitterly. "But that is all right. I don't hold it against you. Every parent has a favorite, I am told. It is my luck that you and Pa both picked Boone."

"We never—" Lillian began, and fell silent.

Epp patted her wrist. "Sit out here awhile yet. I will

have Maria call you when supper is ready." He went inside and closed the door behind him, then leaned against it and grinned. "It is so easy," he said to the air. Squaring his shoulders, he walked down the hall to the kitchen. "How soon until we eat? I'm starving."

Maria was slicing potatoes she had already skinned. "It will be the usual time, Senor Scott."

"Bring my ma in when you set the table so she can wash up." Epp turned to go but looked back. "Any sign of my pa?"

"No, senor," Maria said dutifully. "Not since breakfast. He went out on the range to count the cows."

Epp blinked. "He did what?"

"That is what he told me he was doing, senor."

"But we did a tally at roundup. Why would he want to count the cattle again?"

"He did not say, senor, and I did not ask." Maria dropped potato slices into a pot. "The counting of cows is not something that interests me."

"Remember to get my ma." Epp hurried down the hall to the front door. His hand was on the latch when he changed his mind and retraced his steps to the parlor. The window was open to admit air, as it often was on a summer's eve, and he slipped out without anyone noticing. Instead of going to the front of the house he went to the rear and on past the house and around his mother's lilac bushes. They screened him from the porch long enough for him to reach a gully that presently brought him to within a pebble's toss of the stable.

Epp hunkered and waited. He was not worried about the hands spotting him. Those not out working the range were in the bunkhouse waiting for the triangle to peal so they could hustle to supper. Maria's brother did the cooking for the punchers; his specialty was Mexican food but they didn't mind. As one hand mentioned once, "Food is food and his is damn good."

The sky gradually darkened to gray. Epp consulted his pocket watch and slid it back into his vest pocket. The drum of hooves made him stiffen. He climbed to where he could see over the top of the gully and spied a lone rider trotting toward the corral. The man's face was hid by shadow, but his clothes were familiar, as was his bay with its white stockings.

Epp did not show himself until the man had dismounted and was leading the bay. Careful not to be seen, he came up on the corral from the side. "How was your day, Pa?"

"You," Ned Scott said. "What do you want?"

"I asked you how your day went."

Ned started to strip the saddle, saying, "It went like all the rest have gone since your brother left."

Epp leaned against the corral and folded his arms. "This is tiresome, Pa. Will Ma and you *ever* get over it?"

"When you have a son of your own ask me that." Ned laid hold of the saddle and lifted. "That boy meant the world to me."

"And I don't?"

Ned shot his older son a look of reproach. "I love both of you. I have never favored one over the other. But you have always been more willful than Boone."

"First Ma, now you," Epp said.

"It is true and you know it. I tried and tried to talk

you out of going to Ranson but you wouldn't listen. You like cards and whiskey and the other thing too much."

"The other thing?"

"Don't start with me." Ned placed the saddle over the top rail and reached for the saddle blanket. "I have had a long day and I am not in the mood for your shenanigans."

"Fine. I will talk about something else. What is this I hear about you were out counting cattle?"

"They are my cows. I can count them if I feel like it." Ned led the bay into the corral, removed the bridle and came back out.

"Isn't that what we have a foreman for? Morgan has never miscounted at the roundup, has he?"

"Dan Morgan is as fine a cowman as ever drew breath," Ned said. "What he doesn't know about cows is not worth knowing."

"Then why count them again?"

Ned gripped the saddle and threw it over his shoulder. Carrying the saddle blanket in his other hand, he made for the stable.

Epp went after him, saying, "You haven't answered me."

"I am counting them because of a letter I received," Ned revealed. "A letter from Cramden."

"The cattle buyer for the army? Why would he write to you?"

Ned stopped and faced the spreading darkness to the east. "It seems a man by the name of Hanks offered to sell the army some cattle. Two hundred head. Cramden had this Hanks bring them to be inspected, and at first he thought he was buying a cow-pen herd.

He paid and Hanks rode off. Only later did Cramden take a closer look at the brands." Ned resumed walking. "They had been blotted."

"But what does any of that have to do with us?"

"The brand artist was good, but Cramden was able to make out some of the original brands. By his reckoning, about a hundred of them were Circle V."

"Some of our cattle have been rustled?"

"And now you know why I was out counting today and why I will be out counting tomorrow and the day after tomorrow and for as long as it takes to find out how many the rope and ring man has helped himself to." Ned came to the stable door, and stopped. "If you would like to help, you are welcome."

"You really want me to?"

"What kind of fool question is that? You are my son. When I am gone, the Circle V will be yours. You have as much stake in the ranch as I do."

"I will be happy to help, Pa. It means a lot to me, you asking. Sometimes I get the notion that you don't think as highly of me as I think of you."

"Damn, boy. How many times must I tell you? You mean everything to me. The same as Boone."

"It was wrong of him to run off the way he did. He was ashamed of what he had done, I guess."

"I always credited him with more sense. It goes to show that you just never know about people, not even those closest to you." Ned managed a smile and entered the stable.

Epp wheeled and headed for the house. "Damn you, Blin Hanks," he snarled in a whisper. "Now I have to do it that much sooner."

Sidewinders

It was as hot and dry as a desert, but the ground was rock, not sand.

In the middle of the vast bleakness squatted a structure that the rider mistook for a mirage. It was as brown as the ground and had an unreal aspect, shimmering there in the heat haze as if it had no more substance than the lake he had seen earlier.

The rider shifted uncomfortably in the saddle. His backside was chafed and sore and he yearned to stop and rest, but the compulsion that had driven him to keep on the go was as strong as ever. The sun had burned him so brown that were it not for the color of his hair and eyes, he might be mistaken for an Indian.

Drawing rein, the rider wiped a sleeve across his sweaty brow. He licked his dry, cracked lips and reached for his canteen but stopped himself. "No," he croaked out loud. "I mustn't."

He had taken to talking to himself a lot. He never felt so alone; it helped to hear his own voice. There had been just him and his horse for so many days that the rest of the people in the world might as well be as dead as his past.

The rider touched his spurs to the buttermilk and the weary palomino plodded on, head low.

"I am sorry to put you through this," Boone Scott said.

The building did not dissolve into thin air as Boone approached. Made of planks, it looked like something built by a drunk with a broken hammer and not enough nails. An overhang provided shade for three horses and a mule. None of the animals showed the least interest as the palomino came near. It was too hot to move.

The water trough just out of their reach caught Boone's eye. He eagerly brought the buttermilk over and scowled when he saw that the trough was dry. Tiredly climbing down, he worked the pump lever and was elated when water trickled out. He worked the lever harder and faster and the trickle became as thick as his finger. Cupping some, he gratefully sipped.

"That will be two bits, boy."

Boone turned.

The speaker was a butterball with a face as round as a plate. He had no hair to speak of save for fringe above his ears. His clothes were in as shabby a shape as the building. But there was nothing shabby about the double-barreled shotgun he held. The twin muzzles were pointed at the ground, but his thick thumb rested on one of the hammers.

"Cat got your tongue, boy?"

"Don't call me that."

The man shrugged. "I am easy to get along with. It is why I have lasted as long as I have. But that will still be fifty cents."

"You charge people to drink?"

"It is my water. I found the spring and I built this place and I will by God do what I want with it."

Boone fished in a pocket and flipped the man the money. He tugged on the reins to bring the buttermilk to the trough.

"That will be another two bits for your animal."

Boone looked at him.

"Think what you will of me," the butterball said defensively. "I have to live, the same as everyone else. And not a lot of paying customers come by, as you can imagine."

"Customers?"

The man indicated a sign near the door. The letters were faded but Boone could make them out. PORTER'S SALOON AND STORE, the sign read.

Boone gazed out over the bleak landscape and then at the man with the shotgun.

"I know what you are thinking. I must be crazy, living out here. But this suits me better than a town. I do not like people all that much. I am Ira Porter, by the way."

The buttermilk dipped its head into the trough.

"Fifty cents, remember?" Porter's shotgun started to rise. "The money in advance or your animal can go dry."

Boone's right hand flicked.

"Jesus!" Porter froze, his shotgun not nearly high enough. "Don't shoot me! Please!"

"Take your thumb off that hammer."

"I will do better than that." Porter slowly lowered the shotgun to his side so the stock was on the ground and he was gripping it by the barrel. "There. I can do you no harm."

Boone twirled his ivory-handled Colt into his holster. "You will get your money, but my horse will drink first."

"Whatever you want. I am not about to buck a man who can draw as fast as you can."

Boone resumed pumping, but he did not take his eyes off the butterball. "How long have you lived in this godforsaken spot?"

"Going on twenty years. I was one of the first in these parts."

"The Apaches don't mind?"

"They could have killed me a hundred times over. Six of them showed up shortly after I built the place. I had left the door open and was pouring myself a drink, and suddenly there they were, in the doorway. I about wet myself."

"Yet they didn't kill you."

"I suspect they had been watching awhile, and they were curious. I held out the bottle and one of them came over and took it. Then I did the smartest thing I ever did in my whole life." Porter smiled at the memory. "I had a rifle lying on the counter and I got that Apache to understand it was his if he wanted it. Hell, he could have taken it anyway. I gave him the rifle and I gave him ammunition, and from that day until now, they have let me be. Every now and then a few of them show up and I always give them things so they go away happy."

"You have grit, I will give you that."

Porter was pleased by the compliment. "That will get you a drink on the house if you want one."

"After you." Boone took a step, then stopped and eyed the baked landscape. "Is it safe? My horse, I mean?"

"The Apaches have not stolen one from here in all the years I have been here," Porter assured him. "But once you move on, don't leave your animal alone for a second." He too surveyed the parched terrain. "I don't claim to understand them. They do not think like we do."

Boone followed him in. The place smelled of sweat and booze and smoke. It was not much of a saloon and it was not much of a store either. A long, wide plank atop three upturned barrels served as the bar. To one side were shelves with merchandise, but the pickings were slim: a few blankets, a few canned goods, a few odds and ends. Tables and chairs took up most of the floor space.

At one of the tables sat three men sharing a bottle and playing cards. They looked up, their expressions less than friendly.

"Well, look at this," declared a block of wood with a jaw that would pass for an anvil. "Porter has gone and found a pup."

Porter stopped and frowned. "I wouldn't, were I you, Wagner. He is lightning. As good as Skelman."

All three men regarded Boone with interest. On Wagner's right was a swarthy rodent who had some Mexican in him. He wore a sombrero. On Wagner's left was an ox of a man with a corncob nose and ears that could pass for wings.

"You don't say," the ox rumbled.

The rodent had a laugh that was more akin to a bark. "No one is as quick as Skelman, senor."

"I saw it with my own eyes, Galeno," Porter said. "And I have seen Skelman too, so I should know."

The ox rumbled again, "You don't say."

Porter pointed at him and turned to Boone. "I didn't catch your name, but this big fellow here is Drub Radler."

"Should that mean something?" Boone asked.

Drub and Galeno and Wagner swapped glances and Wagner came out of his chair saying, "Was that an insult, boy?"

"Don't call me that."

Wagner smirked. Galeno sneered. Drub put his big hands flat on the table and said, "Maybe you better not, Wagner."

"Hell." Wagner came around the table. He wore a Bisley revolver on one hip and a bowie knife on the other. "The day I can't handle them this young is the day I turn over a new leaf."

Porter wrung his hands. "I don't want any trouble in here."

"Go polish a glass." Wagner planted his boots as if he was digging them into the floor. "What do they call you, boy?"

Boone did not speak.

"I asked you a question." When Wagner still did not get an answer, color spread from his collar to his hairline. "Maybe you don't know who we are." He gestured at his companions. "We ride for Old Man Radler. Drub, there, is his youngest son."

Drub smiled at Boone.

"Old Man Radler is the top dog hereabouts," Wagner boasted. "He does as he damn well pleases and plants anyone who crosses him. So you will tread light around us, boy."

"I told you not to call me that."

"Do I look like I give a damn?"

"You look stupid enough not to."

The muscles on Wagner's anvil jaw twitched. "I have just explained how things are. We ride for Old Man Radler."

"There is that name again," Boone said. "It means nothing to me." He took a step to the left so Porter was well clear. "Call me a boy one more time. I dare you."

Galeno cackled and smacked the table. "Did you hear, hombre? He throws it in your face."

Drub said, "We should leave him be."

But Wagner was a volcano about to explode. His fingers clenched and unclenched and he showed his teeth in a growl. "For that I will do you myself." His right hand swooped for the Bisley.

Boone drew, cocking the Colt as he cleared leather. But he did not shoot. His trigger finger curled but did not tighten.

"Mother of God!" Galeno blurted.

Drub Radler laughed. "Porter was right. He is Skelman all over again."

Wagner was frozen in shock. The Bisley had barely begun to rise. Splaying his fingers so Boone could see he was not touching the revolver, he held his arms out from his sides. "Hell in a basket."

"Are there going to be any more 'boys' out of you?" Boone asked.

"Not this side of the grave, no," Wagner answered, a note of respect in his voice. "Who are you, if you don't mind my asking?"

"I am no one."

Keen interest animated Wagner as he looked Boone

up and down. "You have enough dust on you to cover this floor. That means a lot of hard riding. And there is only one reason to be riding hard in this heat." He paused. "You are on the dodge."

Boone holstered his Colt.

"That's it, isn't it?" Wagner pressed him. "You are riding the owl-hoot trail. I would not have thought it, as young as you are. But it is plain now. What did you do? Rob a bank?"

"Enough of that," Porter said. "You know better than to pry."

"If he does not want to tell me, he does not have to."

Boone walked to the plank counter and stood so he could watch the three men and the entrance, both. He leaned his left elbow on the counter. His right hand stayed close to his Colt.

Porter ambled around behind the bar. "What will it be, Lightning?"

"That isn't my handle."

"It will do until you give me another. I have seen you draw twice now, and as God is my witness, Lightning fits you as good as anything. Besides, you seem to not want folks to know who you really are."

"You can call me Lighting, then, although it is damned silly." Boone patted his stomach. "Any chance of getting a bite to eat? I am not fussy. Fried lizard will do."

Porter chuckled. "I can do better than lizard. I have a side of beef. How about an inch-thick steak with the trimmings?"

"You are a miracle," Boone said.

"I just like to eat, so I keep my larder filled. Give me ten minutes to fire up the stove." Porter waddled out the back.

Boone went to swipe at the dust on his shirt, but a shadow fell across him. He spun, his hand a blur, then saw that the source of the shadow was holding his big hands in plain sight to show he intended no harm. "What do you want?"

"Just to talk," Drub Radler said. He imitated Boone and leaned on the counter. The planks creaked and sagged. "You and me are about the same age, I reckon."

"What age would that be?"

"I just turned twenty last week," Drub said. "I have an older brother by the name of Vance. He is twenty-four."

"I have an older brother too."

Drub brightened. "That is more we have in common. Do you like horses? I like horses. I like them a lot."

"I have a horse I am powerful fond of."

"There you go." Drub offered his hand. "Can we be friends? I do not have many and I would very much like to be yours."

Boone stared at the big paw and then at the bear it belonged to, and warily shook. "Pleased to meet you. You can call me"—Boone barely hesitated—"Lightning."

"Gosh. That is a good one. I wish my pa had not called me Drub. It sounds too much like dumb."

"What is it you do for a living?"

"Mostly," Drub Radler said, "we rustle and kill people."

Deadly Tally

The butte was a red bull's-eye at the center of a circle of green. It thrust at the blue vault of sky like an accusing finger. The two men searching for cattle were never out of sight of it.

They had been at the tally two days when Dan Morgan came trotting toward them. Ned Scott drew rein, his brow furrowed. "I wonder what Dan is doing out here. He is supposed to be on his way to Tucson to hire new hands."

Epp Scott leaned on his saddle horn and said he was sure he did not know. He stared at their old foreman like a snake would stare at a bird it wanted to eat, then caught himself and plastered a smile on his face.

Dan Morgan started talking before he came to a stop. "So they were right. Chester and Billy said they saw you making a count. I didn't believe them, but here you are with the tally book in your hand." His back became ramrod straight with indignation. "I will quit now and save you the bother of firing me."

"What on earth?" Ned said. "Why would I do that?"

Dan pointed at the tally book. "Because you think I miscounted at the last roundup."

"That is the silliest thing I have ever heard. You are as honest as Daniel Boone."

"Then I am confused."

Ned tapped the tally book with the pencil. "Yes, I am doing a count. But only to be sure our stock is not being rustled."

"The hell you say!" Dan declared. "Why didn't you tell me?"

"You have enough to keep you busy. I intended to let you know when the count was done and I have proof." Ned told him about Cramden, the buyer for the army, and the cow-pen herd that turned out to have blotted brands.

"Hanks, you say?" Dan Morgan pursed his lips. "I seem to recollect a drifter who passed through about a year ago by that name."

"He stopped at the ranch?"

Dan nodded. "I took him for a grub-line rider. He ate at the cook shack and was gone the next morning."

"Anything else you remember about him?"

"I thought maybe he was looking for work, but he told one of our hands that he was on his way to Ranson."

"And that was a year ago, you say?"

"Thereabouts."

Epp pretended to be interested in the news. "Do you reckon this Hanks was passing through our range with an eye to helping himself?"

"Could be," Dan Morgan said. "I will tell our hands to keep their eyes peeled. Strangers are to be confronted, and if they find this Hanks, they are to bring him to me."

"And you are to bring him to me," Ned said. "I do not want you to string him up before I have a chance to question him."

"A hemp social is too good for the bastard. Rustlers are the scum of creation. The only thing worse is a horse thief."

"There are the Apaches," Epp said.

"They have an excuse. I would be fit to kill too if someone was trying to take my land and stick me on a reservation." Dan paused. "No-accounts like Hanks have no excuse. They are money-hungry but too lazy to work for it, so they steal."

"We don't have proof that this Hanks stole any of our cows," Epp noted. "For that matter, he might have bought them from the real rustlers."

"And then resold them to the army?"

"If the rustlers sold them cheap enough to him, he would make a nice profit," Epp said.

That prompted Ned to say, "I hadn't thought of that, son. We shouldn't jump to conclusions. If the ncw tally is short wc will ridc to Ranson and talk to this Hanks."

"Talk, hell," Dan Morgan said.

Ned smiled. "Now that you have solved the mystery, shouldn't you be on your way to Tucson?"

"I will wait for you to get done with the count and then go."

"It is not like you to be contrary. Unless you have a better reason, I must insist. We are two hands short."

"It is on account of your wife," Dan Morgan said.

"What now?"

"She has been crying again. Loud bouts that go on

and on. She doesn't bother to shut the windows and we can hear her, especially late at night. The men don't complain, but it gets to them."

"I thought she was over the worst of it or I would not have stayed away the past two nights," Ned said sadly. "You did right in not leaving. Ride back and keep an eye on her."

"What if—" Dan Morgan swallowed. "What if she goes into hysterics like that one time right after we heard that Boone had shot those men and disappeared?"

"Leave her be. The fit will pass, and after I get back I will take her to visit Doc Baker."

They sat in silence and watched their foreman ride off. Epp was the first to break it, saying, "I will never forgive Boone for what he has done to Ma and you. It was wrong of him to run off like he did."

"I don't care to talk about it."

"I can't help it, Pa. He is my brother. He is your son."

"He is and he isn't," Ned said. "Your ma gave birth to him, the same as she did you, but we did not raise either of you to be killers. To shoot all those people. And then that girl." His voice trailed off.

"I would never have thought it of him," Epp said, adding salt to the emotional wound.

Ned coughed. "Me either. I don't know what got into him. He rode into Ranson and went bad, just like that." He snapped his fingers. "And then he rode out of our lives without a word." He looked at Epp. "Are you *sure* he didn't say anything to you?"

"My ears work fine, Pa."

"Could he have said something that gave some clue but you didn't realize it at the time?"

Epp shammed thinking as hard as he could. "No. Sorry. I have thought about it and thought about it and he did not give so much as a hint."

"All right," Ned said softly. Rousing, he clucked to his sorrel. "Let's get on with the count. The sooner we get this done, the sooner I can comfort your ma."

So far they had counted the cattle on the north side of the butte and the cattle to the west. Now they were south of it, drifting east. Up ahead, the butte's long shadow slashed across the valley. Scattered longhorns, accustomed as they were to cowhands, ignored them.

Epp fell behind his father so he could study the butte without his father noticing. On three sides the butte was sheer cliff. But on the south side, part of the rock wall had buckled ages ago and giant stone slabs crashed onto the valley floor. Many shattered when they hit, but others did not.

Epp nodded to himself, then gigged his mount to catch up. "We should search around the bottom of the butte."

"That can wait." Ned was making for a cluster of twenty to thirty head farther out.

"But we are close to it," Epp said. "Why not search there first and then do the rest?"

Ned considered the suggestion. "I suppose you are right. There might be a few among all that rock." He reined toward the butte. "I want to thank you again for lending a hand."

"I am happy to, Pa."

"I shouldn't tell you this. But your brother has made me so mad, I am considering changing my will."

Another lie tripped glibly off Epp's tongue. "I

didn't know you had one. I just figured that if you and Ma died, everything would go to Boone and me."

"That is what the will says. Your mother had me make it out about five years ago. Now that your brother has turned bad, I am thinking about dropping him and leaving the Circle V to you."

"That wouldn't be fair to Boone, Pa."

"He gave up any claim he had when he turned his back on us."

"I still don't think it is right." Epp paused. "But tell me. If Ma and you were to die, and Boone never comes back, would the ranch fall to me anyway? Without you having to change the will, I mean?"

"I want it in writing so that if he does come back, he can't claim so much as an acre. As soon as this rustling business is settled, we will take your ma to Tucson and while we are there we will visit Shepherd, my law wrangler."

"Maybe we should stop counting and go get the will changed right away," Epp suggested.

"Where would the sense be in that? We are here. We will keep on with the tally."

"Whatever you say, Pa."

They neared the base of the butte. Shattered rock was strewn everywhere. The giant slabs were like so many brown dominoes, lying in a jumble.

"We will split up," Ned proposed. "You go left and I will go right. I will meet you back here when you are done."

Epp reined to the left and rode off. He only went a short way. Then he stopped and shifted in the saddle. The moment his father disappeared around a massive slab, Epp wheeled his mount and trailed him. He kept to a walk and repeatedly rose in the stirrups.

Ned never looked back. He scoured the ground for tracks and checked behind monoliths.

Epp came to where a column of rock twenty feet high and fifty feet long lay on its side. It had buckled in the center when it fell, leaving a gap wide enough for a rider. Ned had gone through the gap. But Epp didn't. Drawing rein, he swung down and led his horse into shadow.

Epp stepped to the gap. On the left the stone had broken cleanly; there wasn't so much as a fingerhold. But on the right were cracks wide enough for his hands and boots. He searched the ground and a chunk of rock about the size of a small melon, with a jagged edge, caught his eye.

It was awkward to climb with the rock in one hand, but Epp managed. He climbed until he was ten feet up. Carefully turning, he jammed his boots into suitable cracks.

Now all Epp could do was wait. The breeze had died and the air was a furnace. He felt slick with sweat. He listened but did not hear the sound he wanted to hear.

A small ant came scuttling across the slab toward him. Epp paid it no mind until a second, larger ant came hurrying after the first. The larger ant quickly overtook the smaller. They merged, antennae waving. The mandibles of the larger ant opened and closed and the smaller ant no longer had a head.

Epp grinned in amusement. "You are me," he said to the large ant. Then he reached over and crushed it with the rock.

The minutes dragged.

Epp licked his lips and swallowed, but he did not have much spit. He spied a Gila monster moving from under one slab to another. In the distance several buzzards flew in circles seeking carrion to feast on.

Drained by the heat, Epp closed his eyes and sagged. No sooner did he do so than the clatter of shod hooves on rock snapped him alert. He craned his neck toward the gap. The *clack-clack-clack* grew louder. The head and neck of his father's horse poked out of the gap and then his father came through, so close that Epp could have kicked him if he wanted. Instead, Epp launched himself into the air. He timed his blow just right and brought the jagged rock smashing down on top of his father's head.

Ned cried out and flung his arms skyward. His horse, startled, bolted, and Ned tumbled to the earth and was still.

Epp came down hard on his hands and knees. Pain speared his left leg, but he gritted his teeth and moved to his father's side. Bending, Epp rolled him over. He started to smile, but the smile died a stillbirth as his father's Colt blossomed before his eyes.

"What are you doing, Pa?"

"Son?" Ned said weakly. A scarlet halo was spreading from under his head.

"What happened? It felt like something fell on me." Ned groaned and trembled and started to lower the revolver.

"It was a rock, Pa." Epp snatched the Colt from his father's grasp.

"What are you doing?" Ned could not seem to stop shaking.

"I wouldn't want you to shoot me. Not after all the trouble I just went to."

"What was that?" Ned blinked, then shook his head as if to try and clear it. Drops of blood flew every which way. Gasping for breath, he stared up at Epp. "What is that in your hand?"

"Your six-shooter."

"In your other hand."

"The rock I smashed your skull with."

"Oh God." Ned moaned and got his hands under him, but the highest he could rise was to his elbows, and that cost him so dearly, he sank down, spent. "This can't be happening."

"Just lie there and die. It shouldn't take too long. I can see your brain through the bone."

Tears welled in Ned's eyes. He tried twice to speak but could only gurgle. Finally he managed, "Why, Epp? In God's name, why?"

"For the same reason I advised Boone that if he came back it would break your hearts. I want the Circle V. I was content to wait a few more months to make my move, but then you went and had to do a tally. You forced my hand. I couldn't let you find out that I had a hand in the missing cattle."

"No, no, no."

"I'll tell everyone a rattler spooked your horse and your horse threw you." In mock sorrow Epp added, "I did all I could but you were too far gone."

Ned used the last of his fading strength to croak, "Your mother! What about her?"

"Don't you worry, Pa," Epp said. "She will join you directly."

Border Ruffians

There were exactly ten of them.

Ten riders who swept out of the night toward Porter's, ten tough men on ten tired mounts. Their slickers and hats and boots were caked with dust. In the pale starlight they appeared to be gray. An onlooker could be forgiven for thinking they were the Confederacy, risen anew. But there were no onlookers. Not in this wild land, at this time of night.

They thundered up on Porter's and climbed down. One of the ten stayed with the horses. One of them always stayed with the horses. It was a rule set down by their leader, and they never broke his rules. Never, ever.

It was their leader who barreled inside ahead of the rest, their leader who nodded at Drub and Wagner and Galeno. Their leader who stopped cold at the sight of the stranger at the table, their leader who said something out of the corner of his mouth that resulted in the rest spreading out as they entered so that they ringed the table and those sitting at it.

"What the hell is this, boy?"

"It is good to see you again, Pa," Drub Radler said.

"I asked you a question."

Drub smiled and gestured. "This here is my new friend. We call him Lightning."

A dust-covered scarecrow next to the leader snorted. He was tall and razor thin and wore a black slicker. Under it were a black shirt and black pants and black boots. Even his belt was black leather. A belt with two holsters that sheathed black-handled Colts. The grips were mother-of-pearl, about the rarest type on the frontier, or anywhere else. Those grips told anyone who was gun savvy that the two Colts were custom models, made to fit the man. And a man who went to that much trouble was more than likely to be more than uncommonly good with them.

The leader scowled. "You know I don't like you making friends without my say-so. I have half a mind to throw him out."

Galeno quickly said, quite politely, "I wouldn't, were I you, Senor Radler."

"No?"

"No, senor," Galeno said. "Not this one." He said those three words with great feeling. Then he looked at the rider with the mother-of-pearl Colts and he said very deliberately, "Not even you should think of doing it, amigo."

That shook them. You could see that it shook them. They glanced at one another and shifted uneasily.

"Is that a fact?" the man with the mother-of-pearl Colts said, and he sounded skeptical.

It was Wagner who answered. "It is more of a fact than any fact you ever knew, Skelman."

The leader studied the boy called Lightning. He might be sixty, he might be fifty; he never said, and no one had the gall to ask. Gray hair poked from under his hat, and his chin was speckled with salt and pepper. But the gray was deceiving. He was not in any way old. His body was well muscled and as durable as rawhide, and when he moved, his movements were those of a man ten to twenty years younger. "I am called Old Man Radler. I reckon you've heard of me."

"No," Boone Scott said.

The rider on the other side of Old Man Radler cracked a grin. He was undeniably handsome, with a shock of black hair and blue eyes the ladies swooned over. "I reckon you're not as famous as you think you are, Pa."

"Shut the hell up, Vance," Old Man Radler snapped, and scratched his salt-and-pepper chin.

Porter came over, wiping his hands on his dirty apron. "What can I get you gents?"

Old Man Radler rounded on him. "What the hell is this?" He did not explain the "this." He did not have to.

"It is a free country," Porter said.

"Don't give me sass. I don't like it when someone gives me sass."

Vance Radler grinned. "He sure don't."

"And I don't like being threatened." Porter held his ground. "Kill me, and where will you stop on your trips to and from the border? Kill me, and where will you get your whiskey and ammunition and whatever else you need without having to look over your shoulder?"

"I would not push it," Old Man Radler said. "You are immune, but you are only immune so far."

Porter nodded at Boone. "He rode in and wanted

a drink, the same as everyone else. I did take my shotgun to him, but he draws faster than I can cock it."

That shook them anew. All of them studied him, the man called Skelman with intense interest.

"Tonight of all nights," Old Man Radler said, and turned back to his youngest. "What exactly do you aim to do with this new friend of yours?"

"I was thinking he could join us," Drub said eagerly but uncertainly. "I haven't had a friend since I was ten and my dog died. Remember my dog, Pa? Remember how he would lick me and play with me?"

One of the other riders laughed in scorn. "God, what a simpleton."

To an onlooker it might have been surprising that Old Man Radler did not tell the man to shut up. Or that Vance Radler did not speak in his brother's defense. But the biggest surprise was when Boone Scott stood. They all saw the ivory-handled Colt then, and a tense air gripped them.

"Say you are sorry."

The man who made the comment was astounded. He was of middle height and compact of build, and he favored a Smith & Wesson worn butt forward on his right hip. "What?"

"You heard me. Apologize to Drub."

"Like hell."

Drub tugged at Boone's sleeve. "He doesn't have to, Lighting. I am used to talk like that. Barnes does it all the time, but he is not the only one."

"We are pards now, aren't we?" Boone said.

Beaming, Drub declared, "Yes, we are. Real and true pards."

"Then he will say he is sorry."

Barnes looked at Old Man Radler. "Are you just going to stand there and let this pup get away with this?"

Old Man Radler glanced at Skelman, who was still studying Boone. "Are we?"

"I want to see him do it," Skelman replied.

Vance Radler laughed. "We sure do stand up for each other, don't we?"

"I won't tell you again to watch that mouth of yours," Old Man Radler warned.

Barnes shifted his weight from one foot to the next and seemed to come to a decision. "You better sheathe your claws, boy. I have killed more than my share."

Boone waited.

"As for saying I am sorry, not now, and not ever. Everyone knows Drub was born simpleminded."

Boone waited.

"In case no one told you, we are the Radler gang, and we don't back down to anyone."

"I was not talking to the rest of your gang," Boone said. "I was talking to you. Either say it or turn tail."

"Why, you miserable snot," Barnes snarled, and his hand swept toward his Smith & Wesson.

The nickel plating on Boone's ivory-handled Colt flashed in the lamplight and thunder boomed.

Barnes staggered back with a new hole between his wide eyes. The Smith & Wesson had barely started to rise from its holster when the shot rang out. His legs buckled and he fell to his knees and slowly keeled onto his side.

"Jesus!" a rider breathed.

Boone twirled the Colt into his holster and turned to Drub. "From here on out, no one insults you when I am around. Pards stick up for each other."

"Pards stick," Drub repeated, and grinned like a kid just given a handful of candy. Facing his father, he said, "Did you see, Pa? Didn't I tell you he is my friend?"

"Son of a bitch," Old Man Radler said.

Vance was agog at the development. "I saw it but I don't believe it. Barnes was no slouch."

All eyes swung to the man called Skelman, who stepped up to the table. "Lightning, is it?" No scorn or ridicule laced his tone. It almost held respect.

Boone shrugged. "It will do as good as any other."

"I am top leather slapper in this outfit. It is not brag, it is fact."

"He is a crack shot," Wagner interjected. "The best I ever did see and I have been about everywhere."

Skelman shifted toward Porter. "Fetch half a dozen empties."

"Hold on," Porter said. "Where do you intend to do it? Outside is better. I don't want holes in my walls."

"They already have holes, and it is dark out." Skelman paused. "Do I have to tell you twice?"

"No, sir." Porter hastened toward the bar.

Drub was gnawing on his lower lip, but he stopped to say, "You're not fixing to shoot my new friend, are you, Skelman?"

"No, Drub."

Drub said to Boone in a half whisper that everyone heard, "I like him, Lightning. He never talks mean to me like the rest do. But he is scary."

"Scary how?" Boone asked.

"He can kill anything. Men, women, even babies. I saw him kill a whole litter of kittens once."

Boone turned to Skelman. "Babies?"

"We came on some wagons that were hit by Apaches. The baby had an arrow in its belly, but it was still alive. I put it out of its misery."

"And the kittens?"

"I hate cats."

"He shoots real good," Drub said. "Pa says he is the best who ever lived."

Porter returned with an armload of bottles. "Where do you want these?" he asked unhappily.

"Put them on a table over by the far wall," Skelman directed. "Line them up in a row."

Scowling, Porter swung toward the others. "Any of you want to help move a table? My hands are full."

No one responded.

"A free drink for those who lend a hand."

Six men sprang and grabbed the table. Two others tried to take hold but were shouldered aside.

Vance Radler hooked his thumbs in his gun belt and swaggered up to Boone. "That business about the insults. It does not apply to me. I am his brother and I will insult him as I please."

"He insults me more than anyone," Drub said.

"It goes for you the same as everyone else." Boone motioned at the crumpled ruin that had been Barnes. "When you feel the urge, think of him. It might help."

"Damn you. Drub is my brother."

"Then you should be nice to him."

"Nice?" Vance blurted, and cackled. "What the hell are you? A Good Samaritan?"

"I am this," Boone said, and patted his Colt.

Now it was Skelman who laughed. Several of the others glanced sharply around, as if they had never heard him laugh before. "Damn, Lightning. You remind me of me when I was your age."

Vance could not let it drop. "I do not like being told what I can say. I do not like it one little bit."

"Feel free to object," Skelman said, and laughed some more.

Old Man Radler had been unusually quiet, but now he stepped forward. "Better rein in that temper of yours, Vance. We have a job to do soon and I cannot afford to lose anyone else."

"Hell."

Old Man Radler thoughtfully regarded Boone. "I like to take a while to judge whether a man is dependable or not, but you have cost me a man and you claim to be Drub's friend so—"

"There is no claim about it," Boone broke in.

"All right. But he goes where I go, and if you want to go where he goes, then you have to join us. And by join I mean you do what I say, when I say, and kill who I say when I want you to kill. And you need to make up your mind here and now. What will it be?"

Just then Porter hollered, "The bottles are all set up. Just don't blow holes in my table, damn it."

Skelman crooked a finger at Boone and they moved to the middle of the room. Setting himself, Skelman swept his slicker back. "When I give the word. You take the three on the right and I will take the three on the left."

"There is no need to do this."

"There is for me if not for you. Don't hold back. Give it your all." Skelman's voice cracked like a bull-whip. "*Now*."

No one saw their hands move. Blurred motion was all.

Skelman drew both of his revolvers simultaneously, each hand equally swift, and his were out and up even as Boone's Colt rose. Six shots thundered and six bottles shattered.

"Wheeeooo!" Wagner cried.

"I never saw the like!" another man exclaimed.

"They tied!" a third said.

"No, Skelman was a shade faster."

"You're loco."

Old Man Radler strode over and said brusquely, "Enough of this tomfoolery." He focused on Boone. "It is time to decide. What will it be? Are you with us or not?"

"Count me in," Boone Scott said.

For Want of Breath

The funeral was grand.

Lillian Scott roused from her emotional lethargy to take charge. She spared no expense on the coffin. She insisted it be of the best wood and have red velvet inside. She also demanded that a red pillow be placed under her husband's head.

Tucson was a day's ride by carriage or buckboard, so the guests had to stay the night. The evening after the burial, Lillian arranged a feast. She had Maria, her cook, call on Maria's sister and cousins and an uncle for help. The dishes were a mix of Mexican and gringo, as Maria liked to call them.

Tables were set up outdoors and everyone was invited to partake. Burying their friend and neighbor had put them in a somber frame of mind, and no one touched the food. Hardly anyone spoke.

Lillian solved that. Dressed all in grave black, she went from table to table, insisting they get up and help themselves and have a good time.

Over a dozen ranchers attended. So did a score of townspeople. Almost all the punchers were present. A band provided music, and to the astonishment of many,

Lillian proceeded to dance and laugh and be as gay as she could be. More than a few thought it strange that she made merry so soon after losing her husband, but they were too polite to say anything.

Epp Scott mingled freely. He too was in good spirits. He smiled as he shook hands and smiled as he was offered condolences. But he did not smile when, midway through the evening, Dan Morgan marched up to him.

"What in hell has gotten into you and your mother?"

Epp took a step back, his glass of whiskey half-raised. He looked around to make sure no one had overheard. "I beg your pardon?"

"We buried your pa not three hours ago, and here you are drinking and carrying on. And your mother!" Dan glared at where Lillian was doing a lively fandango. "I swear. If I live to a hundred I will never understand women."

Epp lowered his glass. "You overstep yourself."

"Do I?" Dan Morgan said gruffly. "I have been foreman since the Circle V started. Your pa was more than my boss. He was my friend. Maybe the best friend I ever had. To see his memory treated this way makes my blood boil."

"Does it, now? Then maybe I should set you straight on a few things. My pa was your best friend. Well and good. But he was my *father*. No one loved him more than me. No one respected him more than me. His death was stupid and senseless and it makes me sick inside just to think about it."

"Thrown from his horse," Dan said in disbelief. "I would never have thought it possible."

"Accidents happen. I blame myself, partly. If I had

been at his side, maybe I could have prevented it. Maybe I could have grabbed hold of his bridle or caught hold of him when his horse reared."

Dan Morgan softened. "Don't be so hard on yourself. Like you said, accidents happen. I have seen more men thrown and hurt than I care to count. It is just bad luck that your pa fell on his head."

"One of those things," Epp said.

"Peculiar how things work out. Your pa was as fine a rider as I ever saw, yet he dies when his horse is spooked by a rattler." Dan paused. "You say you actually heard the snake?"

"I will never forget the sound for as long as I live. I wasn't more than twenty feet away, but I couldn't get to him in time."

"Still," Dan said. "All this laughing and dancing."

"What would you have us do? Wallow in misery?"

"No, but—"

"Look at Ma. Her heart broke when Boone went off and left us. Day after day, all she has done is sit in a chair with tears in her eyes."

"Now your pa dies and she is her old self. Where is the sense in that?"

Epp watched his mother whirl at the end of the Tucson mayor's arm. "If I had to guess, I would say that Pa's death shocked her out of her shell. Come morning, she will probably be a wreck. But right now she is showing everyone she was proud to be Pa's wife. She is being strong like he would want her to be."

"I never thought of it like that."

"No hard feelings," Epp said. "I'm just glad you came to me and not to Ma. It would not take much to bring her down."

Dan Morgan went to walk off. "I will come see you tomorrow so we can talk over how the ranch is to be run now that your pa is gone."

"What is there to talk about? Pa is dead. Boone is gone. Ma is a woman. That leaves me. From now on, the Circle V will be run the way I say it is to be run. Any of our hands who doesn't like it is free to gather up his plunder and his war bag and light a shuck for wherever he wants."

"You don't have to worry about punchers quitting on you," Dan said. "They are loyal to the brand."

"But will they be loyal to *me*?"

"Why wouldn't they? I'll be the first to admit that Boone was more popular. But only because you tended to keep more to yourself and seldom mingled with the punchers like he did."

"That will change." Epp clapped Dan on the back. "All I ask is that you give me the same consideration you gave my pa. I can't fill his boots, but I will do the best I can. You have my word on that."

Deeply touched, Dan clasped Epp's hand. "And you can count on me to back you in anything you do."

"I am obliged." Epp watched the old foreman thread through the crowd, then chuckled and said to himself, "There is a jackass born every minute." Tipping his glass to his mouth, he smacked his lips and joined those watching the dancers.

The fandango was soon over. Epp applauded with everyone else, and while his mother was catching her breath, drifted over. "That was some heel kicking you did, Ma."

Lillian had a black fan and was briskly fanning herself. "I have not done that in years. Your father did not like to dance."

"Let's hope he is not rolling over in his grave right about now." Epp cupped her elbow and steered her toward a table where the drinks were being served. "How are you holding up?"

"I don't rightly know how to explain it."

"Try."

"I am sad and giddy at the same time. Sad to the depths of my soul that Ned is gone. I loved that man, son. I loved him more than I have ever loved anyone or thing. And now God has seen fit to take him from me."

Epp recollected a quote from somewhere. "The Lord works in mysterious ways."

"Exactly." Lillian patted his hand. "You know, Eppley, I am seeing a new side to you, and I like what I am seeing."

"A new side?"

"You have always been the black sheep of the family. Always went your own way. Did what you wanted to do, not caring one whit what your pa or me thought. Take Ranson, for instance."

"My days of gambling and drinking all night are over."

Beaming happily, Lillian squeezed his hand. "I am so glad to hear that. And so sad at the timing."

"How do you mean?"

"Here you have finally grown up and want to do good, and your brother has gone bad."

"I am sure Boone had his reasons for killing all those people."

"It is decent of you to defend him. But he has cut me to the quick and I don't know as I can ever recover."

"You are doing fine tonight."

"I want to honor your father with joy in my heart, not sorrow. Is that wrong of me?"

"Not at all, Ma," Epp said. "Just be careful you don't overdo it. You are not as young as you used to be." He smiled and walked off. He had not gone far when a hand fell on his shoulder.

"I want to offer my condolences, Eppley."

"Doc Baker. Having a good time?"

Baker was white haired and had kindly blue eyes, and never went anywhere without his black bag. He was holding it now. "As good as I can in light of the circumstances. I liked your father. I liked him a great deal."

"Didn't we all?" Epp glanced around, then leaned close and said, "While I have you here, I want to let you know I am worried about my mother."

"What? Why?"

"Have you seen how she is acting?"

"She is doing what she can to cheer everyone up. I call that commendable."

"Not that," Epp said. "I was just talking to her and she complained of chest pains. Has she said anything to you?"

"Chest pains?" Doc Baker said in alarm. "Perhaps I better go talk to her."

"And spoil her mood?" Epp grabbed his arm. "I will bring her into Tucson in a few days and you can examine her then."

"How bad were these pains?" Doc Baker inquired.

"According to her, not bad at all. She thinks it is the stress. But I want to be safe and bring her in to see you."

"By all means." Doc Baker smiled in approval. "I must say, you have risen to the challenge of being the new master of the Circle V quite admirably."

Epp continued to mingle until near eleven, when the band stopped playing and the guests who had not already done so retired. He made it a point to happen on Doc Baker as the aged physician was about to go in, and to say so only the doctor heard, "I will check on my ma before I turn in and make sure she is feeling all right."

"You do that," Doc Baker said.

Epp refilled his glass and relaxed on the settee until the voices and the patter of feet faded and the house was as still as a tomb. Maria came from the kitchen and asked if there was anything else he wanted before she went to bed. He told her no, and remarked that he was going to stay up awhile yet.

The instant Maria was out of sight, Epp set down his glass and hurried to the stairs. He went up them three steps at a bound. The upstairs hall was empty. He glided to his parents' room, quietly opened the door, slipped through and quietly closed the door behind him.

"Who's there?"

Lillian was in bed. She lay with her head propped on a pair of large pillows and a blanket as high as her chin. A lamp, the wick turned low, was on the small bedside table. She reached for it, saying, "I need more light."

"It is only me, Ma," Epp said quickly. Smiling his

best smile, he went over and sat next to her. "I came up to see how you are doing."

"My, my," Lillian said. "I can't recall the last time you were so thoughtful. You never came in here when your father was alive."

"I respected your privacy." Epp put his hand on hers. "How are you feeling?"

"Tired, son. God-awful tired. I hardly slept a wink last night and I was on the go all day."

"You did fine. Pa would be proud."

"What is to come of us, Eppley? Your brother, vanished. Your father, dead. There is just the two of us now. I need your help. I can't run the Circle V by my lonesome."

"I don't expect you to. Don't worry. Thanks to Pa, I know all there is to know about ranching."

"Yes, you do," Lillian said. "And the first thing you must tend to are those rustlers. Your pa was convinced a brand artist is working our range. He even suspected—" She stopped. "No, I shouldn't say without proof."

"What did Pa suspect, Ma? It would help me to know."

"He thought someone here on the Circle V must be in cahoots with them. It is the only way they could take so many of our cattle without us catching on."

"Pa thought that?"

"Yes. We talked about it a few days before he died."

"I'll be damned," Epp said, and then realized what he had said. "Sorry, Ma, for the strong language. What else did Pa tell you?"

"That we should set a trap for the rustlers. We should bunch the cattle so the rustlers have to show themselves to steal some, and when they do, we will have them."

"Pa was smarter than I thought."

Lillian smiled sweetly. "He would be proud to hear you say that. It meant a lot to him, you standing by us when your brother ran off." She made a teepee of her hands. "Lord, watch over my Boone and bring him back to us." Suddenly Lillian grasped Epp by the wrist and pulled him toward her. "You must find him, Epp. You must send men out. Have them cover the whole territory. They are bound to find him, and when they do, they are to let him know we will welcome him back with open arms."

Epp reached around behind her and took one of her pillows and placed it in his lap. "Let me fluff this for you."

"Did you hear me?"

"Yes, Ma. I heard." Epp squeezed her shoulder. "But you shouldn't get worked up like this."

"I can't help it. I am so distraught over Boone, I can't think straight. Promise me you will do as I asked. Promise me you will leave no stone unturned to find him."

Epp chuckled. "Funny that you should mention a stone."

"What? Why?"

"Oh, no reason." Epp bent and kissed her on the forehead. "All in all you have been a good mother. It's not your fault."

"What isn't? Your brother running away?"

"Sometimes people do not turn out as everyone expects. They try and they try, but they just don't see the sense to living like sheep when they are a wolf."

"I don't understand."

"You don't need to. All you need to know is that I am sorry your heart could not take the strain. I am sorry it burst and you died in your sleep, and there was nothing anyone could do."

"What are you talking about?"

"This," Epp Scott said, and jammed the pillow over her face.

Border Ruffians

Hard men in a hard land.

They thundered south, riding with an assurance born of experience and a belief in their own invincibility. No one spoke. No one joked or even smiled except for Drub, who every now and then glanced at Boone Scott and grinned.

The border they were bound for was not much of a border. It was not much of anything besides an imaginary line on a map that divided the country to the north from thc country to thc south. On a map thc border existed, but in reality there were no guards or markers or any signs to show that north of the line was one country and south of the line was another.

The hard men had crossed back and forth so many times that they knew exactly where the border was. They knew it was rarely patrolled, and the times those rare patrols took place. They knew that to the people and government of Mexico, they were gringos. Worse, they were notorious desperados, killers and horse thieves. Men without souls.

The purpose for this raid was to help themselves to a lot of horses. As Old Man Radler explained to

Boone before they left Porter's, "Horse stealing is my bread and butter. I have buyers on this side who will buy all I can get from the other side."

"Do the buyers know the horses are stolen?"

Old Man Radler had given Boone a strange look. "What kind of question is that? Sure they know. So what? They get the horses for less than if they bought them on this side, and I make a profit since I get the horses for free."

"How do the Mexicans feel about you helping yourself?"

"About as you'd expect. Which means you could have your brains blown out if you're not careful. You might be as fast as Skelman, but speed does not make you bulletproof." Old Man Radler had glanced at Drub. "Since my son has taken a shine to you, Lightning, I will give you a word of advice. Be like a cat in a room full of dogs. Have eyes in the back of your head. Because if you don't, I can guarantee you won't make it back."

They rode at night and lay up during the day. It was night when they crossed the border. They always crossed at night and then rode back in broad daylight so they could see whether the Mexicans were after them.

Ten more miles brought them to the Menendez Rancho. One of the oldest and biggest in all Mexico, the Menendez family were famed far and wide for the quality of their horses. They raised the finest anywhere, and were protective of those they raised.

The patriarch of the family, Anastasio Menendez, hired only the top vaqueros. To qualify, a vaquero had to be good with a *caballo* and good with a reata and good with a pistol. That last was important. They had to be very good with a pistol because the vaqueros on the Menendez Rancho were fighting vaqucros.

They fought off Indians, and they fought off anyone who thought they could help themselves to Menendez land, but mostly they fought off rustlers.

This was imparted to Boone by Vance Radler when they came to a ridge overlooking grassy lowland broken by arroyos and sprinkled with mesquite. "I don't much like greasers," Vance concluded, and then grinned at Galeno. "But I sure as hell have a healthy respect for the Menendez vaqueros. If they see you they will shoot on sight, and you better be damn quick shooting back or you will be damn quick dead."

Drub was listening. "Don't you worry about my friend, Vance. He can take care of himself."

"He can shoot bottles," Vance said. "But bottles do not shoot back. How do we know he can handle this?"

Skelman was listening too. "Idiot," he said.

That shut Vance up.

Old Man Radler waved an arm and they descended to the flatland, riding at a walk with their hands on their revolvers, and peering every which way. Dawn was still an hour and a half off and without the moon they might as well be at the bottom of a well.

"This always spooks me," Drub whispered to Boone.

"Hush, you infant," Vance snapped.

Old Man Radler twisted in the saddle to glare at both of them. His mouth worked, but he did not vent the cusswords he plainly wanted to utter. His meaning, though, was clear: *Open your damn mouths again and you will by God answer to me!*

They did not open their mouths again.

It was half an hour before lights appeared. Not

many but enough to tell Boone that they were close to the Menendez hacienda.

Old Man Radler reined to the west and led them another half mile. Drawing rein, he raised an arm and the rest did the same. He motioned at Galeno, who went on ahead. In five minutes Galeno was back. He whispered in Old Man Radler's ear, and Old Man Radler turned.

"This is it, boys. The herd is where we thought it would be. Five hundred or more."

"Are we taking all of them?" Boone asked.

"I wish to hell we could. But we will be lucky if we get half. A dozen vaqueros are riding herd and over thirty more are camped nearby."

"That is a hell of a lot of vaqueros," Wagner said. "Menendez keeps hiring more all the time."

"From here on out, no slacking. All of you know what to do. Lightning, this is your first time, so stay close to Drub. And, Drub, you remember that the vaqueros will be out to kill you. The last time you nearly got a bullet in your brain."

"I'll remember, Pa."

"Good. Let's go."

They moved as silently as their creaking saddles and the dull thud of hooves allowed. Soon they spied the herd, a mass of horseflesh at rest in a broad open area. Around the perimeter rode men in sombreros, the silver conchas on their gun belts, and the silver on their saddles gleaming in the starlight.

Old Man Radler rose in the stirrups and let out with a whoop worthy of a Comanche. At the signal, he and his men crashed out of the brush and smashed into the Mexicans. Two vaqueros were shot from their saddles before they could touch their pistols. Then the *americanos* were in among the horses, yelling and whistling and yipping. Predictably, the horses broke, and it was a credit to Radler and his men that they kept a large bunch of the horses together and drove them in a body to the north.

Vaqueros shouted and swore. Gun muzzles blazed and roared. In the camp, vaqueros were scrambling out from under blankets to get to their mounts and take part. A number of them came charging toward the rustlers on foot, firing at anyone who was not wearing a sombrero.

In the midst of it all, Drub Radler giggled.

Boone, bent low, had his ivory-handled Colt in his hand. But he did not shoot. Not even when lead sizzled the air over his head. Or when a vaquero materialized in front of him, frantically reloading. Instead, Boone reined in close and slammed his Colt against the vaquero's temple.

Drub giggled again.

The horses were in full flight, their heads high and their tails flying. As they swept past the camp, vaqueros tried in vain to stop them.

Radler and his men cut the vaqueros down, shooting as fast as targets presented themselves. Some of the rustlers laughed with glee at the death they dispensed. Skelman shot more vaqueros than anyone, but he did not laugh.

Then they were clear of the camp and racing into the night. They rode hard, risking limb and life, but it was either that or have the vaqueros overtake them, and the vaqueros would not show any mercy. When aroused they were formidable, and nothing aroused them more than to have the horses they were guarding rustled out from under them, and to lose amigos they were fond of to the bullets of the rustlers.

Boone had no difficulty keeping up. Every now and again he patted the palomino's neck.

They rode and they rode, and eventually the eastern sky brightened, and dawn broke. Now that they could see, they slowed and checked their back trail for pursuit.

"They aren't after us," Vance marveled.

"They will be," Old Man Radler said.

It was Wagner who exclaimed, "By God, we must have three hundred head or more!"

He was not exaggerating. They had most of the herd.

Old Man Radler smiled and said, "We will do as we did the last time. Skelman, you take care of it."

They had gone three-quarters of a mile when the sharp-eyed among them spotted dust tendrils to their rear. Skelman began bawling names, six in all. Boone was one of those he picked. Drub stopped too, even though he was not one of those chosen.

"What do you think you are doing?" Skelman demanded.

"What my pard does, I do." Drub smiled at Boone.

"Fine. Just don't get yourself killed. Your pa will never forgive me."

Skelman barked orders. They melted into the brush, spreading out and turning their mounts to the south to await the source of the dust.

"Isn't this fun?" Drub whispered to Boone.

Boone made sure no one was close enough to hear

him whisper in reply, "Taking something that doesn't belong to you is wrong."

"You don't like to steal horses? I have been doing it all my life."

"I don't like to steal anything. I was raised different. My folks would have a fit if I did this."

"My pa would have a fit if I didn't. I have to do as he says or he beats the tar out of me."

"You are big now, Drub. You do not need to take that from him if you don't want to."

"Fight my pa? Are you loco?"

"I am beginning to wonder. If someone had told me a year ago that I would join up with the Radler gang and rustle Mexican stock, I would have thought they were drunk."

"But you said you never heard of him before you met me."

"I fibbed. It seemed like the thing to do at the time. I am young, but I like to think I am not stupid."

"Then you must have heard of Skelman too."

"He has a reputation."

"Yet you're not scared of him, like most everyone else. How come?"

"I have never been scared of anything except losing my ma and pa when they grow old."

"I don't get scared much either. Vance says it is because I am too stupid to know what scared is."

"For a brother he is awful mean."

"What about your brother?" Drub asked. "Does he treat you as mean as Vance treats me?"

"We have our spats," Boone said. "We do not see eye to eye on a lot of things. But he has never been as mean as Vance. Mostly, he likes to go off and drink and womanize and play cards, and leaves me be."

"I wish Vance would go off somewhere and never come back."

Hooves drummed. The vaqueros, unaware of the peril, came galloping toward them, following the trail of the stolen horses.

"Don't shoot until I do!" Skelman commanded, but not so loud that the vaqueros would hear.

"Have you ever done this before?" Drub asked. "I have. We shoot them to ribbons and they fall down and get blood all over everything." He cocked his revolver.

"Stay alive, Drub."

"I'll try. I want to go on being your pard. You are the first true friend I ever had and it means a lot to me."

"Just stay alive," Boone reiterated.

"You too."

The vaqueros, bunched together, were almost on them. In the lead was a handsome man with bandoleers crisscrossing his chest. A trimmed mustache adorned his upper lip, and a pistol was on either hip. He was scanning the brush. Suddenly he hauled on his reins and shouted a warning.

Skelman burst into the open, a black-handled Colt in each hand. He cut loose with ruthless precision, thumbing and firing, blasting vaquero after vaquero. The other rustlers followed his example. Drub too broke from cover to send lead into the mass of Mexicans struggling to control their mounts while getting off shots of their own.

Boone stayed close to Drub. He palmed his Colt

and thumbed back the hammer and he did not squeeze the trigger. Not until a pair of vaqueros came charging toward them, banging away, and Drub said, "Ouch!"

Two shots as swift as thought, and Boone sent both vaqueros into eternity. He turned to Drub, who had clutched his shoulder and was grimacing. Quickly Boone grabbed Drub's reins, wheeled their animals and retreated into the brush, pulling Drub after him.

"What are you doing? We can't leave yet."

"You have been hit."

"It's only a scratch. We should go back before my pa finds out. He is liable to be mad."

No sooner did Drub speak than Old Man Radler was broadside in front of them, barring their way. Boone had to draw rein to keep from colliding with him.

Brandishing his revolver, Old Man Radler snapped, "Where in hell do you think you are going?"

"Your son has taken a slug."

Another strange look came over the outlaw leader. "I don't know what to make of you, Lightning." He kneed his animal up next to his son's. "How bad is it? Can you hold out awhile?"

"Sure, Pa. Don't worry about me. And please don't be mad at my pard. He is only trying to help."

Old Man Radler lowered his six-shooter but glared at Boone. "I will overlook you not doing as I wanted, this time. But it could be I will have to kill you before too long."

Ruler of the Roost

The second funeral was not as grand as the first.

Most of the punchers attended, as did Maria the cook and her family and cousins, and seven ladies came from Tucson, but only two of their husbands could make it. There was no band and no feast although Maria did cook supper for those who stayed over.

Epp Scott wore his sorrow like a shroud. Only when no one else was around did he crack a smile or chuckle and once, up in the bedroom where she had died, he hopped into the air and squealed for joy.

Doc Baker remarked over and over how it was a shame, Lillian's heart giving out the way it did. Ned had meant the world to her, and with him gone she wanted to die. "I see it all the time," he told them, and used one of his favorite lines. "The human heart is a fragile thing."

By ten the next morning Epp had the ranch house to himself. He dismissed Maria and the other servants, saying he would like to deal with his grief alone for a couple of days. Much to Dan Morgan's annoyance, he gave the punchers a couple of days off too, after he assured them that despite the recent tragedies, the Circle V would go on as it always had.

Nightfall found Epp at the kitchen table carving a slice of meat from a slab of beef. He was watching the back door and when someone knocked, he said, "Come on in, you lunkhead."

The man who entered never used soap and water. His clothes were filthy, his boots had never seen polish. A slouch hat hung over bushy brows. The revolver on his hip was the cleanest thing about him. "I came all the way from Ranson like you wanted me to, and I am here when you needed me to be, and what do you do? You insult me."

"I will insult you all I want, Hanks," Epp said. "That was sloppy work with Cramden and I will not have sloppy men under me."

"Hell, we changed the brands as good as they could be changed. That army buyer is sharp."

"We have to be sharper."

"I do my best but I am not you. You are hog fat and axle grease rolled into one."

"I did not send for you so you could flatter me," Epp said flatly.

"Why *did* you send for me? I thought you were going to wait awhile before you bared your fangs."

Epp was about to fork a piece of meat into his mouth. "You are dumber than a stump."

"And you are prickly tonight. I only meant that no one on the Circle V has any idea what you are really like. They will be some surprised when they find out."

"You are a lunkhead *and* a jackass."

"Here, now. I will only stand for so much of that kind of talk. If I am doing so poorly, cut me loose."

"I finally have the Circle V all to myself and you want me to throw it away. The foreman and the punchers must never suspect. If they do, they will treat me to a strangulation jig." Epp bit the meat off the fork and jabbed the tines at Hanks. "There will be no baring of fangs until I say, you hear?"

Hanks spread his hands in a gesture of innocence. "When have I ever gone against your wishes? Thanks to you, I stand to make more money than I've made my whole life long. Do you think I would do anything to jeopardize that?"

"Tell it to the army buyer. You are lucky he caught on after you sold those cows to him, and not before."

"I never did savvy what you were up to," Hanks said. "Why have me and the boys rustle your own cows when you could just as well have sold them to the army yourself?"

"My pa did all the selling. Oh, he probably would have let me if I'd asked. But then he would want to know why I needed the money and I couldn't very well tell him I was selling them to make good on a few gambling debts."

Hanks snickered. "So you stole your own cows. Don't you beat all?"

"What did I tell you about the flattery?"

"I can't help it. You have more sand than most ten men."

"I will need it for the next step," Epp said.

"So soon? You just planted your ma."

"Why waste time? I aim to roll in money up to my armpits, and I don't mean five years from now."

"You could sell the Circle V and make a heap of it," Hanks said.

"That there is why you will always take orders and I will always give them. Yes, I can sell. But the money won't last forever, and when it is gone I will have nothing."

"You will still have your holdings in Ranson."

"But they are not respectable. I need the Circle V to help me hide my other activities. In the long run I will make more money by holding on to it than I would by selling it. Which brings us to why I sent for you."

"I am all ears."

"It is time to extend our rustling. Pay the Bar Thirty a visit, and the Box T. Round up as many of their cows as you can. But be damn sure you cover your trail."

"I do not want to get caught. They are salty outfits. But what about your own hands?"

"I am the big sugar now. My punchers will do as I say or they will look for work elsewhere."

"Just so they don't get curious and nose around."

"Let me worry about that."

"Begging your pardon," Hanks said, "but it is my hide they will perforate. I can't help but worry."

Epp began to slice another piece from the side of beef. "How many men have you rounded up?"

"Seven, besides me."

"Good men?"

"If they were good they wouldn't be fit for the job, would they?" Hanks cackled, showing teeth as yellow as pus.

"Warn them against itchy trigger fingers. Rustling is one thing. We can get away with it for a good long while if all we do is steal cows. But kill a rancher and the whole territory will be up in arms. Or you will have the law after you."

"After us," Hanks amended.

Epp scowled as he chewed. "We are lucky Arizona has so few tin stars. If this was Texas, we would have Rangers behind every bush."

"We'll be careful," Hanks promised.

"Off you go. Report to me when you get back. Just come to the back door any night between eight and ten."

Hanks placed his hand on the latch. "I am glad to be working with you. I won't let you down."

"You better not." When the door closed, Epp laughed. He sliced more meat onto a plate, and, taking it with him, he left the kitchen and bent his steps to his father's liquor cabinet. His father had always kept it locked. The key was on a hook next to the cabinet, but no one was to touch it without permission. "Look at me, Pa," Epp said to the ceiling. He opened the cabinet, selected a bottle of Cyrus Noble and deposited his food and drink and himself on the settee in the parlor. Once again he raised a mocking grin to the ceiling. "How about you, Ma? Remember that time you smacked me for eating Saratoga chips in here?"

Epp ate with relish, smacking his lips as his mother would never let him do. He washed each mouthful down with the Noble. He was enjoying himself so much that when a knock came on the front door, he almost didn't answer it.

"I hope I am not disturbing you," Doc Baker said. He had his hat in one hand and his black bag in the other.

"Not at all." Epp stepped aside so he could come in. "I figured you would be back in Tucson by now."

"I was halfway there and turned back." Doc Baker sniffed as he walked past. "Unless I miss my guess, I could ask you for a drink and the bottle would be handy."

Epp slowly closed the door. His brow knitted but otherwise he was composed as he ushered the aged physician into the parlor. "Have a seat, why don't you? I will fetch a glass."

"That is all right," Doc Baker said. Going over, he drank several quick swallows straight from the bottle and set the bottle down again. When he turned, his face was flushed. "I needed that."

Epp crossed to the settee and reclaimed his seat. "What is on your mind, Doc?"

"You."

"Me?"

"Don't bandy words with me," Doc Baker said. "I want to know why, Eppley. Your folks were two of the finest people I know. They were good to you and your brother, and raised you proper. Why did you murder them?"

"Hell," Epp said. "If it ain't chickens, it's feathers."

"Don't try to deny it. You pulled the wool over my eyes for a bit, but I sensed something wasn't right about your father's death and I had my doubts about your mother's."

"So you are accusing me on a guess?"

Doc Baker stepped to a chair and tiredly sank down. "Hear me out, Eppley. That is all I ask."

"I would not make you leave now for anything. I

am not easily surprised, but you have surprised the skin off me."

Placing his left ankle on his right knee, Doc Baker held his black bag in his lap. "I have been a doctor for fifty-two years. Did you know that?"

"I knew it was a long time."

"I have seen all the hurts and wounds and diseases there are. I have mended more broken bones than you can count. I have healed more sores and blisters. I've delivered more babies. In range parlance, I am an old hand at what I do."

"There is a point to this," Epp said.

"Men fall from horses all the time. They break arms, they break legs. Every so often a man lands on his head. Concussions are common. Fractured skulls happen a lot. But it's rare for a man to die from the fall."

"It does happen, though."

"Yes, it does," Doc Baker conceded with a nod. "But here is the thing. In all the falls from horseback that I am acquainted with, not one rider fell on his head the way your father did."

Epp said irritably, "A head is a head. Make sense."

"Bear with me." Doc Baker opened his black bag and took out a large magnifying glass. "Do you know what this is?"

Epp frowned. "What do you take me for?"

"Of course you do. It is not an instrument a doctor uses much, but my eyes are not what they used to be. It helps when I lance a boil or need to stitch a cut." Doc Baker paused. "Or when I examine a wound like your father's."

Epp went on frowning.

"You see, when a man falls from a horse, usually there is a lot of bruising. Your father hardly had any. And when a man takes a tumble like his, usually he lands on the back of his head or on the side of his head or the front of his head, not smack on top of it. For your pa to hit the way he did, he would have to be upside down when he fell."

"You make it sound impossible but it's not."

"True. But then there is the other thing. His skull was caved in a good three inches. I measured it. And with my magnifying glass I found bits of stone embedded deep in the wound."

"So?"

"So you claimed he hit his head on a boulder. Boulders are harder than bone. They don't splinter." Doc Baker fiddled with his bag. "I took your word about how he died. But it bothered me, Epp. I couldn't stop thinking about it. Couldn't stop wondering if maybe he didn't die the way you said he did." The physician took a deep breath. "Then your mother gave up the ghost."

"You told everyone her heart gave out."

"It was the logical conclusion. After all, you told me she was having chest pains. But when I examined her, I saw something in her throat. Something so far down, I almost missed it. I fished it out and didn't say anything, because at the time my doubts had not become a certainty."

Epp clenched and unclenched his fists. "What was in her throat?"

"A feather."

"A what?"

"A feather. The kind you find in a mattress. Or in

a pillow. A feather that had no business being where I found it."

"That is plumb ridiculous. Maybe she swallowed it when she was thrashing around on the bed."

"You said there was no sign of a struggle. She died as peaceful as could be. Your very words."

"I could have been mistaken." Epp picked up the whiskey bottle but put it down again without taking a drink. "All of this amounts to a lot of hot air. I am insulted you think I would do such a thing."

Doc Baker was silent a bit. Then he cleared his throat. "You are right. I can't prove a thing. But I know you did it, and I am going to keep an eye on you from here on out. If anyone else dies under peculiar circumstances, anyone at all, I will take my suspicions to the United States marshal."

Epp started to come up off the settee, but Doc Baker's hand suddenly rose out of his black bag, holding a derringer.

"Stay where you are."

"You are a bundle of surprises, Doc."

"I never go anywhere without this."

"And you, a healer. What would people think?"

Doc Baker rose. "I no longer trust you, Eppley. I will see myself out. Don't try to stop me. Don't come after me. I told several of your funeral guests I was coming back, so if I turn up missing you will get a lot of attention you might not want." He backed toward the hall, the derringer steady in his varicose-veined hand. "Be seeing you."

Epp did not stir until the front door slammed. Then he swore and said, "You can count on it, old man."

Curly Wolves

They had pushed the stolen herd hard and were well north of the border. Old Man Radler allowed only brief rests. When their mounts tired, they switched their saddles to stolen horses.

Finally, Old Man Radler consented to stop and make camp, but only because Drub Radler was pale and sweaty and his right sleeve was stained bright with blood.

"You are a damned nuisance," the father told the son as Drub sat glumly on a boulder.

"I am sorry I got shot, Pa."

"Don't apologize, damn it. How many times have I told you a man never says he is sorry? Take what life throws at you and don't whine."

"It hurts an awful lot," Drub said.

Vance Radler's cruel features split in a smirk. "What an infant. How we can be related I will never know."

Suddenly whipping around, Old Man Radler slapped him. "Shut your mouth, boy. Your ma was too scared of me to ever lie abed with another man."

"Hell, Pa," Vance said, rubbing his cheek, "I know she was a lady. I was only joshing."

"Some things shouldn't be joshed about."

Boone Scott had taken a folding knife from his saddlebags. The blade was six inches long and honed sharp; the hilt was a deer hoof. Unfolding it, he examined Drub's shoulder. "You need to take the shirt off or I will have to cut it."

"I will take it off. I only have the one." Drub clumsily pried at the buttons.

"Slow as a turtle," Vance said.

Boone switched the knife from his right hand to his left. "You might want to find something else to do besides insult your brother."

Vance looked at his father, and when his father did not say anything, he growled, "Oh, hell!" and tromped off.

"Thank you, Lightning."

"Keep unbuttoning."

The slug had caught Drub high in the right shoulder. It missed the bone and lodged in thick muscle. But it did not go clean through, and he had a bulge in his skin the size of an acorn.

"This will hurt some," Boone said.

"Do what you have to, pard. I can hardly lift my arm and I need it for eating."

Old Man Radler watched as Boone carefully made a slit and lightly pried with the tip of the blade. "I don't know what to make of you, Lightning. I truly don't."

"What did you mean back there about maybe having to kill me?" Boone casually asked. The tip scraped metal and he parted the skin for a better look.

"I can't have weak sisters in my outfit," Old Man Radler replied. "To put it simply, you are too nice."

"And nice is bad?" Boone asked while inserting the tip so it was between the slug and sinew.

"Nice is stupid. The world isn't nice. It bites us and chews on us and swallows us whole if we don't watch out."

Boone looked up. "I will get a few shots off before I am swallowed. I can promise you that."

Old Man Radler glanced at Boone's ivory-handled Colt. "That is something to keep in mind."

"My ma is nice and she is not stupid."

"Women can afford to be. They do most of the kid raising, so it is natural for them. But for a man it is a weakness. If we aren't hard, life grinds us under like a miller's wheel grinds flour."

"You have a colorful way with words."

Old Man Radler reacted as if he had been slapped as hard as he had just slapped Vance. "Don't you ever do that again, you hear me?"

"Do what?"

"Give me praise. That is a woman's trick. Get it through your head I don't want to know you or like you or be your friend. The only worth you have to me is as a pistol with a body attached."

"I will keep that in mind." Boone twisted his knife and the slug popped out into his open palm. He held it for Drub to see. "Here. Your arm should be good as old in a week or so."

Grinning, Drub inspected it. "Hard to believe puny things like this kill so many folks. It is no bigger than the marbles I used to play with."

"Your pa let you have marbles?" Boone asked, with a sideways glance at the father.

Old Man Radler colored, and swore. "Don't make more of it than it was. I needed to stop him from yapping."

"Can I keep it, Pa?" Drub asked.

"Not a lick of sense." Old Man Radler spat. Suddenly snatching the slug, he threw it far away.

"What did you do that for?"

"Because I know you, Drub. You would show it to people and they would ask how you got shot, and you, with your head so full of mud, would tell them you were shot rustling horses down in Mexico."

"But I was."

Old Man Radler hissed like an angry rattler. "Damn it. How many times must I tell you?" He put his hand on Drub's other shoulder. "Pay attention, boy. Is what we do legal or not?"

Drub's face scrunched up. "Not."

"And if it's not legal, what is the law liable to do to us if they catch us?"

The furrows on Drub's face multiplied. "Dangle us from cottonwoods."

"Good, son. You remember."

"But why can't I tell folks about the slug? I won't tell it to anyone wearing a badge. I can be smart, Pa."

"Then try to be smart now. What happens if one of those you tell goes and tells it to a tin star?"

"Oh," Drub said.

Old Man Radler sighed and turned to Boone. "Do you see what I have to put up with?"

"Yet you put up with it. As hard as you are."

"You can go to hell." Old Man Radler walked off, glowering at the world and everyone in it.

"You made Pa mad."

"He is mad at himself, not me. You should wash the bullet hole and then button your shirt back up."

"Can't waste the water," Drub said. "Pa says we

are only to use it for drinking, and then only a little bit at a time. That's so we don't die of thirst."

"Your pa takes good care of you."

"He does?" Drub's face did more scrunching. "He doesn't talk like he does. But he hasn't shot me yet, so that is something." He paused. "He shot my cousin, Thad."

"No fooling?"

"Thad used to ride with us. One day Pa saw him talking to a sheriff, and that night when we were camped Pa walked around behind him and shot him in the back of the head. It shook me so much, I about spilled my coffee."

"I can imagine," Boone said.

Grimacing, Drub shrugged into his sleeve. "We are never to talk to lawdogs. Don't forget that or Pa will shoot you too."

"Your pa probably thought your cousin was about to turn him in for the reward."

"You know about that?"

"Everyone in Arizona must know about it. Five thousand dollars is a lot of money."

"That's why Pa has to be so careful. Anyone is apt to shoot him in the back. Except me. He told me once I am the only person in the whole world that he trusts not to do that."

"Yes, sir. Your pa is as hard as flint."

Wagner and the others had gathered wood and Galeno had kindled a fire. Coffee was put on to brew and beans were poured into a pot.

Drub sat with his big hands to the flames and grinned from ear to ear.

"What the hell are you so happy about?" Vance snapped.

"My shoulder doesn't hurt no more."

Old Man Radler was poking the ground with a stick. "Tomorrow we start to sell off the horses. If all the buyers have the money in hand like they are supposed to, by the end of the month we will be back at the canyon."

"The canyon?" Boone said quietly to Drub.

"Our secret place."

Old Man Radler had gone on. "That is where we will divide up the money. Then all of you can go off and do as you please." He pointed the stick at Boone. "You are one of us now, so you get an equal share."

Drub chuckled in delight. "Do you hear that, Lighting? You are one of us!"

"Get married, why don't you?" Vance said.

Boone was up and around the fire in two swift bounds. No one had time to react except Skelman, whose hands swooped to his mother-of-pearl Colts. Boone's own Colt flashed up and out and caught Vance Radler on the temple, felling him like a poled ox. For a moment Boone stood over him, and then he stepped back and twirled his Colt into his holster.

Galeno, grinning, reached over and slapped Vance. He kept slapping him until Vance groaned and groggily sat up.

"God, my head hurts." Vance blinked in confusion. His eyes alighted on Boone and he swore and started to stand but apparently thought better of it. "You had no call to do that."

"I warned you about the insults. On your feet."

"What?"

"You heard me."

"The hell I will." Vance looked around for help,

but no one answered his mute appeal. He swallowed, and sat back. "I won't let you goad me. If I draw on you, you will kill me."

"It will be fair. Skelman will count to three."

Skelman looked up. "I don't recollect being asked."

"Three or four or none, it is all the same," Vance said. "I am not getting up."

"The insults will stop?"

Vance glared at Drub and his mouth became a slit. "You have heard the last of them."

Boone turned to their father. "Was that hard enough for you?"

Old Man Radler snorted. "Hard, hell. Hard is never giving the other bastard a chance. Hard would have been to shoot the fool dead."

"Thanks, Pa," Vance said.

"I am not your umbrella, boy. You bring rain down on your head, you are bound to get wet."

Drub chose that moment to wriggle with glee and say, "This is more fun than I've had in a coon's age."

Dawn found them on the move. The lingering cool of night gave way to the inferno of day. The dust they raised hung in the air as if reluctant to fall back to earth.

Boone was riding drag when a figure in black came around the trailing end of the horse herd and reined in alongside him.

"We need to talk," Skelman said.

"I don't recollect being asked."

"You are not nearly as hilarious as you think you are."

"I try."

"Old Man Radler was right. You are not hard enough. And I don't see you getting any harder."

Boone flicked his coiled rope at a bay that was inclined to dawdle. "Maybe I will surprise you."

"You can fool the others but you can't fool me or Old Man Radler," Skelman said without looking at him.

"I am not out to fool anyone. I am just me."

"He tolerates you because of Drub. But he does not like you. Don't make the mistake of thinking you can be his friend, because you can't. If he gets the hair, he will kill you, and you won't see it coming."

"Why are you telling me all this?"

Skelman pulled the black brim of his hat low over his eyes. "After you get your cut, light a shuck. Everyone else will head off to seek entertainment. They will be back, but if you are smart you will never show your face in this part of the country ever again."

"You didn't answer me."

"Don't prod me."

Shimmering particles of dust settled over them. The horses were plodding dully along, heads drooping. They needed water and they needed graze and they needed both soon.

Skelman let out a sigh. "I have been at this a good long while and I aim to stay at it awhile more. Some might call me loco for liking to ride the owl-hoot trail, but it is in my blood. I like the killing more than anything. It is the one thing I am good at."

"That is the first time I have heard you brag."

"You have seen for yourself. Don't accuse me when I am only stating fact." Skelman raised his reins.

"Now I have said my piece. Whether you take my advice or not is up to you."

"You still haven't told me why you went to this bother."

"Use your head for something other than a hat rack. When the time comes, Old Man Radler might not do it himself. He might have one of the others do it. Or he might ask me."

"I think I savvy."

"At last."

"You don't want to have to kill me."

"Damn, you are as stupid as Drub," Skelman said, and rode off.

To Tree a Sawbones

Doc Baker was a kind man. Good and kind, everyone said. The salt of the earth and a blessing to the community, was the opinion of its churchgoing members. Everyone knew him or knew of him.

His snow-white hair and ever-present black bag were common sights in Tucson and along the dusty country roads and rutted tracks he traveled in his buggy day in and day out, year after year.

People liked to joke that Doc Baker had helped give birth to more babies than God. He had been there for half the mothers in the territory in their time of trial, and the ladies who benefited from his presence praised him to high heaven.

Doc Baker had stitched knife cuts and bandaged bullets wounds. He had treated bite marks and set practically every bone in the body that could be broken. And he always did his work with that warm smile of his, and always with a kind word for the stricken and afflicted.

He was a constant in their lives, like the sun and the moon. He was steady of mind and habit, a rock in a sea of life's uncertainties, as dependable as a human being could be.

So when he started to change it was all the more startling.

Abby Harker out to the Harker Ranch was the first to notice. She was eight months along and sent for Doc Baker because of stomach discomfort she was having. She was outside taking a stroll when his familiar buggy came up the road. Some of the punchers waved, but Doc Baker did not wave back. He brought the buggy to a stop near the white picket fence and stiffly climbed down.

Abby hurried to greet him. "Than you for coming so quickly," she began gratefully. She had more to say, but the sight of him so shocked her that she did not say it. Instead, she asked, "Are you all right?"

Doc Baker pushed open the gate. He wore his usual suit and hat and had his black bag. But his face was unnaturally pale and slick with sweat, and he had dark rings under his eyes. "I am fine," he said brusquely.

"You don't look fine."

Doc Baker motioned toward the house and she fell into step by his side. "I have been under the weather for the past week or so. Even doctors come down sick, you know."

"What is wrong?"

"A touch of something or other."

Abby tried to make light of his pallor. "You a doctor and you don't know what it is?"

"I have been a trifle restless and keep having headaches," Doc Baker revealed. "Suppose you diagnose what I have."

"Pshaw," Abby said. "You are the doctor."

"I trust you will remember that. It is probably the onset of a cold. I rarely get them, but when I do they tend to lay me low."

"Try chicken soup," Abby said. "A physician I know recommends it to all his patients."

"If it is the physician I think it is, I wouldn't listen to anything the old quack says."

They repaired to the privacy of Abby's bedroom and Doc Baker took out his stethoscope and carefully examined her. He asked questions as he moved the stethoscope across her swollen belly and twice probed gently with his fingers. When he was done, he sat back on the stool.

"If you were any healthier you would be a horse."

"Thank you, I think," Abby said as she did up her stays and buttons. "Why am I having so much discomfort?"

"There is bound to be some. Have you been taking the remedy I prescribed the last time I was here?"

Abby went to a cabinet and brought over a large bottle. "See for yourself. It is almost empty."

A label on the bottle proclaimed that it was DR. KILMER'S FEMALE REMEDY. THE GREAT BLOOD PURIFIER AND SYSTEM REGULATOR. SYSTEM VITALIZER. INVIGORATOR. DESTROYER OF ALL KINDS OF BLOOD HUMORS. SPECIALLY ADAPTED TO FEMALE CONSTITUTION.

Doc Baker shook the bottle and said, "Yes, I can see that you have." He handed it back. "What about your diet? Any peculiar cravings?"

"Just pickles."

"That is normal. God knows why, but more women

crave pickles when they are in your condition than anything else."

"I like the big fat sour ones. I have my Tom bring me a dozen at a time when he goes into Tucson. Then I sit at the kitchen table and stuff myself. I dip them in mustard so it makes me pucker with each bite and—"

"Wait," Doc Baker said. "You do what?"

"I dip the pickles in mustard. I have always been fond of mustard but not very fond of pickles, so I dip the pickles in the mustard to take away the taste of the pickles."

"Land sakes, woman."

"What?"

"You are lucky you have not exploded." Doc Baker closed his black bag. "From now on eat the pickles alone or the mustard alone but do not mix them."

"But my craving."

"Then put up with the stomach discomfort and don't send for me when there are people I must visit with real ailments."

"Oh!" Abby said, putting her hands to her cheeks. "I'm sorry. I didn't mean to upset you."

Doc Baker pressed his hand to his own brow. "No. I am the one who is sorry. I should not be short with you. It is this infernal headache."

Abby walked him out and as he climbed into his buggy she said sincerely, "I hope you get to feeing better."

"So do I," Doc Baker said.

Four days later young Pedro Rodriquez was trying to bust a mustang, but the mustang busted him. It bucked him against the corral so hard he broke a rail and his leg and his family did not know what else, so they sent for Doc Baker. Although a gringo, Doc Baker was highly thought of by the Spanish-speaking segment of the citizenry. He treated everyone regardless of race or skin color. White, Mexican, black, it made no difference to him. He even treated the few Indians who came to him for help.

Ten-year-old Arturo Rodriquez rode his skewbald pony near to exhaustion to fetch Doc Baker out to the Rodriquez Rancho. Pedro was in bed, near delirious with fever. The family had done the best they could, but the jagged tip of the shattered femur stuck a good four inches out of Pedro's skin.

Calmly, efficiently, Doc Baker set to work. It was Senora Rodriquez who noticed the ghastly shade of his skin and the beads of sweat that dotted his forehead and upper lip. She noted too how several times he winced as if in pain. When he was done and washing his hands in a basin, she made bold to make mention of what she had observed.

"I am feeling a little poorly, is all," Doc Baker informed her. He said it harshly.

"Is there anything I can do?" Senora Rodriquez asked.

"Put me out of my misery." Doc Baker laughed too loud and too long.

"You should see a doctor."

Doc Baker glanced sharply at her, but when he saw she was not being facetious, he smiled and said, "How little you know about physicians. Doctors never go to other doctors. If we can't heal ourselves we have no business trying to heal others."

"That is ridiculous."

"I know. But knowing it and being man enough to go see another sawbones is something else." Doc Baker wiped his hands on the towel she had provided. "I suppose if I get any worse, I will have to take your advice."

"What is wrong? Or is it too bold of me to ask?"

"Not at all." Doc Baker began rolling down his sleeves. "I can't hardly sleep anymore. I pace the floor at night, my body all aquiver. Even hot milk doesn't help. I have a constant headache." He mustered a wan smile. "I am at the point where I might need to start taking some of that remedy Abby Harker is so fond of."

"There must be something you can do," Senor Rodriquez optimistically offered.

Doc Baker explained that he had tried Hostetter's Stomach Bitters, but that gave him cramps so he switched to Pricklyash Stomach Bitters, but that gave him worse cramps. He figured something more mild would do and took extract of sarsaparilla for a few days, but that had no effect whatsoever. "I am trying laudanum now," he concluded. "It seems to lessen the headaches but not enough to suit me."

"What will you do next?"

Doc Baker shrugged. "There is always opium. I have never used it myself, but from what I have seen and heard it can work wonders."

"I am sorry for you." Senora Rodriquez squeezed his hand. "I wish I could help you as you have so many times helped me."

Doc Baker walked himself out and climbed into his buggy. He had not gone a quarter of a mile when he broke out in a cold sweat and experienced a severe bout of dizziness that gave him a profound scare. Eventually the world stopped spinning and his insides stopped churning, but now he felt as weak as a newborn kitten. He sat back and let Mabel have her head. The old mare knew the road as well as if not better than he did and could find her way home with no help from him.

"What is the matter with me?" Doc Baker asked aloud. He pressed a thumb to his wrist, checking his pulse. His heartbeat was erratic, weak. He tried to swallow but had no saliva. Settling back, he closed his eyes and groaned.

The ride that Doc Baker normally enjoyed became an ordeal. The cold sweats came and went. A hammer pounded inside his head, pounding harder and harder as time went by. He had bouts where he was short of breath.

"Maybe it is my age catching up to me," he told Mabel. "No one lives forever. Not even doctors."

Tucson had grown so much in the past ten years that he reached the outskirts long before he reached his office. Eight thousand souls and growing, according to the *Arizona Daily Star*. The arrival of the Southern Pacific Railroad had a lot to do with the surge in growth. New buildings were going up faster than summer corn. A new courthouse was being constructed just down the street. Local politicians were crowing about how Tucson would soon be the crowning jewel in all of Arizona.

Doc Baker was glad when Mabel finally came to a stop. He climbed out slowly, his muscles sore, his joints stiff. Afraid of another dizzy spell, he climbed the outside steps holding to the rail. Once the door was shut and locked, he moved down the hall with his left hand against the wall for support. His legs were so weak, he did not know if they would bear his weight. He placed his bag on his desk and sat in his chair and thought about his wife, long dead, and his son, killed at Gettysburg, and his daughter, drowned in a flood, and his eyes grew moist. Sniffling, he said to the walls, "I will be damned if I will sit here feeling sorry for myself."

Doc Baker got up and went to a mahogany cabinet where he kept his medicines, but it was not a bottle of medicine he selected. It was his pet passion: a bottle of brandy. Every night before he turned in he had a glass of brandy to soothe his nerves and his stomach. For forty years he had stuck to the habit without fail.

Tonight Doc Baker dispensed with a glass. He sat at his desk and drank straight from the bottle. He was on his tenth or eleventh swallow when the cramps hit him so bad, he doubled over. The room spun and his body grew numb. He sucked in deep breaths until the spell passed. Then, spent and queasy, he looked up.

Epp Scott was in the doorway, smiling.

"What the hell?" Doc Baker said, his tongue feeling as if it were covered with wool.

Epp walked over and sat on the edge of the desk. "Surprised to see me? You shouldn't be."

Doc Baker tried to stand but had to sink back into his chair. "What are you doing here?"

"How is your brandy these days? I have never been all that fond of the stuff. Too sweet for my taste. But everyone knows you partake before you turn in, and I figured the sweet would hide the bitter."

Clutching the edge of the desk, Doc Baker steadied himself. "I want you to leave. I am not feeling well."

"As much as you have had, it is a wonder you are still breathing," Epp said. "You are tougher than I gave you credit for."

"What is this? Some childish prank to get back at me for the accusations I levied the last time I saw you?"

"I never treat dying as a prank. I always take it as serious as can be."

"Did you say dying?"

Epp nodded. "You have been taking it for weeks now. That's what comes of not latching your windows. I slipped in one day while you were off on a house call and mixed it with your brandy. But you have been taking too damn long to die, so last night I snuck in again and added five times as much as before. Then today I have been keeping an eye on you, waiting for you to keel over."

Doc Baker's grip on the desk was not enough. He slumped back against the chair, struggling for breath. "What is this *it* you keep talking about?"

"Oh. That's right. I haven't shown you yet." Epp reached into a jacket pocket and brought out a small cobalt blue bottle that had a porcelain label with gold trim. In bold letters were NATR. ARSENIC.

"Dear God."

"Recognize the bottle?" Epp asked. "You should. It is yours. I was going to stab you, but when I saw this, the brandy idea occurred to me."

"You didn't."

"It is better this way. More natural. They will think your heart gave out. In three days they will bury you, and my secret along with you."

"So I was right about you and your parents?" Again

Doc Baker struggled to rise and again he fell back, but this time the chair slipped from under him and he landed on his back on the floor. He attempted to lift his right arm, but the numbness had spread with frightening speed. He could not move anything except his mouth. "You have killed me."

Epp Scott smiled. "That was the idea."

Sassy Tree

Early one morning the rustlers passed through thick swaths of mesquite and paloverde. A short climb brought them to manzanitas. Higher yet, and they were in oak. Now and again a prickly pear cactus reminded them they were still in desert country. By noon they were amid woodland of piñons. By one o'clock they were riding among tall ponderosas. The forest went on for miles. They were grateful for the shade and a faint breeze.

Then came a forest of fir. The moss on the trees seemed out of place, more suitable for Oregon or Washington than Arizona.

They rode alertly. By now they were convinced they had shed the vaqueros, but they were in Apache country and there was no predicting Apaches. They had enough men and guns—particularly guns—to discourage a war party. But the Apaches might decide those guns were worth the risk of an attack. So they rode with their hands on their revolvers or had rifles across their saddles.

Finally, they reached the rim. From its heights they beheld a breathtaking spectacle of endless canyons and bluffs, sprinkled here and there with the green of valleys.

"Where are we bound?" Boone Scott asked his new friend.

Drub Radler yawned. "Let's see. We have been to two ranches and sold off some of the horses. The next one will be—" He stopped, and a broad smile spread over his face. "Why, the next will be Sassy Tree."

"If that is a town, I have never heard of it."

Galeno was next to them, and he threw in, "It is no town. It is a ranch, Senor Lightning." He had taken to calling Boone that, and when he did, he always smirked.

"Hell," Wagner said. "Calling it a ranch is being charitable. It is no more a ranch than I am the president."

"That means it doesn't amount to much," Drub told Boone.

"I know what it means."

"Ben Drecker owns it," Wagner continued. "And if we are lucky, he will be sober when we get there."

The trails they took were not the trails most men took. Old Man Radler had been a rustler for a lot of years and he knew game trails and Indian trails that no one else did.

The valley they came to was small and isolated, but it had water, and in Arizona water was everything. Enough grass for a fair-sized herd and an oak woodland lent a picturesque quality. From a distance the cabin with smoke curling from its stone chimney and the stable and corral looked respectable enough. But up close the illusion was shattered.

The cabin had been put together by someone who

could not cut logs the same length if his life depended on it. The chinks had been filled with clay, but only here and there, so that on cold nights the fireplace would be put to good use. The corral rails had not been completely trimmed. The stable consisted of old planks with cracks and holes and looked fit to come down if someone sneezed on it.

Old Man Radler drew rein and the rest of them did the same. He pushed his hat back on his head and leaned on his saddle horn. "You in the cabin! Are you awake in there? You have visitors."

Burlap covering the window moved and a rifle poked out. "That there is far enough, stranger."

"Drecker, you damned idiot! How long have you known me?" Old Man Radler returned. "I have come with the horses you told me you wanted. And if you have wasted my time, by God there will be hell to pay."

The rifle was pulled in and a moment later the cabin door creaked open on leather hinges. Framed in the uneven doorway was an unkempt man of fifty or so. His clothes were little better than nothing at all, his boots were ventilated with large holes and the rifle in his hands was an old Sharps. "Radler! I had about figured you weren't going to show. It was, what, seven months ago you stopped here last?"

"If you can remember that far back, you are off the booze, which will make this easier."

"I am not off it by choice. I ran out of money."

Old Man Radler stopped in the act of dismounting. "The hell you say. Then why did I bring horses?"

"Oh, I have my stash for those," Drecker quickly answered. "I was not about to touch it, not after we shook and all."

"Then you *do* have some common sense." Old Man Radler alighted. "We will camp yonder." He pointed at oaks fringing a spring. "Mosey on over and we will dicker. Bring that sprout of yours if you want. I can use a laugh and she is always worth plenty."

"She?" Boone said to Drub.

"Sassy," Drub said with a vigorous bob of his chin.

Ben Drecker asked, "What was that about dickering? I thought we had set how much they would be?"

"Come talk," Old Man Radler responded.

They stripped the saddle horses, and the stolen horses were put under guard and a fire was kindled and coffee put on. In a friendly frame of mind because everything had been going so well, the rustlers sat around talking and joking. Skelman did not talk much, and he never told a joke, but when he did speak the others listened.

Drecker joined them, hunkering by the fire with Old Man Radler and Vance.

Boone and Drub were seated with their backs to trees a short distance away, along with some of the others.

It was Wagner who snorted and said, "Look at that old goat. Talking business. As if he can afford more than four."

"Four is more than none," Drub said. "Even I know that."

"Four makes for a great horse herd. Why, in ten years he might build it up to eight or ten."

"You don't think much of Drecker?" Boone asked.

"Hell, I don't like or dislike him. He is an old drunk who will never amount to much except in his head.

But he does let us stop over when we are passing through, and that girl of his is a delight."

Boone looked around. "She must be lying low."

"Likely as not she is off hunting," Drub said. "That is what she does the most." He paused and then said almost shyly, "I like her, Lightning. I like her a whole lot."

"You like puppies and kittens too," Wagner said.

"Don't you?"

Boone rose. "I am going to stretch my legs. We have been in the saddle for so long, I have plumb forgot how to walk."

Drub cackled and slapped his big thigh. "I will have to remember that one to tell Pa."

Wagner swore in disgust. "The world is full of simple—" he started, and then his eyes darted toward Boone's ivory-handled Colt. "That is, I reckon I will take a nap."

Boone strolled off. As he went deeper into the oaks, birds chirped and warbled and somewhere a jay squawked. A doe bounded off. He saw sign of other wildlife that used the spring. Bear tracks caused him to dip onto a knee to study them. They were in a patch of bare dirt, and the claw marks were as clear as could be.

"That would be Methuselah."

The voice startled him. Not so much because Boone had not realized he was no longer alone but because it was female and of such pitch and tone that it sent a shiver down his spine. He glanced up and was thunderstruck.

She was no more than five feet tall, but every inch of her was superb. Sandy hair cut below her small ears and swept back added a dash of pixie to a face that was as smooth as a baby's bottom but as bronzed as an Apache's. Eyes the same green as the forest peered at him with interest. She had a small, perfect nose, and a small, perfect mouth. Her clothes were a duplicate of her father's, only hers were cleaner. She was barefoot. Cradled in her arms was a Spencer rifle. "How old are you?"

"What?"

"Don't your ears work? I asked how old you are."

Boone rose. "I don't know as I should say."

"Why not?"

"Some think I am older than I am and I would like to keep it that way," Boone explained.

She nodded toward the spring. "By some do you mean the Radlers and the rest of those serpents?"

"They gave me the impression they are friends of yours."

"I like Drub. He is the only worthwhile one in the bunch." She waited, then said, "Well?"

"Well what?"

"Are you going to tell me or not?"

"Why do you want to know?"

"Damn, you are contrary. But you look to be about my age and I hardly ever meet anyone as young as me. I am sixteen."

"Promise to keep it a secret?"

"May I be shot if I don't."

"I am the same age as you."

The girl smiled and stepped boldly forward and offered her small hand. "Sassy Drecker. What is yours?"

Boone opened his mouth, then hesitated.

"Don't tell me you have forgot."

"It is another secret."

"You sure as hell have a lot of them."

"And you sure do cuss a lot. My ma says that ladies should not cuss like men do."

"If you want your mother I am wrong for the part. So will you tell me or should I make a name up? Because if I have to make a name up, I think I will call you Silly. How would that be?"

"I am called Lightning but my real name is Boone. Boone Scott."

"Lightning?" Sassy said, showing teeth as white and even as teeth could be. "Why in creation would anyone call you that?"

Boone's hand moved, and the ivory-handled Colt performed its magic. "This is why."

Sassy's green eyes widened in appreciation and she whistled softly. "Land sakes. I am impressed and I do not impress easy." She looked him squarely in the eye. "There is a lot about you that impresses me."

"The way you talk." Boone coughed and twirled the Colt into his holster with a flourish. "What did you mean by Methuselah?"

"That is the name of the bear. He is big and fat and getting on in years and I always wave to him when I see him."

"You named a wild bear?"

Sassy gazed fondly at the surrounding oaks and undergrowth. "I give a name to every critter. They are my friends."

"A bear is no friend to anyone. Aren't you afraid he will decide you make a tasty meal?"

"I have this," Sassy said, patting the Spencer. "And I am a damn good shot, if I say so my own self."

"There you go again."

"There I go again what?"

"Cussing."

"Are you a preacher or something?"

"Hell no."

They looked at each other and laughed.

"Why don't you come for a walk with me and I will show you around?" Sassy suggested.

"I can think of nothing I would like to do more."

Sassy's cheeks tinged pink as she turned and headed away from the spring and the cabin. "These wilds are my home. We came here shortly after Ma died. Pa took to the bottle and has not climbed back out. Most of the time I am all alone, if you don't count the Apaches."

"Apaches?" Boone said in sudden alarm.

"I find their tracks and camps from time to time," Sassy said. "I suspect they know we are here, but I reckon we are not worth their bother or they would have gouged out our eyes by now."

Boone had a thought, an ugly thought, and his trigger finger twitched. "When you are a little older maybe they will not think you are so worthless."

"There is that," Sassy said, and placed a hand on the knife at her hip. "But I will slit my own throat before I let any man, red or white, do that to me without my say-so."

"God, you are frank."

Sassy bestowed another smile on him. "Do I scare you?"

Boone looked at the ground and at the sky and finally said, "More than anything has ever scared me in all my born days."

"Good," Sassy said. "Can I tell you something?"

"Will it scare me more?"

"Probably." Sassy did not wait for him to give his consent. "I am glad we met. More glad than I have been about anything in all my born days." She laughed, and her laughter was music.

"Are you poking fun?"

Sassy stopped, so he stopped. She put a hand on his arm and leaned close and said so quietly he barely heard her, "I would never do that. Not now. Not ever." Her hand stayed there. "Don't you feel it?"

"Feel what?"

"Feel what I am feeling?"

"Oh, hell," Boone Scott said.

"And you say I cuss a lot. If your ma were here I would tell on you." Sassy grinned and they walked on, her hand brushing his.

Boone Scott broke out in a sweat that had nothing to do with the heat.

A Secret Place

Boone Scott had not smiled this much since that awful night in Ranson. He walked with a lighthearted tread, his arm occasionally touching Sassy's. Or her arm would touch his.

Sassy knew the valley from end to end, every tree, every boulder, every shadowed nook and shaded cranny. She showed him a tree the black bear she had named Methuselah liked to scratch, and a squirrel nest, and a fox den. She showed him where grouse liked to roost and the tracks of wild turkeys. She took him to where deer liked to lie up, and the trail the deer used when they went for their evening drink at the spring. She showed him, in short, everything there was to know about her valley.

Boone lost all track of time. He listened to her wonderful voice, and drank in the sight of her with sly glances, and he was content.

They came to the far end of the valley. A cliff wall loomed, a barrier that kept the wildlife from drifting into the mountains beyond, and Sassy suddenly clasped his hand.

"I have a treat for you."

"You can take me anywhere," Boone said.

Sassy pulled him toward the cliff. "It's my special place. The place I come to when I want to be alone. I have never brought Pa or anyone else. I have never wanted to."

"I am honored."

"You should be."

Soon they emerged from the oaks. Above them reared the cliff, sheer and unbroken, reaching to the sky.

"Is this it?" Boone asked.

"No, silly. What is so special about here?" Sassy grinned and pulled him to the right.

For a good five minutes they hiked along the base of the cliff. Then Sassy stopped and pointed. "What do you think of those?"

Boone looked, and was puzzled. Hand and footholds had been carved into the rock face. Their rounded edges suggested they had once been well used. They were old, very old, maybe as old as the valley itself. "I'll be." Stepping back, he craned his neck and saw that they went up the cliff for as high as he could see. "Who made them?"

"How would I know?" Sassy shrugged. "Indians, I reckon. They are long gone." She slung her rifle over her back by the rawhide cord that was tied to the barrel and the stock, then began to climb. "Come on. My special place is higher."

"Is it safe?"

"Are you yellow?" Sassy teased, gripping the next niche.

Had a man said that, Boone would have pistol-whipped the culprit.

Now he grinned and said, "I will show you how yellow I am." And he followed her.

They climbed until they were higher than the oaks, and went on climbing. Boone glanced down once and did not glance down again. When a bird swooped past his head, he nearly lost his grip.

Sassy was not the least concerned. Several times she looked down at him and smiled. "It is not much higher," she said at one point.

Presently Boone heard a scratching noise. He glanced up and was startled to find she had disappeared. "Sassy?"

There was no answer.

"Sassy?" Boone said again in concern.

"Not so loud. This high up, voices carry. Do you want them to hear you at the spring?" A hand appeared, beckoning. "Keep on. You are almost there."

Boone climbed quickly, not caring that if he slipped, he would plummet to his death. He reached up, and instead of another niche his fingers closed on the rough edge of what he took to be a ledge. But when he raised his head above it, he was shocked.

Sassy clapped her hands and laughed at his expression. "Isn't it something?"

Before them was a fair-sized cavern. Worn by erosion, the sides and ceiling were smooth, so that it resembled a bowl tipped on its side. Filling the bowl, to Boone's amazement, were houses. Made of sandstone and mortar, they were stacked one on top of the other like boxes. The dust of great age covered them, and there were other signs of antiquity. He climbed up and stood, agog.

"Have you ever seen the like?" Sassy asked breathlessly.

Boone shook his head. "I have heard tell of places like this. My pa saw one once. If I recollect right, it was bigger but not as old." He moved past her and then turned and gazed out over the valley. "How is it we couldn't see it from down below?"

"It is in shadow during the day. Almost as if whoever lived here did not want to be found."

"A whole village in the cliff," Boone marveled.

"I was out hunting one day and I spotted those cut marks. I went on hunting, but I got curious, so I came back." Sassy motioned. "This is what I found. I never told Pa."

"Why not?"

"He wouldn't care. And he hates Injuns. Hates them worse than he hates anything."

"I wonder what happened to the people who lived here."

"That is a mystery," Sassy said. "Maybe their enemies drove them off. Or maybe they got tired of toting water up here." She took his hand. "Come on. I want to show you something."

In places the sandstone had crumbled and there was other evidence of the stress of centuries.

Boone was dubious about entering, and said so.

"It has not collapsed on me yet," Sassy said as she bent slightly to go in a doorway.

The dust smell was strong. Openings permitted enough sunlight to filter in to see by, but it was too dark for Boone's liking. He kept his right hand on his Colt.

Sassy moved with the sure tread of familiarity. "See these?" she said, pointing.

On the plaster walls were paintings rendered in shades of yellow, green, white and red. Many were scenes that depicted the life of the Indians who had lived there. One showed women making baskets. Another depicted warriors fighting a mountain lion. Still others were of symbols.

Sassy was leading them down, not up. She went along a narrow passage and turned right and walked down another, bringing them at last to a large circular chamber. Sunlight streamed in slits high up. She moved to the center and spread her arms wide. "Isn't this glorious?"

Looking at her and not at the paintings or the ceiling, Boone said, "It is more than that."

"I would live here if Pa would not have a fit. It is so quiet, so peaceful." Smiling, Sassy turned in a circle. "That is silly, I reckon."

"Not if you want it, it isn't."

Sassy faced him and bit her lower lip, then asked, "Be honest with me. Do you have a girl off somewhere you are powerful fond of?"

"I would never lie to you. And no, not unless you count my ma."

"By girl I meant sweetheart or wife."

Boone laughed. "I am too young to be married off." He quickly amended, "That is, I haven't met the right girl yet."

"Are you particular?"

"What kind of question is that?" Boone rejoined. "But since you ask, I reckon I am."

Sassy's mouth curled down. "Oh."

"I would like for her to have all her teeth. And to be able to cook. And it would be nice if she was real pretty although she doesn't have to be if she is sweet and nice."

Brightening, Sassy said, "I can be nice when I put my mind to it." She looked down at her feet and poked at the dust with a toe. "Do you find me at all pretty?"

"You are a sunrise and a butterfly rolled into one," Boone answered before he could stop his mouth from moving.

"Really?" Sassy moved a few feet away so her back was to him. She coughed and did more dust scraping. "That is just about the best thing anyone has ever said to me."

"If you lived in a town you would have suitors crawling out your ears," Boone predicted.

"The hell you say."

"There you go again." Boone walked up behind her. He started to reach for her but lowered his hands.

"Would you be one of them?"

"I would be the first and only," Boone said hotly. "There are two things in this life I will not share. One is my horse. The other is my girl."

"Do you think you could grow to care for me?"

"It is too late for that."

Sassy turned. Her eyes were limpid pools of worry and confusion. "Too late how?"

"You can't tell?"

"Oh." Sassy bowed her head. "Oh," she said again, and her bronzed face grew darker. "I bet you say that to all the females."

"Not ever!" Boone replied, more loudly and harsher than he intended. "There has only ever been one girl who—" He caught himself, aghast.

Sassy's head jerked up. "Another girl? But you said there wasn't one. Who is she?"

"Was," Boone said. "She is dead. Her name was Lucy. I hardly knew her, but she was nice and she died taking a bullet meant for me."

"Was it a lawman's bullet?"

"Why would you think that?"

"You ride with the Radler gang. Every tin star in the territory is on the lookout for them. Twice that I know of the Radlers have shot it out with posses and been lucky to get away."

"I am not an outlaw," Boone said. He began to explain how it was that he was with them, and once he started, he couldn't stop. He told her everything. About the Circle V. About going to Ranson. About Jarrott. About Condit. About drifting to Porter's, and the rustling in Mexico. "And here I am." He ended his account with a gesture at the chamber made ages past by a tribe long dead.

Sassy had not said a word during his recital. Her eyes, alive with interest, grew bright with something else. "Then you are not really one of them."

"They act like I am but I am not. I only stayed with them because I like Drub."

"So do I."

Suddenly Sassy grabbed his hand again and wheeled toward a doorway on the other side. "There is one spot left to show you. The most special spot of all."

The next passage was lined with clay pots. Some were cracked. Others lay in shards. A mouse went skittering away in fright. Soon they were at the foot of a wooden ladder that reached up into darkness.

"Will it hold us?"

"It has always held me. But to be safe we will climb one at a time."

The ladder creaked and shimmied. Boone stood ready to catch her should it collapse. Sassy disappeared into the shadows and a few moments later called down out of the ink.

"Your turn."

Boone placed his right boot on the bottom rung and carefully applied his full weight. "Will wonders never cease?" he muttered, and cautiously ascended. A square of pale light at the top turned into an opening onto the roof.

Sassy was over at the edge, hands on her hips, staring down at the cliff homes and the valley beyond. "Isn't the view wonderful?"

"It is more wonderful than anything."

Curling her legs under her, Sassy sat and patted the roof. "Have a seat. I reckon we should rest a spell before we start down."

Boone did not need to rest, but he sat cross-legged with his elbows on his knees. The sun was streaming into the mouth of the cavern, but at such an angle he doubted anyone on the valley floor could see the secret village.

"What now, Boone Scott?" Sassy asked.

"There is no need for you to be so formal," Boone answered. "We are friends, aren't we?"

"Are we friends? Or are we more than friends?"

Boone did not answer. His tongue had tied itself into knots.

"I took it for more but maybe that is me. I do not have much experience at this." Sassy paused. "Hell, I do not have any experience at all."

"One more hell out of you and I will take you over my knees and spank you," Boone was able to joke.

Sassy leaned toward him, her breath warm on his cheek. "Would you? I might like that."

"The things you say. I never heard a girl talk like you. But damn me if I don't like it."

Sassy put a hand on his leg. "I want you to like me. I want you to like me as much as I like you."

"God help me."

"We have to work out how it is to be with you and me. Old Man Radler will leave in the morning. He will expect you to go with him."

"He has no say over what I do."

"Then what will it be? I need to know your intentions. If I am too forward I am sorry, but I have never felt this way." Sassy leaned so close that her lips practically brushed his. "I want you, Boone Scott. I want you to want me. I want for you to take me with you when you leave. I will go anywhere you say, do anything you want me to do. But only if you feel the way I do. If you don't, tell me now. There will be no hard feelings. I promise. Just tell me true." She stopped, and her next words were a whisper. "What will it be?"

Layers of Deceit

For the Circle V it was not life as usual.

The foreman and the hands and everyone else tried to shake off the deaths of the owner and his wife, but the wounds were too fresh. Ned Scott had been well liked. He was a working owner, not one of those who sat on his porch and gave orders but never sat a saddle. Lillian was fondly recalled for her many kind words and for her cookies and pies. Their dough puncher didn't mind. As good as he was—and it was the Circle V's boast that their cook was the best in the territory—neither his cookies nor his pies were the equal of Lillian's.

Dan Morgan did what he could to draw the men out of their funk. He had been a working cowboy at fourteen and a foreman by twenty-three, and he was employed in that capacity at three other ranches before he came to work for Ned Scott. Dan knew cows and Dan knew men. It was said that what he did not know was not worth knowing. He had peers, but no one anywhere was better. He was wise but practical. He was tough but fair. And he never missed a thing. He could pull two and two out of thin air and get four.

For all his savvy and ability, Dan was hard pressed to restore the Circle V to where it should be. The freak mishap that claimed Ned Scott was bad enough; to have his wife die so soon afterward was a shock. A few hands muttered about a jinx, but Dan nipped that in the bud by announcing that anyone silly enough to believe such nonsense had no business working at the Circle V.

Dan tried tactics that never failed him in the past. He gave the men extra days off. He practically booted some of them in the general direction of Tucson with the admonition that they better have a good time, or else. He told the cook to whip up extra treats. He did all this, and more, and it had no effect on morale.

Dan was about at his wits' end the morning he came out of the tack room and discovered his new boss waiting for him. "This is a surprise. What can I do for you, Mr. Scott?"

"I have told you before about being formal. Call me Epp or call me Eppley, but for God's sake do not call me Mr. Scott."

"It was good enough for your pa."

"I am not him. You will treat me as me. And what is so surprising about me being in my own stable?"

Dan Morgan shrugged. "We have not seen much of you of late. I reckon you are busy with the books, and all."

"There is that." Clasping his hands behind his back, Epp moved down the aisle between the stalls, and the foreman naturally went with him. "I needed to talk to you."

"My ears are yours any hour of the day or night," Dan said amiably. "It is what you pay me for."

"I know I can always count on you, just like my pa could. If he told me once, he told me fifty times that without you the Circle V would fall apart."

"That was kind of him, but it was not true. I can name half a dozen men who can do as good a job as me."

"I am content with you. I trust the reverse is true?"

"I am still here," Dan said, and smiled.

They emerged into the harsh glare of the summer sun. Epp squinted at the horses in the corral and then at Red Butte in the distance. "How would you say the ranch is doing?"

"I am not sure how you mean that."

"Let me rephrase the question. In your opinion, is the Circle V as prosperous as it can be?"

"We could run a few more head, I suppose. But where is the need? The Circle V has been in the black since I signed on. Your pa never complained about a lack of profits."

"Oh, the ranch is still earning well enough," Epp said. "I just happen to think it could earn more."

They were near the corral. The bronc buster was working, and too busy with a bronco to do more than nod.

"Earn more how?" Dan Morgan asked. "Tell me what you want me to do and I will get it done."

Epp turned his back to the rails and leaned against them, his legs crossed in front of him. "My idea does not involve you and the men. My idea involves our grass."

"If I were any more lost I would be booze blind," Dan said. "You are fixing to cut and sell hay?"

Epp grinned and shook his head. "I am fixing to rent out our range."

"Rent?" Dan Morgan said the word as others might say "warts" or "toe fungus."

"Rent," Epp said again. "The Circle V is one of the largest ranches in the territory. We have plenty of range. More than we use at any one time."

"A ranch can never have enough graze."

"True, true," Epp said quickly. "But I was thinking of that section to the southwest. The barrens. We never use it, but there is good grass and water."

Who first coined the name, no one could remember. The barrens consisted of five square miles of washes and low bluffs. A spring watered enough grass to keep a small herd fed. But choked thick with thorny brush, the barrens were more hospitable to deer and mountain lions than to cows.

"Who would want to live in the barrens?" Dan asked in some amazment.

"I did not say live. I said *rent*," Epp corrected him. "Anyone driving cattle north would be glad to have a place to rest for a day or two. We could let word get out. Say that for a fee, a dollar a head, they can use our grass and water and then move on."

"I never heard of such a thing."

"I have. Down to Texas and elsewhere it is common."

"If this is what you want," Dan said uncertainly.

"I would not bring it up if it wasn't. In fact, I have already talked to a man about it and he will be bringing in a small herd next week. His name is Hanks."

"Do you want me to ride over with a few of the

hands and see that—Hanks, you say?—keeps his cattle where he should? We don't want them drifting out of the barrens and mixing with the Circle V cows."

"That won't be necessary. He is aware of the problem that would cause." Epp watched the buster dab his rope on the bronc. "I want you to have a talk with the men. Explain to them that until I say otherwise, under no circumstances are they to go anywhere near the barrens. I would not like it if someone came poking around our herd and I am sure whoever rents range from us will not want our hands poking around theirs."

"I will spread the word."

"It is settled, then." Epp turned toward the house but stopped when the foreman cleared his throat. "You have something on your mind?"

"This Hanks you mentioned. It wouldn't be *Blin* Hanks, would it? I have heard of him. I even saw him once. By all accounts he is unsavory."

"No, the man I talked to is Edgar Hanks. I ran into him when I was in Tucson. He is a small rancher trying to grow bigger."

"I've never heard of him."

"I would imagine there are a lot of ranchers we haven't met or heard of," Epp said.

"How many head will he be bringing through?"

"I don't rightly know yet. Somewhere between two and three hundred." Epp smiled. "Don't forget to tell the punchers. Never let it be said the men at the Circle V don't have manners."

Dan Morgan stood still for a full minute after Epp had walked off. "Manners, hell," he finally said. "He must think I was born yesterday."

"Who?" the bronc buster asked.

Dan had not seen him standing by the rails. "No one. I was talking to myself. Old ranahans like me do that a lot."

"The hell you say," the buster responded. "You are no more feeble than me, and I am half your age."

"You are a braggart, is what you are." Dan walked off smiling, but the smile faded. He went into the stable and down the aisle to the tack room, and once he was alone he placed both hands flat on the wall and bowed his head and shook as if with the ague. "Damn him anyway," he said bitterly. He closed his eyes and the lines in his face deepened. "What do I do about it? That is the question. And I will be a maid in waiting if I know the answer."

It was ten minutes before Dan came out of the tack room. He had composed himself and he went on about his duties without anyone suspecting the turmoil he was in. That night, in the shack he had all to himself, he sat with his head in his hands for more than two hours. Finally he stood and said, "All I have done is give myself a headache."

But Dan also remembered: an incident here, a word there, an oddity or two that had pricked him but not enough to create suspicion. Now, though, after stringing the incidents and the words and the oddities together, he saw everything differently.

The horror of it all shook him.

Dan Morgan thought of Ned and Lillian Scott, and young Boone, and he did something he had not done in more years than he would admit to; he wept. He cried softly and silently until he did not have a tear left to shed, and then he shook himself as would a bear coming out of hibernation.

"I will be damned if I will fall for it," he told the four walls.

Day followed hot day and night followed warm night, and Dan kept a horse saddled behind his shack after the sun went down, and did not tell anyone. He sat by his window with the lamp off and watched the ranch house until his eyelids were too heavy for him to keep his eyes open.

His patience was rewarded when a rider approached the ranch house along about ten, and rode around to the rear.

Dan was ready. He grabbed his Winchester and hurried out. The cribber he had chosen was gnawing on his shack, but it stopped when he shoved his Winchester into the saddle scabbard. Stepping into the stirrups, he reined to the south. He swung wide of the outhouses and was waiting off in the dark when Epp Scott and another man came out. They shook hands and for a few moments were bathed in light spilling from the open doorway.

"I knew it," Dan Morgan said to himself, with all the bitterness of a man who had been lied to by someone he would have died for if called to.

The night rider climbed on his roan and departed.

Dan let him get a good lead but not so good that he would lose him. A crescent moon made the following easier. Thankfully the rider did not stop but made a beeline for the barrens.

Hours went by. Dan would not be able to make it back to the ranch by dawn, but that was all right. He had told a puncher by the name of Frank Lloyd, a ranny Dan trusted, that if he was not there in the morning to rouse the men and set them to work;

then Lloyd was to do it. And if Epp Scott happened by and wanted to know where Dan was, Lloyd was to tell him he had gone into Tucson to pick up supplies.

Dan was surprised he was not nervous. If he was right—and by the looks of the man who had paid Epp Scott a visit, he was—then he was riding into a viper's nest. But he needed to prove his suspicions were justified and he refused to endanger anyone else in the proving.

By the middle of the night they were well west and south of Red Butte. They passed bunches of cattle that had bedded down.

The barrens were the horror Dan remembered, the thornbrush impenetrable unless a man knew exactly where to find the few trails that led in and out.

Dan had been in the barrens often enough after strays that he was more acquainted with the maze than most. He knew where Epp's visitor was headed, and rather than keep following and risk being spotted, he reined wide and rode in a loop that brought him up on the basin, as it was called, from the west. Ten acres of grass in an oval hollow. Plenty for a small herd, and a campfire could be hid from prying eyes.

Dan drew rein fifty yards out. He remembered to take his spurs off and shove them in his saddlebags so the jingling did not give him away. He smiled as he stalked forward. He had not done anything like this since he was a youth. The young were always headstrong and thought they were invincible.

The last sixty feet, Dan crawled on his belly, the Winchester in front of him. He expected sentries and he was not disappointed. One at each end of the basin, the man near him constantly yawning and shaking his arms to stay awake. Another man was by the fire and three or four were under blankets.

It was the cows that interested Dan, the cows he had come so far to inspect. Two hundred head, more or less. Many were longhorns, but a lot were not. A few open-faced cattle were mixed in, and that told Dan, as surely as anything, that his hunch had been right.

Still, Dan waited, and when the nearest sentry drifted in the other direction, he slipped into the basin.

The cows had been driven so long and so hard that they were too exhausted to do more than look at him with dull regard. Dan crouched and quietly moved among them, patting necks and rumps and speaking softly. A torch would help to read the brands, but he did not need his eyes when he had his fingers and could trace the brands by touch. It helped that most of the brands were on the left hip. Those that were elsewhere were added evidence that the cows came from more than one ranch.

None of the brands had been changed. It occurred to Dan that maybe they were going to do the altering right there on the Circle V, and that made him so mad, he almost stood up and started blazing away. Caution prevailed, and when he was satisfied he made his way to the top of the basin and got out of there. He was not spotted.

Anger and sadness waged war inside him as Dan made for the outskirts of the barrens. He had added two and two correctly. Vile deeds had been done, deeds so terrible, Dan could scarcely embrace their enormity.

He was working for a monster.

The question now, the big question, the only question, was one Dan voiced out loud. "What in God's name do I do?"

Lightning Rod

Old Man Radler and his wild bunch had been on the go since dawn, and it was now pushing noon. They were wending north across terrain as rugged as any on the continent. Riding the high lines came with a price, and part of that price was comfort. The withering heat, the choking dust, the prospect of an Apache ambush, had everyone on edge.

Boone Scott had been on drag since sunup. Removing his hat, he wiped his face with his sleeve, then jammed the hat back on and twisted in the saddle to scan their back trail.

"Why do you keep doing that, Senor Lightning?" Galeno was the other rider on drag, and he had made no bones of the fact he hated it as much as he hated anything.

"Doing what?"

"Don't take me for dumb, because I am not. You keep looking back. Who or what is back there?"

"No one," Boone said, "if you don't count Apaches."

Galeno started and twisted in the saddle, his hand dropping to his six-shooter. "Apaches? Have you seen them?"

"No. But that doesn't mean they aren't there."

"You are, as you gringos say, jumpy."

"One of us should have a look-see," Boone proposed, and without waiting for a reply, he wheeled his palomino and trotted back along the trail of pockmarks. The moment he was out of Galeno's sight, he slowed and whispered, "Sassy?"

She appeared from behind a boulder, riding one of the horses her father bought from Old Man Radler. She wore the same clothes as before, only now she had on scuffed shoes instead of going barefoot.

"Are you all right?"

"You haven't heard me scream, have you?" Sassy grinned.

Boone did not find it funny, and said so. "I don't like this. I don't like it at all. I don't see why we couldn't have left in the middle of the night when Radler was camped in your pa's valley."

"We have been all through that," Sassy said. "My pa would have noticed I was gone when he woke up, and come after me. By me sneaking off like I did, I bought myself a whole day. Likely as not he didn't realize I was missing until that night."

"He still might show up. Our trail is not hard to follow."

Sassy shook her head. "He won't leave home, not with those new horses. He'll be too afraid the Apaches will steal them."

"I still don't like it."

"Because it was my idea?"

"I don't like you alone back here. Apaches could jump us at any time and then where would you be?"

Sassy wagged her Spencer. "I have this. If I see any, I will give a holler and you can come on the run."

"By then it might be too late."

Sassy kneed her horse next to his. "You gnaw on a thing like a pup gnaws on a bone. I will stay close until Old Man Radler makes camp for the night. Then you can slip away and join me and we will go off and be together for as long as we draw breath, so help us God." She giggled.

"I do not find it funny."

"Are you going to be this way the rest of our lives? Because if you are, I should go back to Pa. I do not want a man who is grumpy as he is. I do not want a fretter."

"I can't help it. Not after w—"

Sassy held a hand up. "Stop right there. That was special and we will not talk about our special times, ever. Talking about them spoils them."

"How in God's name—?"

"Stop right there, again. If I am to stop cussing like you want me to, then you can't take the Lord's name in vain. I may not amount to much, but that is one thing I have never done and I am proud of it."

Boone stared at her.

"What?"

"There is more to you and me than I reckoned. I know so little about you and you know so little about me."

"Have you changed your mind?" Sassy asked, her voice quavering slightly. "It all happened sort of sudden, so I wouldn't be surprised if you have come to your senses."

"Hush," Boone said.

Sassy's horse stamped and she appeared ready to kick, herself. "This is a fine note. You said you are not bossy. You said I am free to think what I want and say what I want."

"You are. But I am not ten years old. I do not change my mind with the changing of the wind. We have pledged to stick by each other, so stick I will until you pry me loose and throw me away."

Sassy smiled sweetly. "That was downright poetical."

Boone opened his mouth to say more, but someone snickered behind him. Whirling, he stabbed at his Colt.

"It is only me, senor." Galeno snickered again. He had come unnoticed around the bend and his hands were empty of anything save reins. "I do not mean you or the senorita any harm."

"How much did you hear?"

"Enough to know you have snuck her away from her father. Ben Drecker will want you dead, and Old Man Radler will not be happy either." Galeno laughed and slapped his thigh. "I admire your grit, senor. You spit in the face of death."

"Are you fixing to tell Radler?"

"Why should I?" Galeno retorted. "That would make you mad, and I would rather have him mad at me than you. I have seen you draw, remember?"

"Then what?" Boone said.

"I will keep my mouth shut and you two can carry on." Galeno's expression became crafty. "But it would help to still my tongue if you were to give me, say, a hundred dollars out of your cut after we divide up the money."

"I could shoot you and not have to pay you a cent."

"True, senor. But how would you explain it to Old

Man Radler? That I was mad and tried to shoot you? But what would I be mad about? No excuse you make will be believed. He knows me too well."

Sassy offered her opinion. "I say give him the hundred dollars. It is not much to pay for our happiness."

"Listen to the senorita, senor," Galeno coaxed. "A hundred dollars is—how do you gringos say it?—a pittance. It is nothing. Your cut will be much more. Do we have an agreement?"

"I think it is a mistake."

"Please," Sassy coaxed.

"Yes. Please," Galeno said. "What do I care if you two want to be together? There is no reason for me to tell Radler if I do not want to."

"A hundred dollars," Boone said. "And you are not to mention what you saw or heard to a living soul."

"You have my word, senor." Galeno wheeled his pinto.

Boone lowered his voice so Galeno couldn't hear. "I don't trust him, but I reckon we have no choice. Stay close. I will sneak away first chance I get and we will light a shuck."

Galeno was waiting at the bend. "I suspected you were up to something, senor, when you came back from your walk yesterday. You could not stop smiling, and you are not a man who smiles much."

"Does anyone else suspect?"

"No one has said anything to me."

They used their spurs and soon came on two of the stolen horses. The animals had stopped and the herd had gone on without them. Boone and Galeno reined to either side and drove the pair on. They had not gone far when Vance Radler appeared.

"Where the hell have you two been?"

"I don't like your tone," Boone said.

"And my pa won't like that you two dropped back. You are supposed to be riding drag."

"We dropped back after these two." Boone nodded at a pair of horses. "Or would your pa rather we let them run off?"

"It took both of you to catch them? What do you use for brains? Didn't my pa make it clear that one of us must be on drag at all times?"

Galeno acted sheepish. "We made a mistake, for which I apologize. We would be grateful if you keep this to yourself. And we promise it will not happen again."

"It better not." Vance gazed past them. "Have you seen any sign of Apaches?"

"No, senor," Galeno said. "But you know how Apaches are when they do not want to be found."

Vance grunted and turned his mount. "Remember. One of you always stays on drag no matter what."

"Damn," Boone said.

"Your senorita is safe. Vance believed us."

"But if he tells his pa—"

"What if he does? We caught the two horses. They are all Old Man Radler will care about."

Boone rode uneasily on. About two in the afternoon Drub trotted back to spell him, but Boone said he was fine.

"You can spell me," Galeno said. "I have eaten enough dust for one day." He touched his sombrero.

"It is you and me now, Lightning." Drub beamed. "What would you like to talk about to help pass the time?"

Boone did not answer right away. When he did, he

chose his words with care. "Do you like this kind of life, Drub?"

"Like it how? I don't much care for the heat. Cold is better, but Arizona is short on cold unless you go up in the mountains and play in the snow."

"Do you like stealing horses and cattle and being wanted by the law?"

"It is all I have ever done."

"But do you *want* to do it?"

Drub rubbed his chin. "No one has ever asked me that before. Pa decides what I want to do, not me."

"If it were yours to choose," Boone persisted, "would you go on rustling or start a new life?"

"You mean be on my own? Without Pa? Without Vance? Just me and only me?"

"Yes."

Drub squirmed on his saddle. "Would you go along, pard? I wouldn't want to go alone. It would scare me to be on my own."

"A big man like you?"

"Sure, I am big. Bigger than most and stronger than most. But I'm not very smart."

"You are smart enough," Boone said.

"That is kind but it is not true. And not just because my pa has always told me how dumb I am. I *know* I'm not smart. I know it by how I think and how I talk. I am slow as a turtle and other people are rabbits."

"Don't be so hard on yourself."

"It is not being hard. It is seeing things as they are. You wouldn't want me to lie to myself, would you?"

"No, Drub, a man should never lie."

"I would start a new life if we started it together. You and me and no one else? We could go to California. Pa keeps saying it is awful nice out there. There is an ocean and everything. I am not much at swimming, but I think it would be fun." Drub was growing excited. "What do you say? You and me, pard?"

"Drub, listen. I would—"

"We can cut our fingers and mix our blood and be blood brothers. How does that sound? That way you will be my brother and not Vance." Drub chortled. "It would serve him right. He doesn't deserve a brother, as mean as he is."

"Drub," Boone said again. "I would like nothing better than to go to California with you. But I can't."

"Why not?" Drub was upset and didn't hide it. "Was all that talk about being my pard just talk?"

"You *are* my pard. But things are complicated. I have plans. Plans that involve someone else."

"Oh."

"Don't look like that. You can come with us. We will all go to California. Once we get there you can srike off on your own and live your life as you see fit and not as your pa makes you live it."

"No, thanks," Drub said.

"Don't be so contrary. I wouldn't ask you to come if I didn't want you along."

"So you say. But you are just like all the rest. You pretend to be nice but deep down you aren't really my friend. You only say that so I will be nice to you."

"You are mistaken."

"And here I was so happy. I thought I had a real friend at last. But you want nothing to do with me."

"Damn it, Drub. That is not what I said. You are putting words in my mouth."

"We are not pards anymore." Drub jabbed his spurs

and broke into a gallop, leaving swirls of dust in his wake.

Boone called to him, but Drub did not answer or stop and presently Boone was alone. He almost reined around then and there. Instead, he said to himself, "Night will be better. We will be far away before they realize I am gone." He patted the palomino. "Between you and me, I hope I didn't just make the worst mistake of my life."

Accident Prone

The first time was an hour after dawn.

Dan Morgan ate breakfast with the punchers. Most continued to be glum over the deaths of Ned and Lillian, and Dan did what he could to lift their spirits. He talked about how well the ranch was doing. The cattle were fattening nicely and the next bunch they sent to market promised to bring in more money than ever. He talked about how although it was hot, as every summer in Arizona was hot, they weren't suffering from drought, and for that they should give thanks. Dan had lived through two droughts and he hoped to God he never had to live through another.

Dan talked about Boone Scott. The punchers all liked the boy. His disappearance had affected them as deeply as the deaths. Dan mentioned that they still might hear from him, and that maybe, just maybe, Boone would get homesick and drift back to the Circle V.

It was at that point that a puncher called One Thumb Todd spoke up and said how he hoped Dan was right and Boone came back and put an end to the jinx the Circle V was under.

That got Dan good and mad. He cussed One Thumb and said that all of Todd's brains had been in the thumb Todd lost when a bull tromped on it and smashed it to pulp. Dan reminded them that a jinx was nothing but superstition. Jinxes did not exist. He had warned them a while back that the next man to mention a jinx would be fired.

At that, One Thumb Todd blanched and said how sorry he was.

Dan forgave him, but he was not in the best of moods as he walked to the stable to saddle his horse. His habit of late had been to spend a couple of hours out on the range right after breakfast. It showed the men he was devoted to his job and to the Circle V. That he was not one of those foremen who sat around doing next to nothing while everyone else did the work.

The stable doors hung open, but that just meant the stable hand had been in to feed the horses and sweep out their stalls. Dan moved down the center aisle to the stall that held his favorite horse, a dun as easy on the backside as an easy chair. He gave it a pat and was turning toward the tack room when something struck him on the shoulder so hard he was sent staggering and nearly fell.

There was a tremendous *thud.*

"What the hell!" Dan recovered and stared at the bale of hay that had missed his head by a few inches. Then he jerked his head toward the hay loft above and dropped his hand to his revolver. "Who's up there?"

No one answered.

Dan stepped to the ladder. His shoulder was throbbing and it throbbed worse as he climbed, but it wasn't broken as near as he could tell. He reached the loft and peered over and for the second time said, "What the hell?"

Dozens of bales were neatly stacked, as always, but otherwise the loft was empty.

Dan climbed all the way. Drawing his Colt, he went the entire lengh of the loft, searching among the bales, but did not find a soul. Perplexed, he went back to the ladder. As he was standing there trying to make sense of how the bale fell on him, he noticed that the hay loft door was open. He went over. The rope to the winch was down. Ordinarily, it was kept coiled on the loft until the winch was put into use.

Dan poked his head out. Several punchers were moving about, and over at the ranch house a servant was hanging out newly washed clothes. He saw no one who should not be there. He saw no one slinking from the stable.

"Damn it," Dan said. He pulled up the rope, closed the loft door and descended. His shoulder stayed sore, but it didn't pain him when he moved his arm. Soon he had the dun saddled, and rode out of the stable.

The glare of the morning sun caused Dan to squint. He trotted to the south, still mulling the problem of the bale. Once he was clear of the buildings and on the open range, he slowed to a walk.

For over an hour Dan checked on cattle and talked to the hands he ran into. One puncher mentioned how he had liked Dan's talk at breakfast, and he agreed with Dan that the jinx business was so much nonsense.

Dan was happy to hear it. They parted company, and Dan drifted in the general direction of the ranch buildings. He passed a knot of cattle and had just brought the dun to a gallop when the world was yanked out from under him.

It happened without warning. One moment Dan was tall in the saddle, riding hard. The next, he and his saddle were pitched headlong to the hard earth. He threw up his arms and managed to hit on his shoulder and roll. But it was the same shoulder the bale fell on, and when he sat up he could barely move his arm.

Next to him lay his saddle and saddle blanket. Dumbfounded, Dan pushed to his knees and rolled the saddle onto its side. The cinch was busted. It had not come undone; it was split clean through. The edges were frayed, as they should be if it broke and wasn't cut.

Even so, Dan bent lower. He ran a finger over the break. It was hard to tell, but he was willing to swear that someone had cut the cinch just enough to ensure that it would come apart on him when he rode hard.

"First the bale. Now this." Dan stood and brushed at his clothes. Thankfully his hat had stayed on and his Colt was still in his holster.

The dun came back to see what was going on. Dan patted it, then shucked his rifle from the saddle scabbard, transferred his saddlebags to the dun and climbed on bareback.

The first puncher Dan came on, he sent the man to fetch his saddle and blanket. He also instructed him not to say anything. Word of the busted cinch would only fuel the jinx talk.

Dan glowered as he neared the buildings. He did not reply to a hail from a cowboy and he did not return a wave from the blacksmith. Instead of going to the stable, he rode to the house and dismounted with the sharp movements of a man close to losing his temper. He climbed the steps and knocked on the front door.

A servant answered. Dan was admitted and waited with his hat in hand. It was several minutes before Epp Scott came down the hall.

"Dan. Good to see you again. What can I do for you?"

"You can stop trying to kill me."

Epp stopped and glanced behind him as if to make sure none of the servants had heard. Putting a hand on Dan's shoulder, Epp opened the front door and ushered him out on the porch. Only after Epp had closed the door did he say, "What is this nonsense about killing you?"

"You have tried twice since daybreak. If there is a third time I will come for you with my revolver out."

"Have you been drinking?"

"Don't you dare," Dan said. "I rarely touch liquor and you know it. So does everyone else. Try to spread a rumor that I have turned into a drunk and no one will believe you."

"Why else would you talk so crazy?"

"The barrens," Dan said.

"What about them?"

"I know about Blin Hanks. I know about the stolen cattle." Dan allowed himself a grim smile. "I went there. Snuck right in and right out and your rustler friends never caught on."

"I don't have the slightest idea what you are talking about."

"Pretend if you want but it will not fool me."

Epp motioned toward the bunkhouse. "If all this is true, why haven't you told the men? Why keep it to yourself?"

"Are you complaining? Would you rather I did?"

Epp did not reply.

"I have not told them yet because it will crush them. On top of all that has happened, to find out you are a rustler will be the last straw. No puncher worth his salt will ride for a brand-blotting outfit. They will pack their war bags and go. Word will spread, and that will be the end of the Circle V."

"Your devotion to the ranch is a trait I have always admired."

"Go to hell."

Epp straightened. "I will overlook that because you are upset. You have jumped to conclusions and accused me falsely, and I forgive that too."

"Go to hell twice over."

"Think for a minute. Here I am, the owner of one of the biggest and best spreads in the territory, with plenty of cattle and plenty of money. Why would I jeopardize all that by rustling?"

"Some people never get enough. No matter how much they have, they always want more."

"Let's look at this another way," Epp said. "Suppose for a minute you are wrong. Suppose that whatever filled your head with this nonsense is not what you think it is. For instance, Blin Hanks. Who is he?"

"You know damn well who he is. He paid you a visit."

"The man who owns the cattle in the barrens? I told you before. His name is Edgar, not Blin. At least, that is what he told me."

Some of Dan's conviction evaporated. "He said his name was Edgar?"

Epp nodded. "I had no reason to doubt him. He paid in advance for the use of the barrens and gave his word he would only stay a few days."

"I suppose he could have lied."

"Now you have been out to the barrens and you say the cows are rustled? If that is the case, then we must call in the law. I will not have the Circle V's reputation tarnished."

"And you are serious?"

"Damn it, Dan. How could you think so poorly of me? You, of all people. The one man I count on the most. The man who keeps this ranch running smoothly. The man who was a good friend to my father and my mother, and who I thought was a friend to me. Was I wrong? Was I mistaken about you? Have I trusted you all these years and you have not trusted me?"

"I don't know what to say."

"Then I will say it for both of us. We need to clear the air. We should talk this out over supper tonight. Come about eight. I know that is late but I have a lot to do today and it can't be put off. What do you say?"

"I reckon that's best."

"Thank you." Epp clapped Dan on the shoulder. Fortunately, it was Dan's good shoulder. "Eight o'clock it is. I can't tell you how happy you have made me. The last thing I want is to lose your confidence."

"I feel like a fool."

Epp smiled and ushered him to the steps. "Don't be so hard on yourself. Isn't that what you told me after my pa died? Take the rest of the day off. Relax.

Sort out your thinking. Take a look at things from my point of view and maybe you will see them differently."

Dan went down the steps. "I will be here at eight and we will hash this out like you want."

"I want nothing more than to set things right."

"If I am wrong, and it is beginning to look as if I am, I apologize in advance."

"We all make mistakes." Epp hurried back inside.

Dan stared at the door awhile; then he bent his boots toward his shack. "The benefit of the doubt," he said to himself. "I have not given him the benefit of the doubt."

Once inside, Dan kicked the wall and kicked the table and then sat with his chin in his hands and did more thinking. He went over the little incidents that led him to believe Epp was rotten to the core. Doubt crept in. He got up and paced, and when that did not relieve the tension he was feeling, he walked to the stable to see whether his saddle was there. It was, and the cinch was being repaired. He took a chance and asked the stable hand, an old puncher whose bones and joints were no longer up to punching, if he thought the cinch broke or had been cut.

"My eyes ain't what they used to be, but I would say it busted. Do you think different?"

"I was just asking." Dan got out of there and for a spell walked in aimless confusion among the buildings.

The day dragged. Dan did not see anything of Epp. He was in his shack changing into clean clothes when a noise drew him to the window. The buckboard had been brought out and the team was being hitched. Maria and her cousins were on the porch, watching.

Dan finished dressing.

At the appointed hour Dan headed for the house. He left his six-gun behind. It wasn't fitting to go to supper armed.

Twilight was falling. Most of the punchers were in the bunkhouse, the horses in their stalls and some in the corral, the chickens in the chicken coop.

"I am glad you came. It will be good to get this out in the open."

"I have been thinking and I admit I might have been wrong about you," Dan said.

Epp smiled and led the way down the hall to the kitchen. "I can't tell you how happy this makes me. I need your trust. We must work together if the Circle V is to prosper."

"I have always been loyal to the brand."

"That you have. No one is more loyal than you."

"Tomorrow I will show you just how loyal. I'll take ten of our hands and ride to the barrens to confront Hanks."

"There is an idea."

"You'll come along, won't you?"

"I wouldn't miss it for the world." Epp held the kitchen door open. "After you."

Dan walked past him. He felt a searing pain in his chest and looked down at a knife hilt jutting from his body. Shock seized him. Then he saw Blin Hanks. Dan went to cry out and a hand came from behind and clamped over his mouth. He struggled, but his legs were mush and the next thing he knew he was on his back and the world around him was fading to black.

A face filled his vision. A cruel face. A mocking

face. "You were right about me. I always want more. And if the only way to get it is to get rid of you, all I can say is—"

Dan Morgan did not hear the rest. He did not hear anything at all.

Plans Awry

Minutes had never dragged so slow in Boone Scott's life. At last the sun perched on the brink of its daily extinction, blazing red in farewell and splashing the sky with orange and yellow.

Old Man Radler called a halt in a wide canyon. Charred embers, a pile of dry brush and old tracks showed they had been there before. A new fire was kindled and coffee put on to brew.

Boone left the palomino saddled and joined them. Drub was across from him and would not meet his gaze.

The coffeepot hissed and steam rose from the spout.

"We have one more ranch to visit and then we can split the money," Old Man Radler announced.

"I can't wait," said a rustler named Roerig. "I want a shave and a bath and a woman and whiskey."

"Give me bug juice before anything else," said another, and smacked his lips. "I miss that the most."

"Keep that up, Aten, and you will end up like Ben Drecker," Old Man Radler told him. "You will be so far down in the bottle, you will never climb out."

"Why say a thing like that?" Aten asked.

Old Man Radler turned to Boone. "How about you, Lightning? Is there anything you miss?"

"No."

"Oh? I could have sworn you had taken a fancy to Drecker's daughter, Sassy. Or doesn't she count?"

Boone grew cold inside. "Talk like that can get a man bucked out in gore."

"Quick is not everything," Old Man Radler said.

"Meaning?"

"Smart will beat quick if the smart is done right." Old Man Radler nodded at Skelman, who stood with his hands close to his black-handled Colts. Old Man Radler nodded at Vance, and Vance shifted the rifle he was holding in his lap so the muzzle pointed at Boone. Old Man Radler nodded a third time, and Drub put his hand on his six-shooter, but he didn't draw it. Old Man Radler frowned.

"What is this?" Boone snapped.

"I don't want you flying off the handle when Galeno and Wagner get back," Old Man Radler said.

Boone glanced around the campfire and gave a start. He began to rise, but a flicker of movement from Skelman froze him in place.

"See what I mean?" Old Man Radler said. "Smart will beat quick if the smart is done right. You might want to work on being smarter and then you will be twice as dangerous. Provided you live that long."

"You had no right."

"Did you really think you could keep it a secret? That Galeno would keep his mouth shut if you paid him? Hell. Trusting him is like trusting a rattler not to bite you. He came to me straightaway and I sent him and Wagner to fetch her."

Something in Boone's expression prompted Skelman to say, "Don't try it. You might get two or three, but we will sure as hell get you."

"Listen to him, Lightning," Old Man Radler said. "If I had wanted you dead, you would not be breathing."

"Then what?"

"I like that girl. I have known her since she came to my knees. And I can't think of anything more stupid than to let her ride alone through Apache country."

"She has stuck close to us," Boone said before he could stop himself.

"And that will stop Apaches? Damn, boy. If you weren't so young I would have you shot for being so dumb. Have you ever tangled with them? I have. And they are smart *and* quick. If they spot her they will snatch her and either make her one of their women or do things to her that would turn your stomach."

"You care what happens to her?"

Old Man Radler glowered. "What the hell? Why wouldn't I? Have you been listening to a word I've said?"

"I just thought . . ." Boone said, but he did not go on.

"What *do* you think of me? Yes, I am a rustler. It is my trade. But have you ever heard of me robbing banks? Or killing folks just to kill them? Or murdering women and children?"

Boone looked down.

"You son of a bitch," Old Man Radler said. "I have not been this insulted since Hector was a pup. Give me one good reason why I should not snap my fingers and have you shot to pieces."

"I can give you several. You just said you don't kill for the sake of killing. Then there are the two or three I will take with me, one of which will be you. And then there is Sassy."

Old Man Radler drummed his fingers on the ground. "If you don't beat all, I don't know what does."

Vance said, "I say we shoot him, Pa."

"When I want your opinion, which I never do, I will ask for it." Old Man Radler gazed into the gathering twilight. "Unless I am mistaken we are about to have company. There will be no more talk of killing unless I do the talking."

Hooves drummed and into view came three horses but only two riders, Galeno and Wagner. Galeno was leading the riderless animal by the reins.

Boone was on his feet before they got there, and he was not the only one. Old Man Radler hurried past him.

"Where is she? Why bring her horse and not her?"

"The horse is all we found," Wagner said.

"We yelled and yelled for her, senor," Galeno reported. "But she did not answer us."

"Were there tracks?" Old Man Radler asked. "Anything that might give you a clue?"

"Not a sign, senor."

"She wouldn't go off and leave her horse," Wagner said. "Something must have happened to her, and it wouldn't surprise me if that something was Apaches."

No one tried to stop Boone from dashing to the palomino. No one tried to stop him as he gripped the saddle horn and swung up. "Where exactly did you find her horse?"

"Half a mile back in some boulders. I can show you if you want," Wagner offered.

"I want," Boone said.

Old Man Radler had other ideas. "Hold on." He ran up and seized hold of Wagner's bridle. "No one goes anywhere without my say-so."

"You better give it quick," Boone said.

"Don't go off half-cocked. That might be what those red devils want. It could be they took her as bait. Apaches know how white men think. They know that when they steal our females we will move heaven and earth to get our womenfolk back."

Vance added, "There are too many of us and we are too well armed for the Apaches to jump us without losing a lot of warriors. So they took your girlfriend to draw some of us out."

"It worked," Boone said, and applied his spurs. Shouts were flung after him and Old Man Radler bawled for him to stop, but Boone was not about to draw rein this side of the grave. He lashed the palomino, calling on all the speed it possessed. Soon he was out of the canyon, galloping headlong. He was keenly aware that night was about to fall, and with it any hope he had of finding Sassy quickly.

"Dear Lord, spare her," Boone said. He rose in the stirrups, seeking the boulders Wagner mentioned. He vaguely recollected passing them with the herd.

From behind him the drumming of more hooves was added to those of the palomino. A glance showed four men coming to help. Drub was one, Wagner was another. The third was Skelman. Why Skelman should care about Sassy, Boone could not begin to guess. But the fourth rider was the biggest surprise; it was Old Man Radler.

The four were well back and had no chance of overtaking Boone before he reached the boulders. And there they were, some as wide as Conestogas and others big enough to conceal a cabin.

"Sassy!" Boone shouted, reining in among them. "Sassy! Can you hear me?"

The silence taunted him.

Boone came to the end of the boulders and was about to rein around to go back and search for tracks when a lithe form hurtled at him from out of the shadows. In pure instinct Boone's hand flew to his ivory-handled Colt. It was up and out before he knew he had drawn, the *click* of the hammer a prelude to the blast to come.

"Don't shoot!" Sassy squealed. "It's me!"

Shock rooted Boone to his saddle. Then her hand was on his arm, and instantly he swung her up behind him. Her Spencer gouged his back. "I thought the Apaches had you."

"I will explain after we are safe," Sassy said in his ear. "Hurry. This may be our only chance to get away."

"But your horse—"

"We are more important. For God's sake fan the breeze before it is too late."

Boone did as she wanted. He was so happy she was safe that for a few minutes he drifted on a tide of pure relief. Then reality crashed down, as it always did. "Where are we going?"

"Anywhere so long as it is away from the Radlers."

As ideas went, hers smacked of panic. But Boone would like to be shed of the Radler gang too, so he knuckled down to riding. Her arm slid around his waist and held snug, and he grew warm all over.

Nightfall was upon them. The dark was their ally; it would cloak them from white and red alike.

Boone glanced over his shoulder. Old Man Radler and the other three were nowhere to be seen. He lashed his reins harder.

Half a mile they fled, with no sign of pursuit. Boone would have gone farther, but by then the palomino was winded. He hauled on the reins and they came to a sliding halt, dust rising from under its hooves.

"Why did you stop?" Sassy anxiously asked. "They are still back there somewhere."

"Somewhere but not here." Boone twisted and her nose almost bumped his. "How did they get your horse?"

"I saw they had made camp so I hunkered in those boulders to wait for you," Sassy said, her eyes dancing with a secret light. "When I heard someone coming I figured it was you and ran to see. But it was Wagner and Galeno. They were almost on top of me, but I ducked down and they went on by and found my horse. I stayed hid until they were gone, and here we are."

"We need a horse for you," Boone said. "We can't go all the way to California on mine."

"There is something else," Sassy said.

"If it is bad news I don't want to hear it."

"I think I saw an Apache earlier."

"You *think*?"

"It was a face, and it was watching me. But when

I saw it the face disappeared and I did not see it again." Sassy nervously licked her lips. "I am pretty sure it was an Apache."

"From the frying pan into the fire." Boone was not making a joke. Impulsively pulling her close, he glued his mouth to hers.

"Goodness. What was that for?"

"It might be our last."

"Not if I have anything to say about it." And Sassy molded her lips to his and kept them there until he pushed her back. "You don't like to kiss me now?"

"Your kisses are my heaven. But now is not the time."

"Listen to you. We are not hitched yet and here you are, taking me for granted."

Boone thrust a hand over her mouth and whispered in her ear, "I heard something."

In deathly stillness they waited, the only sound the palomino's heavy breathing.

After a while Sassy broke the brittle shell of their dread by whispering, "Whatever it was must be gone."

Boone nodded, and then because he was not sure she saw him, he said in her ear, "I wish we were anywhere but here. Apaches are ghosts and I can't shoot a ghost."

"That is silly talk. They are flesh and blood, the same as we are."

"Maybe so. But they don't die easy."

"We can't let them get their hands on us. If it comes to that, you must shoot me. Do I have your word?"

"I would rather shoot myself."

"You can do that too. But first shoot me. I have

heard what they do to white women. Promise me, Boone."

"I am not sure I can. Shooting you would be like shooting my own heart."

"That is a hell of a thing for you to say. If you care for me you will put a window in my skull."

"I will not make a promise I don't know if I can keep." Boone was straining his eyes to pierce the gloom, to no avail.

"I would put a bullet in your brain if you were the woman and I was the man."

"That doesn't make me feel any better," Boone said. "But I will try to kill you if there is no other way."

"That is all I ask. Let's hope it doesn't come to that."

No sooner were the words out of Sassy's mouth than the palomino whinnied and shied.

The next moment a shape swiftly sprang out of the night at them.

Devil's Brood

Sassy started to scream and clamped a hand over her mouth.

In a twinkling Boone had his Colt out and level. He came within a whisker of firing.

Then the young buck went bounding past, and with a startled snort it was gone.

"I'll be!" Sassy declared.

"Just a deer." Boone let out a long breath and slid the Colt into his holster. "He must have happened by and we spooked him." Deer did most of their foraging at night, making it harder for predators to prey on them.

"He sure spooked me," Sassy said, and laughed. "I thought we were goners."

Boone spread his arms and held her, her face pressed to his shoulder. He breathed deep of her scent.

"What now?" Sassy asked.

"We get you a horse."

"But the only horses to be had for a hundred miles are those with Old Man Radler."

"Then that is where we will get it."

Sassy pulled back, her face a mask of anxiety. "Can't we wait and get one somewhere else? So what if we have to ride double for a few days?"

"If that face you saw was really an Apache, we stand a better chance if we both have mounts."

Sassy nuzzled his neck with her warm lips and said softly, "I am a burden, aren't I?"

"We do what we have to, and right now that means getting you a horse, pronto."

Boone reined back the way they came. Sassy had one arm around his waist and was holding her Spencer between them, her head on his shoulder blade.

"It doesn't seem real at times," she said.

"What doesn't?"

"This. Us. Together." Sassy sighed. "I dreamed of the day when a man would come along and claim my heart, and now that my dream has come true, I am so happy I could bust."

"I will do the best I can by you. I want you to know that."

"I do," Sassy said. "You're not no-account like my pa." She sighed again. "I will miss him but not that much, and less as times goes by."

"It is a shame I can't take you to meet my folks. They would like you a whole lot."

"Why can't you?"

"I told you about Ranson, about what I did. I imagine my pa is sorry he ever sired me. And Ma must have cried until she did not have tears left to shed."

"We could stop long enough for you to say your good-byes."

"And put them through more pain?" Boone shook his head. "No, thanks. I would spare them that."

They lapsed into silence. The dull clomp of the palomino's hooves were punctuated now and again by the yip of coyotes. Once a mountain lion screeched, far off, the cry so much like a woman's, it brought goose bumps to Boone's flesh.

The North Star made it easy for him to tell direction. He had to watch for boulders and other obstacles and twice reined aside just in time. Every now and then he rose in the stirrups and scoured the sea of dark for a pinpoint of light.

They had been riding for half an hour when Sassy said in a small voice, "Boone?"

"I am right here."

"Thank you."

"For what?"

"For saving me."

"Shucks. I did not want Radler to get his hands on you. He claimed to want to protect you, but he is as trustworthy as a rabid wolf."

"No, not that," Sassy said. "I want to thank you for saving me from the emptiness. I was so lonely."

"You had your critters and your woods and your secret place in the cliff," Boone reminded her.

"Critters can't hug like you do, and woods do not make me laugh, and those Indian ruins only made me lonelier. So thank you."

"I am the one who should do the thanking. I have drifted from the straight and narrow, as my ma calls it, and might have gone completely bad if you had not come along when you did. You brought me out of myself. You reminded me there is more to life than feeling sorry for oneself."

"We were meant to be. God brought us together at just the right time. Maybe it is him we should thank."

A sound off in the dark caused Boone to draw rein. "Did you hear that? It was a hoof on rock."

"Apaches," Sissy whispered, her body tensing against his. "If they have heard us we are in for it."

The sound was repeated, and multiplied. Horses were coming toward them from several directions. Boone placed his hand on his Colt and was about to jab his spurs when a raspy voice called out.

"Lightning? Is that you?"

"Oh God!" Sassy whispered. "Old Man Radler."

Skelman's voice came from their right. "It is him. He has the girl." Seconds later he materialized at their side. "We have been looking all over for you."

Old Man Radler, Drub and Wagner converged, the former saying, "It is good to see you safe, girl. You pulled a damn fool stunt, following us like you did."

"What the hell happened?" Wagner asked Boone. "Where did you get to?"

"We hollered and hollered," Drub said. "But you didn't answer."

"An Apache got her," Boone lied. "He was on foot and I chased after him, but Lordy, could he run!"

Sassy's fingers tightened on his arm in a reassuring squeeze.

Old Man Radler grunted. "They say an Apache buck can go sixty miles in a day and not tire. I don't know as they can, but they sure as hell can outlast a white man."

"They aren't human," Wagner remarked.

"I finally got close to him," Boone said, continuing his lie, "and he dropped Sassy and ran."

"They will do that when there is a chance they will take a bullet," Old Man Radler said.

"They are yellow," Wagner declared. "They only attack when they have an advantage."

"I can see my sons aren't the only idiots in my gang. That isn't yellow. That is smart. Apaches are as brave as you or me and maybe more so in your case."

"Here, now," Wagner said.

Drub kneed his horse in close to the palomino and reached over to touch Sassy's shoulder. "I am glad you are all right. I was scared for you." He looked at Boone coldly.

"Is something the matter?" Sassy asked.

"No," Drub said, but he was a terrible liar.

"Enough of this jawing," Old Man Radler said. "I want to get some sleep tonight and we have a ways to go." He reined about and the rest of them brought their mounts into step on either side.

Sassy gave Boone another squeeze, then said to the old curmudgeon, "It was kind of you to come after me. You have always treated me decent and for that I am grateful."

"Why wouldn't I?" Old Man Radler rejoined. "I had a wife once. She bore me my two boys and never gave me much cause to complain. Then she went and died on me. Consumption, the doc said. At the last I held her hand for three days straight while she slowly wasted away. It was an awful way to go."

"Do you ever miss her?"

"If a man asked me that I would shoot him," Old Man Radler said in disgust. "There are some things a person should not talk about, and losing a wife or a child is one of them."

"I never saw this side of you."

"What side? The side that brought up two sons? We are all of us more than we seem to be. I rustle and I have killed, but that does not make me worthless."

"May I ask you something?"

"So long as it is not about my wife."

"Why did you take up horse stealing for a living? Why live on the wrong side of the law when it is less trouble to live on the other side?"

"That is a fair question and I will answer you." Old Man Radler paused. "When I was Drub's age I didn't know any better. I took up with a rough bunch. They made their money the easy way. They stole it or rustled it. That is where I learned the trade and I have stuck with it in part because I do not know how to do anything else and in part because I like it."

"You like taking stock that doesn't belong to you?"

"Careful, girl. I am fond of you but I will not be pricked. As for the rustling, it is root hog or die in this world. A man does what he has to or he doesn't last."

"You never feel any guilt?"

"Hell. Let me tell you something. Ravens and jays steal eggs and hatchlings from the nests of other birds. Do you think they feel guilt? Rabbits help themselves to the vegetables in a garden. Do they feel guilt? A wolf will leap into a pen, take a lamb in its jaws and leap out again. Does the wolf feel guilt? It is the same with me."

"You are mixing people and animals."

"So? It is in their nature and it is in ours. If you ask me, we are nothing more than animals in clothes."

"It is not in my nature to hurt things," Sassy said.

"Oh?" Old Man Radler bared his teeth in a grin.

"Tell that to your pa. You ran out on him, didn't you? Left him there all alone with his bottle. If that is not hurt, I don't know what is."

Wagner laughed.

"I left him. I didn't kill him. And we were talking about rustling. What I did is not anywhere near the same and don't pretend it is. You are only saying that to annoy me."

"I am saying that deep down people are more alike than those like you are willing to accept. We are none of us perfect. Yet you make up excuses when you do something that you don't think is right so you can pretend to be."

Drub said, "You sure do think good, Pa."

"Someone in our family has to. Your brother never thinks of anything except himself, and you are lucky if you have a thought a day."

"Ahhhh, Pa."

That ended the talk for a while. Until Sassy started it up again by clearing her throat and saying, "I want to ask you something else, Ezekiel."

Old Man Radler rounded on her with a low growl. "Don't ever call me that again, girl. Only my wife could."

"It is just a name."

"It is *my* name and it will not be used if I don't want it used. Go ahead and ask what is on your mind."

"What are your plans for Boone and me?"

"Who?"

Boone felt Sassy stiffen. He looked over his shoulder and smiled to show he was not upset.

"Lightning, I mean."

"That is not what you called him." Old Man Radler focused on Boone. "Is that your real name?"

"I don't use it much, just like you don't use yours."

"I have heard it somewhere."

"It is not uncommon," Boone said. "Maybe you are thinking of Daniel Boone. Everyone has heard of him."

"I've heard it somewhere else, and not all that long ago." Old Man Radler shrugged. "If it is important it will come to me." He turned back to Sassy. "My plans for you, you asked? I don't have any. Once we sell the rest of the horses we will divide up the money. You and Lightning or Boone or whatever you want to call him are free to go where the wind carries you."

"How long will it be?"

Old Man Radler chuckled. "Don't worry. It won't take a month of Sundays. We have one more ranch to visit. Ten days or so to get there, another two or so to collect our money and off you can go."

"I can't wait," Sassy said.

"That is, if all goes well," Old Man Radler amended.

Boone decided to take part. "Why wouldn't it?"

"The man we have to deal with is one of the worst I have ever come across. I don't trust him any further than I can throw a buckboard."

"Worst how?"

"People think I am bad, but I am an angel compared to him. He works in secret, letting folks think he is upright and law-abiding. If they knew the truth they would take the law into their own hands."

"How is it I have never heard of him?"

"Didn't I just say he works in secret? You would

never know it to look at him that he is wicked to the bone. He practically runs a town called Ranson—"

"Ranson?" Boone repeated.

"Heard of it, have you? As vicious a nest of side-winders as you will ever find, and the man I have been telling you about is the top serpent. When we meet with him let me do the talking and don't turn your back on him or anyone who is with him."

Sassy chuckled. "Does this demon have a name or should we call him Satan?"

"Poke fun if you want, girl."

"His name," Boone said when Old Man Radler did not go on. "I would like to know his name."

"The worst hombre in all of Arizona Territory goes by the name of Epp Scott."

Claws of the Schemer

For the third funeral they did not have much to bury. The head was in the coffin, minus the scalp. So was one arm, without the hand, and both legs, with the feet. Some of the chest had to be scooped up with a shovel.

The scalping pointed the finger of blame at the Apaches, exactly as Epp knew it would. Poor Dan Morgan, he told everyone.

Only two people came from Tucson, and they were old friends of Morgan's. The punchers attended, to a man, and Maria was there, dressed in a black dress she now kept at the ranch, along with her family and cousins.

The parson spoke about how Dan Morgan was now in the hands of the Lord and would be smiling down on them from beyond the pearly gates.

Epp said a few words, but only because they were expected. About how awful it was that a good man like Dan Morgan had been jumped by stinking redskins. About how lucky they were that a puncher had noticed buzzards circling out on the range and gone to see why. About how the Circle V now needed a new foreman and he had picked a man named Blin Hanks, and he hoped the hands would treat Hanks with the same respect they had treated Dan Morgan.

The punchers were puzzled. When cowhands weren't herding cows, they talked about cows, and everything that had to do with cows. They talked about roundups and what made a good cow horse. They talked about other outfits and the big sugars of those outfits. They talked about cooks, and argued over who was best. They talked about the men who made good foremen and the men who did not.

The Circle V punchers were puzzled because in all their talk none of them had ever heard of a cowhand or a foreman or anyone connected with cows by the name of Blin Hanks.

Hanks installed himself in the foreman's shack. He ate with the men that evening and stood up to say that he was looking forward to working at the Circle V, and how he heard that the hands there were some of the best anywhere. When a puncher asked what other outfits he had worked for, Hanks smiled and said he would tell them all about himself in due time.

The next day Hanks called all the cowhands together and Epp Scott came from the ranch house to address them. Epp had an announcement to make.

"To continue to prosper the Circle V must grow. Before Dan Morgan's untimely end, he and I had talked about how best to do that. He agreed with me that a good start would be to bring in more cattle. We don't use nearly enough of our range. I intend to use more. Every square foot will be put to use from here on out."

The punchers looked at one another. To overgraze

a range was to risk disaster. But they did not say anything.

"More cows means more work for you," Epp continued. "It also means I will be hiring new hands to help out, and I trust you will make them feel at home at the Circle V."

The punchers assumed it would be a while before the new hands showed up. Normally, an announcement was placed in the Tucson newspaper, and as word spread, men looking for work drifted in. But the very next day two new men were added, and three more the day after. Four more were signed on a bit later, from where the punchers couldn't guess.

Right away the Circle V hands noticed a few odd things about the newcomers. They kept to themselves and always worked and ate together. The new foreman did not mind. In fact, when a herd of new cattle was brought in, Hanks put the cows in charge of the new hands.

Resentment flared. The old hands did not like the special treatment given the new hands. They especially did not like it that some of the new hands put on airs and swaggered around as if they owned the Circle V.

Then something happened that took their minds off the new punchers and set tongues to wagging about their boss.

A woman arrived at the Circle V. She came in a buggy early in the afternoon, a pink parasol shielding her from the sun. She wore a dress that was much too tight and showed too much cleavage. Several trunks came with her. To the collective amazement of the punchers, she was promptly installed in the ranch house, in the very bedroom Lillian had slept in.

Her name was Alice Thorpe and she hailed from New Orleans. That much Maria the cook learned, and passed on the information. How and where Epp Scott met Alice Thorpe was a mystery until Maria overheard Alice say to Epp that she had her doubts about giving up the excitement Ranson offered for the boredom of ranch life.

The discontent grew when Blin Hanks did not do as much work as the punchers felt he should. Hanks certainly did far less than Dan Morgan. He seldom ate with them and seemed to take it for granted that they knew what to do and would do it without bothering him. Hanks spent a lot of time at the ranch house.

Maria was the source of the news that the second night after Alice Thorpe showed up, Epp and Thorpe and Hanks drank enough to put a regiment under the table. Maria also hinted of carryings-on of which Maria did not approve. She would not go into detail.

Then a puncher was shot.

His name was Bob Carver and at seventeen he was the youngest. He was out working the south range and happened to drift toward the barrens in search of strays. Bob never saw who shot him, but he heard the shot and felt the pain of the slug when it cored his shoulder. He reined around to flee and another shot nearly took his head off.

When another puncher found him, young Bob was still in the saddle but so weak from loss of blood he was barely conscious. The puncher brought him to the bunkhouse and Epp Scott was sent for. Epp was none too happy. With Hanks in tow, he examined the wound, oversaw the bandaging and listened to Bob's brief recital of how he was wounded.

The punchers expected sympathy and outrage.

Instead, Epp snapped, "What in hell were you doing near the barrens anyway? I gave word that no one was to go near there. Weren't you told?"

"We were told not to go in them," Bob weakly answered.

"In. Near. It is all the same. See that you never go near them again."

And that was it. Epp did not investigate. He did not gather the men and race to the barrens to find the culprit. He acted as if the shooting was of no consequence.

That was when the muttering started. The punchers spent every spare minute huddled in bitter resentment of the state of affairs. And the more they muttered, the more bitter they became. The discontent was a disease that spread from hand to hand.

A pall of gloom hung over the Circle V. At mealtimes the punchers ate mostly in silence, picking at their food with little enthusiasm. They went about their daily work with even less.

Their unhappiness did not escape notice. They were at supper one evening when the door opened and in strode Epp Scott. Hanks, as usual, was at his elbow. Epp came straight to the head of the table.

"I want to know why I haven't seen any of you smile in days."

An older puncher called Pete was the only who answered. "We are eating."

"I can see that. But it is not your stomachs I came

here to talk about. It is the long faces I keep seeing out my window. I would swear we were about to have another funeral."

"If that was a joke it was in poor taste," said a cowboy by the name of Jeffers.

"Start talking," Epp said.

"Do you want it all at once or in bits and pieces?" From Pete.

"I am a grown man. I can take it whole."

Pete looked at the other punchers and several nodded. "All right. Since you asked." He did not hold back. When he was done an expectant hush fell, with all eyes on Epp.

"If that is how you and some of these others feel, I have this to say." Epp raked them with a glare. "Pete, you are fired. Gather your plunder. First thing in the morning throw your war bag in the buckboard. I will pay you what is due and you will be taken to Tucson. The same with anyone else who does not like the changes I have made."

Many a sun-weathered faced mirrored shock.

"Only those who want to ride for the Circle V need stay on. Freaks are not welcome. Those who whine make life miserable for those who don't, and I will be damned if I will put up with it."

"I have been here seven years," Pete said.

"Then you should know better than to air your lungs behind my back," Epp said. "Do you think I don't know what has been going on? My house has windows, and some of the other hands have talked."

"You mean the new ones," Jeffers said.

"I will not name names. Make up your minds, all of you. Either you work for me without griping or you will be on the drift. It is up to you." Epp pivoted on his boot heels and strode out, Hanks slightly behind him.

"How many do you reckon will quit?"

"Two or three at most," Epp predicted.

"That's all? You were awful hard on them."

"I had to shake them up. Make them realize I am the big sugar and I will by God not stand for their shenanigans. Nip it in the bud, as the saying goes."

"How long before those who stay become suspicious?" Hanks asked.

"Never, if we do this right. They will work the legal cows and you and your men will work the rustled herds. So long as your men keep their mouths shut, there should not be a problem."

"My boys know what to do. Don't you worry."

Epp stopped so suddenly that Hanks nearly walked into him. "If I don't, who will? Worry is what keeps me from making mistakes. It shows me where we need to improve. Worry is good." He walked on.

Hanks waited until they reached the porch to ask, "Wouldn't it be easier to get rid of all those who worked for your pa and bring in an entire new outfit?"

"The punchers we cut loose would talk. And before long people would start to wonder why I let them go. It might raise suspicion where we do not want suspicion raised."

"You think of everything."

"I try but I am only one man. There are things I would do differently if I had them to do over again." Epp opened the front door.

"What, for instance?"

"I would have busted my pa's skull with an ax and

not a rock and claimed Apaches were to blame so Doc Baker did not get curious. I would have made my ma suffer more. And I would not have let my brother leave Ranson alive."

"That did surprise me some."

"I paid Jarrott to do the job, but he proved worthless. I forgot how quick my little brother is. That is the only reason he is still breathing. It is a mistake I would fix if I could, but he has disappeared. Damn him."

"You have men looking?"

"Of course. I sent Tinsdale and Rufio out over two months ago. I told them they are not to come back unless they bring me my brother's trigger finger wrapped in a handkerchief."

"Have you heard from them?"

"One note from Tinsdale. He can't spell worth a damn and his writing is chicken scrawl, but I made out that they heard my brother drifted down into the border country."

"Maybe he will drift into Mexico and not come back."

"If only I was that lucky." Epp frowned. "But he won't stay away forever. Sooner or later he will miss my dear, departed parents, and have a hankering to see the Circle V again."

Blin Hanks grinned. "And when he does you can end it once and for all."

Epp nodded. "He was always the good son. Always the one my ma and pa liked best. Always their darling." Epp moved down the hall toward the kitchen. "I wish he had been here when they died. I would have given anything to see the look on his face."

"You hate him that much?"

"I hate my brother more than I hate anyone," Epp declared. "He is younger than me, but I have had to live in his shadow." He punched the wall, but not so hard as to hurt his hand. "Not anymore, by God. I have the Circle V and I run Ranson and before I am done I will run the whole territory."

"That is what the governor is for," Hanks remarked.

The kitchen was immaculate. Maria did not allow a speck of dust.

Epp took a cup and saucer from a cupboard. He filled it with fresh-brewed coffee and sipped. "Don't kid yourself that the politicians run things. The rich and the powerful do from behind the scenes. The politicians are puppets. The rich and the powerful pull their strings."

Shoes clapped down the hardwood hall and Alice Thorpe sashayed into the kitchen. "Here you are. You were supposed to give a holler when you got back. How did it go?"

"Good," Hanks said.

"I will reserve my opinion until we see how many stay on." Epp took another sip and noticed Alice Thorp was staring at him. "What?"

"You could be a gentleman and pour a cup for me."

"Are your hands broken?"

"Damn you, Eppley," Alice said. She had a high, squeaky voice, an hourglass shape and lips like ripe strawberries. "Would it hurt you to show a lady a little respect?"

"Show me a lady."

Alice stiffened. "I will be in my bedroom if you

want to say you are sorry." Her lower lip quivering, she whirled and flounced out.

"I think you hurt her feelings," Blin Hanks said.

"I don't care. She better learn to watch what she says or she will end up like my ma and pa."

Blin Hanks chuckled. "That is what I like most about you. You are one coldhearted son of a bitch."

"You don't know the half of it," Epp Scott said.

Snakes in the Grass

The caravan of dust-caked figures plodded toward the ramshackle oasis of drink and rest that was Porter's. The weariness in the men and their mounts and the plodding fatigue of the horses they had rustled in Mexico testified to the trial that was Arizona in the worst heat of the summer.

The exception was Sassy Drecker. She had dust on her but not as much as the others. Her face glowed. The reason was apparent whenever she looked at Boone Scott. It showed in her eyes, and in the curl of her lips in a caring smile.

Everyone noticed. Old Man Radler, Skelman, Vance and Drub, Wagner and Galeno and the rest of the rustlers. But no one said a thing. No jokes were cracked. No sarcastic comments were made. The girl was somehow immune.

The only comment made to Boone Scott was by Wagner one night. Wagner looked across the campfire at him and said without rancor, "God, how I envy you, you miserable, rotten, stinking, lucky son of a bitch."

Boone bristled and started to rise, but Old Man

Radler held out a hand, motioning for him to sit. "Don't you know a compliment when you hear one?"

Sassy was immune to something else. No one bothered her. No one leered or made suggestive remarks or groped her when she walked by. The hardest men in the territory, men branded scum by their more civilized brethren, did not molest or harm the girl in any way. She was treated as a princess. She was treated better than many married women were treated. It had nothing to do with Boone and his ivory-handled revolver, and everything to do with the fact that she was an innocent. She had not been tarnished by the taint of that which sent the rustlers down the dark road of violence.

That the rustlers saw the difference and responded to it was demonstrated one morning by none other than Skelman. They were in the mountains, in a barren stretch where water was scarce and vegetation next to unknown, and they came upon a solitary flower, a tiny dot of blue all by itself in the vast expanse of brown. The men looked at it as they rode by. And when it was Skelman's turn, he suddenly swung over the side of his horse, Comanche fashion, and with a flick of his arm, plucked the flower from the ground. A jab of his spurs brought him up next to Sassy and without saying a word he held the flower out.

"For me?" Sassy looked into eyes as blank as a slate. "Oh, goodness. You shouldn't have."

Skelman did not reply.

Sassy held the tiny blue flower up. "It's so pretty. The only life we have seen for miles. And now it will wither and die."

"It is you."

Sassy looked at him again, and cupped the flower in her palm. "I will keep it for as long as it lasts."

"They never last long."

Sassy carefully slid the flower into her shirt pocket. "Thank you for your kindness."

"I should be thanking you. I don't often get the chance." Skelman used his spurs to catch up to Old Man Radler.

Now here they were, with only half a mile to Porter's. Boone and Sassy rode side by side. The glances she gave him rivaled the sun for warmth.

"It scares me when you do that."

"Whatever for?" Sassy asked.

"It scares me that I might not prove worthy. I am new to this and do not know what to think and do sometimes."

"I am new to it too." Sassy bobbed her head at the island of human habitation. "I have been here once. With Pa, years ago. It has not changed much."

"I will pay Porter for the use of his bed if you want."

Red crept from Sassy's neck to her hair and she sounded as if she had a cold when she said, "I must get used to that, I reckon. But you are usually not this blunt about it."

"What?" Then Boone imitated a beet and quickly declared, "Not for *that*. For you to have a bed to sleep in, is all."

"Oh. Well, I am not sure I want to sleep in any bed that Porter has used. As I recollect, he is not much for cleanliness."

Two horses were at the hitch rail. One had a Mexican saddle with more silver than a silverware set.

Wariness crept over the rustlers. Old Man Radler stared at the two horses and put his hand on his six-shooter. "Porter has visitors."

"Just so they are not tin stars," Vance said.

Spurs jangling, swatting dust from their clothes, they filed inside.

Boone and Sassy were the last to go in. He was walking past the two horses at the hitch rail when he abruptly stopped and placed a hand on one of them. "I'll be damned."

"What is it?"

Shaking his head, Boone let Sassy go in ahead of him.

Porter was behind the bar. He smiled and greeted them and answered the question in their eyes by nodding at the corner table and saying, "Those two showed up about four days ago. They say they want to join up with you."

"Do tell." Old Man Radler studied the pair. "They look salty, don't they?"

"They are not infants."

"Start passing out bottles." Old Man Radler took one, and he and Vance and Skelman moved toward the corner table.

Drub held out a big hand.

"You too? You don't often drink."

"It is not for me." Drub carried the bottle to another table and thrust it out. "For you."

Boone stared at it and then at the gentle giant. "I thought you were mad at me."

"I have stopped. I want to be your friend again." Drub grinned eagerly. "Please."

Accepting the gift, Boone pushed out an empty chair with his foot. "Join us if you want to."

"I do." Drub had to wriggle to fit in the chair. "I am sorry I was mad for so long. I do that sometimes."

"What were you mad about?" Sassy asked.

"I wanted him to go to California with me but he wouldn't. I didn't figure out why until last night." Drub pointed a finger as big as a railroad spike at her. "He couldn't because of you. That's right, isn't it, Lightning? That is why you turned me down."

"That's why."

Sassy said, "We could all go together. I have heard it is a wonderful place. Flowers grow all year long." She touched her shirt pocket.

"You would do that? Take me with you?" Drub lit like a lantern. "You wouldn't mind my company?"

"Don't be silly. We will go as soon as your pa sells off the last of the horses and Boone and you get your share of the money."

Boone frowned and burst their bubble of delight with "I have something to do before we can go anywhere."

"What?"

"I can't say."

Sassy sat back in dismay. "You are keeping something from me? I thought we agreed. No secrets, ever."

"I will tell you when the time is right to say."

"Why not do it now?" Sassy asked.

Boone gazed across the saloon at where Old Man Radler was talking to the two strangers in the corner. "It is not you I am keeping the secret from."

"I would never tell—" Sassy caught herself. "Oh."

"I would never tell either, Lightning," Drub said.

Boone opened the bottle and tilted it to his mouth, then coughed. "God, this stuff tastes awful. I could never be a drunk."

Sassy covered his hand with hers. "That is fine by me. I have lived with one all my life and I am not hankering to live with another."

"I wouldn't tell," Drub said again.

"I know." Boone slid the bottle toward him. "But Galeno has ears that can hear a pin drop and he is over at the bar. I will wait for now. Besides, it is personal."

Sassy set him straight. "There is no personal between us."

Vance came over and without being asked plopped into an empty chair. He helped himself to a swig and smacked his lips with pleasure. "See those two men?" he said to Drub.

"The Mex and that other one with the scar?"

"They want to join up with us. The Mex says he has done rustling south of the border and Tinsdale is a curly wolf if ever there was one. Pa wants us to keep an eye on them just the same. He never trusts anyone until they prove they can be trusted."

"That Mexican sure likes silver. He has more on his clothes than on his horse."

"For you that is a good one, brother."

They all looked when Boone's chair scraped. He stood and loosened his Colt in its holster. "Stay here," he told Sassy.

"Hold on. Where are you going?"

Boone smiled at her. "I hope you will still love me after this. But I have it to do."

"What are you talking about? I am confused."

Boone regarded Drub a moment. "If you are my friend again, I have a favor to ask. Keep her at this table. Do not let her get up no matter what. Do you hear me? No matter what."

Drub did not ask why. He placed a big hand on Sassy's wrist, and grinned. "We are pards again. Don't you worry. She will stay put."

"What the hell?" Vance said.

Sassy tried to stand, but Drub pulled her back down. "Consarn it! Let go of me. What is this? Tell me what you are up to."

"Sometimes we don't see what is right in front of our face," Boone told her. "I have been so stupid I should shoot myself."

"You are making no sense." Sassy struggled, but Drub's hand was an iron clamp.

Boone stalked toward the corner table. Some of the rustlers noticed, and froze. Old Man Radler and Skelman were talking to the two new men and it was Skelman who saw Boone coming and took a few steps to one side, his brow knit with interest.

"I hope you work out," Old Man Radler was saying. "I can always use good men. They are hard to come by and harder to keep. None of us live a long life in this trade."

"You have," said the man with the scar.

Boone stopped six feet from the table. "You might want to get out of the way."

Old Man Radler glanced over his shoulder. "Eh? Oh, Lightning. I want you to meet Tinsdale and Rufio. They will be riding with us."

"No, they won't."

"Since when do you say who does and who doesn't?" Old Man Radler went to turn, and stopped. "What is going on here?"

"This is between them and me." Boone took a half step to his right so he could see the pair clearly.

Rufio pushed his sombrero back on his head. He had a thick mustache and ferret eyes. "Do we know you, senor?"

"I am sure he described me."

"Who?" Tinsdale casually asked. But his scar twitched and his hand eased toward the edge of the table.

"Those are good horses you have."

"Our horses, senor?"

"At the hitch rail. The ones with Circle V brands. Did he give them to you or sell them to you?"

Tinsdale's scar would not stop twitching. "I don't have any damn idea what you are talking about."

"How about you?" Boone asked the Mexican. "Do you want to play dumb too?"

"I have no need to play dumb, as you call it, so long as I have my pistola, senor."

"You are that sure of yourself?"

"I still breathe, senor."

"And the horses?"

"As you say, they are good animals. Better than the ones we were riding when we went to your rancho. He had many good horses in the corral." Rufio paused. "I did not think about the brands."

"How much is he paying you?"

"Five hundred. Each. And a good horse."

Tinsdale twisted toward his companion. "Damn it to hell. Tell him everything, why don't you?"

"He has already guessed. What good would lying

do?" Rufio had not taken his eyes off Boone. "Is there anything else, senor?"

"Not unless I can convince you to change your minds."

"I am sorry, senor. I am more fond of money than I am of a good horse. Will you permit us to stand?"

"No."

"That is a pity, senor. It is harder to draw when sitting."

"I know."

"You are clever for one so young."

"I still breathe," Boone said, and grinned.

Rufio smiled. "I would like you if I did not have to kill you. You are nothing like him, senor."

"Let's get on with it, shall we?"

The pair glanced at each other and then both heaved out of their chairs and clawed at their hardware. Rufio was faster and he almost had his pistol out when Boone slammed two shots into his chest. Shifting, Boone fanned another two into the man with the scar. Gun smoke wreathing them, the pair oozed back down and sprawled onto the floor.

For the first time since Boone met him, Skelman laughed. "I wish I could see that again."

"Are you going to tell me what that was all about or not?" Old Man Radler demanded.

"No," Boone Scott said.

Good and Evil

The sunset was spectacular. A golden orb, balanced on the brink of the world, splashing the sky with rainbow stripes and candy swirls.

The breeze carried a hint of the coolness night would bring. The land was dry as the land always was in Arizona in the summer, but here and there spots of green testified to the vitality of the plant life.

Boone Scott and Sassy Drecker stood hand in hand on the lip of a dry wash a hundred yards from Porter's and watched the earth take a bite out of the golden orb.

Sassy glanced over her shoulder at the saloon. "This is far enough. We can talk in private. And after what you just did, we have a lot to talk about."

"I would rather not." Boone had his other hand on his Colt. He raked the wash for sign of tracks and then the surrounding flatland for sign of life.

"You just killed two men. I have seen men die before but never like that. One was a patent medicine man the Apaches got hold of. Another was a farmer whose buckboard overturned on him."

"I had to do it."

"What else?" Sassy asked. "Or do you expect me to accept that the man I am in love with and want to be with the rest of my life goes around killing people for the fun of it? There has to be more."

"There is."

Sassy clasped his hand in both of hers, raised his fingers to her lips and kissed him on the knuckles. "I am waiting."

"I would rather not say just yet. Maybe after we meet with the man who is to buy the last of the horses."

"Don't you dare treat me like this. I have given my heart to you and I expect better." Sassy let go of his hand and placed both of hers on his shoulders. "Look at me. Look me in the eye. I need you to understand how it is between us. If you don't, there won't be any us. We will go our separate ways and I will have plenty of hard feelings for you misleading me as you've done."

"What don't I savvy?"

Sassy motioned at the wash, stepped down and sat. Boone eased down beside her and draped an arm across her shoulders. "I love you, you know," he said.

"And I love you. But there are different kinds of love, and I am not sure now if you love me as I love you or whether you love me another way."

"What other way is there?"

"Maybe you only love me because you get all hot inside when you look at me. Maybe you only love me for the kissing and the hugging. That is one kind of love and it is not the love I feel for you."

"You don't?"

"Don't sound so hurt. Of course I want to kiss and

hug you, silly. I like to do that more than anything. But that is not all there is to love, or shouldn't be to a love like ours." Sassy pressed her hand to his chest over his heart and pressed her other hand to her bosom over her heart. "I want our love to come from in here. I want our love to be deep and true."

"So do I."

"For it to be that way, Boone, we must be open with each other. There can't be secrets. I have to understand you and you have to understand me. Not just what we like to eat and the kind of clothes we like to wear. But how we are deep down. How we are in our heart. Does that make sense to you?"

Boone gestured. "Sort of."

"Think of it this way. The more we share what goes through our heads, the deeper we can see into our hearts."

"Damnation. How did you come up with all this? I always thought of love as just love."

"Don't cuss. You got on me about it and I have stopped, so now you must stop cussing too. And there is no *just* to love." Sassy stopped a moment. "As for how, when you only have yourself for company, you do a lot of thinking. I expected one day to fall in love. Most folks do. So I thought about what it would be like, and what it *should* be like."

"Am I what you expected?" Boone asked.

"You are close as close can be. You would be perfect if you stopped keeping secrets. I have opened my heart to you and for this to work you must open yours to me." Sassy gazed into his eyes. "What will it be? Do you keep your secrets or do you keep me?"

"My brother Eppley is out to kill me."

"Why? I remember you saying how you went with

him to Ranson. How after you shot the man who killed that girl and some others, he convinced you to light a shuck."

Boone shared his new suspicion, leaving nothing out. "I couldn't figure out why Jarrott tried to bed me down permanent. I thought Condit had something to do with it, although I didn't know the man and there was no reason in the world for him to want me dead."

"And now you credit your brother with the brainstorm?"

"It had to be someone who wanted me dead so much he was willing to pay to have it done. Someone who knew Condit and Jarrott and where I would be that night."

"You own brother?"

"I figured he cared for me. When he suggested I make myself scarce, I thought he did it to spare my folks the misery my turning into a killer would cause them."

"What changed your mind?"

"When I found out Old Man Radler is selling the rest of the stolen horses to Epp. Although what he wants with so many horses is a mystery. Our ranch already has plenty."

"Do you think he plans to resell them for more money?"

"I will ask him when I see him. But what matters more is that Old Man Radler says my brother is the most vicious coyote in all of Arizona. Coming from him, that says a lot." Boone stopped. "It woke me up. It made me see my brother in a whole new light." He looked at her. "How can we be so wrong about someone? I grew up with Epp. I thought I knew him. Sure, he was wild, and sure, he was partial to the company of those on the wrong side of the law. But he's my *brother*. We have the same parents. We grew up on the same ranch. How can he have turned out so different from me?"

Sassy pondered, then pointed toward Porter's. "And those men in there? How did they fit in?"

"They were riding horses with Circle V brands. But our remuda is for Circle V punchers only. We take cattle to market, not our horses. We never sell them. So either those two were stolen or someone gave the horses to them. And the only one who would give them two of our horses—"

"Is your brother," Sassy finished for him.

Boone nodded. "It proves Epp did try to have me shot in Ranson. And then he sent those two to finish what Jarrott couldn't do."

"Why are you so pale all of a sudden? Are you afraid he will try again?"

"I know he will. But it is not that." Boone swallowed and dug his fingers into the dirt. "It just hit me. I'm worried about my folks. If Epp has done this to me, what will he do to them?"

"Maybe nothing. Maybe it is just you he hates."

"But why? What have I ever done that he would want me dead? I have racked my brain and I can't for the life of me come up with anything."

"Like you said, you can ask him when you see him."

"I will do a hell of a lot more than that."

Sassy smiled sweetly. "Don't cuss."

"You are not going to try and talk me out of it?"

"After what that son of a bitch has done to you? I say kill him, and good riddance."

Boone leaned toward her. "Have I mentioned lately how much I love you?"

A half-full whiskey bottle was on the kitchen table. An empty bottle was on the floor. Of the three people drinking only the woman in the too-tight dress was tippled.

Epp Scott refilled his glass, raised it and swirled the whiskey. "I hate ranch life. I hate cows and I hate branding and I hate the god-awful long hours."

About to reach for the bottle, Blin Hanks opened his mouth but closed it again.

"What?"

"I have known you a good long while. Ever since that first night you showed up in Ranson. And since that night I have wanted to ask you something. But I know how mad you get when someone pries, so I am asking if it is all right to ask you now."

Alice Thorpe giggled. "He slapped me once for asking the reason he hired Jarrott to kill his brother."

"Is that what you want to ask?" Epp said to Hanks.

"My question is bigger than that." Blin Hanks poured and took a gulp. "I want to know why, Epp."

"Why what?"

"The why to all of it. Why do you rustle? Why do you kill? Why do you gamble and run girls in Ranson?" Hanks motioned at the walls. "This is a fine ranch. Your pa and ma were well-to-do. You never wanted for money your whole life, never wanted for clothes, never had to worry about where your next meal was coming from."

"So?"

"So you had everything. Or at least more than most. Yet it wasn't enough. You had to have more."

"There is your answer." Epp slowly sat up. "I have never been happy with what I had. I have never been content. When I was little I always wanted the things my ma and pa would not let me have."

Hanks went to say something, but Epp held up his hand.

"You got me started, so hear me out. As I recollect, I was seven when I killed our cat. The damn thing scratched my hand. It hurt so much I damn near cried. So when Ma and Pa went to the stable, I got the broom out of the closet and snuck up on the cat while it was sleeping and beat it to death."

"You killed a kitty?" Alice giggled some more.

"I took the body out the back and stuck it in the wood shed under a pile of logs. Since it was summer no one went into the shed until months later when the weather turned cold and by then most of the stink was gone."

Alice giggled.

"I was ten when I killed our dog. It was old and could barely walk, but my ma made me take it out every day so it could go. One day I had enough. I walked it to the stable. None of the punchers were around, so I got hold of the pitchfork. The dog barely let out a whimper. I dragged the body out to the corn patch. When my pa finally found it, he blamed coyotes."

Alice threw back her head and yipped like one.

"When I was fourteen we had a maid named Sally. She was seventeen. She came from a poor family over to Tucson. She was heavy and had lips as thick as sausages, but I got it into my head that I wanted her. So one day when my folks were gone I cornered Sally upstairs and had my way with her."

"You raped your maid?" Alice smacked the table in glee.

"She was my first. She tried to fight, but I was big for my age and I pinned her arms and there was not much she could do. After I was done she lay there and cried and cried until I was fit to take an ax to her head."

"Did you?"

"No, you damned painted cat. I was smart. I offered her a hundred dollars to keep quiet and she took it." Epp held his glass toward the lamp and swirled the whiskey again. "I learned the most important lesson of my life that day."

Alice let out a loud snort. "That a man has to pay for it one way or another?"

Ignoring her, Epp went on. "The next time I had to buy my way out of trouble was when I was sixteen. I went with my pa to Tucson. While he was meeting with a cattle buyer, I went to a bawdy house a friend had told me about. I was having a grand time, but I drank too much and I got into an argument with the girl I had picked. I don't remember what it was about. But she made me so mad, I broke the whiskey bottle and cut her."

"That was you?" Alice said. "I knew her. Caroline was her name, and I saw her after you got done with her." Alice shuddered. "You nearly took her nose off. The doctor did the best he could stitching her up, but she had a hard time finding work after that."

"Where do you think she got the money for the

doc? I paid for him to work on her and I gave her a thousand dollars besides to keep quiet."

"That was generous of you seeing as how you ruined her for life." Alice wagged a finger at him. "You really are a miserable bastard, do you know that?"

Epp drained his glass and set it down. "To raise the thousand dollars I had to sell some of my pa's cows without him knowing."

Blin Hanks stirred. "Was that how you got your start rustling?"

"That was the first time, yes. I went on living high on the hog, but I had to be careful my parents didn't catch on or they were likely to throw me out." Epp stood and stretched.

Alice tittered. "Too bad for them they didn't toss you out on your ear. They still might be alive."

"No. They wouldn't. Because it came to me that I was going to all that trouble to keep what I was doing secret when I didn't have to. Not if the Circle V was mine." Epp moved to the stove and picked up the coffeepot and shook it. "We need a new batch."

"Don't look at me," Alice said. "I am not your servant. I only came because you promised me that we would have more fun here than in Ranson. But you lied. I am bored to death."

Epp set the coffeepot down, stepped to a shelf near the stove and selected a cast-iron frying pan. Hefting it, he came back to the table.

"What are you going to cook with that?" Alice asked.

"Brains," Epp said, and smashed the frying pan over the top of her head. The *crunch* of bone was louder than her bleat of surprise, and then she was sliding from her chair to the floor with her dull eyes fixed on the frying pan that had crushed her skull. Epp placed the pan on the table. "Did I answer your question?" he asked Blin Hanks.

"You answered it just fine."

Nest of Vipers

More riding. More dust to eat. More days of the relentless Arizona sun baking the rustlers and the horses into exhaustion.

Boone Scott and Sassy Drecker were together every minute they could be. When he rode drag, she rode with him. At night they sat apart from the others but so close to each other that in the dark they seemed to be one person and not two.

Drub spent a lot of time in their company. Now that he had made up with Boone, he tried to show he was the best pard a man could be.

One afternoon Old Man Radler came back to ride with Boone and Sassy. The land around was stark and dry. Radler took off his hat and moped his brow with his sleeve, saying, "This infernal heat. At least I will be used to it when I get there."

"Get where?" Boone asked.

"Hell. They say it is as hot as this if not hotter. A preacher told me there is a lake of fire. That will be something, swimming in fire."

"I never have understood that," Sassy said. "Hell, I mean. How can God make such a place?"

"Don't ask me, girl. This world makes no kind of sense that I can see. We are born just to grow old and die. And along the way we sweat and struggle and suffer. If you ask me, the Almighty was drunk when he made all this. Either that, or he had a headache and wanted everyone else to have one too."

Boone chuckled. "I have never thought of it like that."

"It is worse when you are a parent. Look at Drub. He will never be any smarter than he is right now. I will never forgive God for him being born a tree stump."

"That isn't God's fault," Sassy said.

"If not his, then whose? All of this is his, not ours. We are flies to him. Any time he wants, he swats us down and crushes us underfoot."

"Goodness gracious, that is an awful way to look at life. A body would go around glum all the time."

"You don't see me smiling much except when I am drunk." Old Man Radler jammed his hat back on. "But I did not join you to talk about how loco this world is." He looked at Boone. "I wanted to thank you."

"Me? What did I do?"

"For what you have done with Drub."

"I haven't done much except be his friend."

"That is more than enough right there." Old Man Radler rubbed the stubble on his chin. "He has never had one before. He is so big and so dumb that no one ever wants anything to do with him."

Sassy said, "I think he is sweet."

"You are female and do not count. Females are as fond of simpletons as they are of kittens and puppies."

"I wish you would not talk about your own son like that. Drub is neither dumb nor a simpleton."

"Don't sugarcoat him, girl. You do him no favors." Old Man Radler swatted at a fly. "I first noticed it when he was four or five. He would not learn his words. Vance had been frisky at that age, waddling around and poking his nose into everything. But Drub just sat there with a stupid smile on his face."

"You did good raising him," Sassy said. "Some parents would not have stuck with him, but you did."

"It was my wife's doing more than mine. And when she died, she asked me to go on taking care of him." Old Man Radler looked at Boone. "So I thank you. It has made him happy having you as his friend. He told me last night that he wants to go off to California with you two."

"We do not mind him coming along."

"Then you are fools, girl. What will you do? Hold his hand every hour of the day? That is what it will take to keep him out of trouble." Old Man Radler shook his head. "No. I can't allow him to go. I will hold off telling him to spare his feelings."

Boone said, "He is big enough to make up his own mind."

"An ox is big too. But you don't let it do what it wants. You lead it around by the nose and show it where to eat and drink and keep it penned up at night so it doesn't wander off and get lost. That is Drub. He is an ox. He needs constant looking after. One day you will have a family of your own and Drub will be nothing but a nuisance."

"Do not put words in our mouths," Sassy said. "I think he is sweet and I will stick by him if he comes."

"That is the female in you. And like I just said, he isn't going. But I am grateful for you treating him so nice." Old Man Radler lifted his reins. "I also hate the both of you."

Boone was startled. "Wait. Why?"

"Because you bring out a part of me I have kept buried for so long, I almost forgot it is there. I do not like being reminded. I am not Skelman."

"Skelman?"

"Haven't you noticed, Lightning? He is the only one of us who never lets his feelings show. Not ever. He can kill anyone at any time and not bat an eye."

"It is nothing to brag about," Sassy said.

"It is when you ride the owl-hoot trail. I cannot afford scruples. Skelman has none and is the better for it."

"He gave me a flower once."

"And I thought for sure the world would come to an end. But that only shows that you females can ruin even the best of us."

"Honestly, now."

"Don't use that tone on me, missy. Even if I am wrong I am right. You can say I have blinders on, but I would rather see the world my way than let life trample me worse than it already has." Old Man Radler gigged his mount and moved up the line.

"I feel sorry for him."

"I feel sorry for Drub."

Their winding course from spring to tank continued. Around the campfire one evening Old Man Radler tapped his tin cup to get their attention.

"We are close enough to Ranson to pay it a visit. I know some of you would like to. I would too. But we will keep the herd hid, and three of us will stay with the horses at all times. I wouldn't put it past some of those bastards to try and take the herd away from us."

"We should keep on going," Sassy said. "Ranson is a wretched place."

Vance snickered. "Wretched to some is fun to others."

Wagner grinned and nodded. "Me, I can't wait to have a dove in my lap, a bottle in one hand and cards in the other."

"We have earned the treat," Old Man Radler agreed. "Besides, Ranson is where I am to meet with the man who wants to buy the rest of the horses."

Boone sat up.

"He is supposed to meet me at the Acey-Deucey any of the next three nights. We could not set an exact date because I had to allow for delays in getting here."

"Is there a dress shop in Ranson?" Sassy asked.

All eyes swung toward her, twinkling in amusement.

"How in hell would we know?" Vance said. "Do any of us wear dresses?"

"There's one," Skelman said. "On the outskirts to the north."

All eyes shifted to him, and many of them grinned.

Skelman patted his mother-of-pearl Colts. "There are twelve beans in these wheels. Enough for all of you with some left over."

The eyes found somewhere else to look.

"Be on your guard," Old Man Radler told them. "More people die of lead poisoning in Ranson than anything else." He turned to Drub. "You especially. They eat babies like you for breakfast."

"Ahh, Pa. I am a growed man."

"Listen to me. Their cemetery is filled with sheep they have sheared and roasted."

"People don't eat people, Pa. Even I know that."

"In some parts of the world they do, boy. Cannibals, they are called. They would tie you to a pole and roast you slow and easy over a fire like you would a suckling pig."

"You are making that up, Pa."

"Suit yourself, boy. But don't blame me if they take a bite out of you."

A wide-open town like Ranson wasn't like other towns. It didn't roll up the boardwalks at sunset. People didn't file to their homes after a long day of toil and quietly eat their suppers and then turn in early so they could be up with the crow of the cock. In a wide-open town like Ranson, the boardwalks were never rolled up. Sunset was when its inhabitants came out of their burrows and dens to partake anew of the raw and lusty delights dangled before them like so many tempting sweetmeats.

A wide-open town was a magnet. From miles around it drew those who preferred to live life rather than sleep and work it away. Liquor as their water, revelry their food. Instead of containing their passions, they let them bust loose. The only limits were those that spared them from a bullet or a blade.

The rustlers could not wait to get there. Yipping and yelling and waving their hats, they thundered toward the den of vice with delight writ on every face.

Except for the herd guards, only Boone and Sassy were left. Boone took his time saddling up and held the palomino to a walk once they were under way.

"Are you nervous?" Sassy asked.

"What would I have to be nervous about?"

"Your brother. What will you do when you run into him? Shoot him on sight? Your parents would be heartbroke, one son killing the other."

"He has tried to kill me twice."

"Two wrongs do not make a right." Sassy reined closer. "I have an idea. Let's forget about Ranson. Let's ride clear to the Circle V and let your folks know you are alive and tell them what your brother has done."

"No."

"They deserve to know."

"You forget why I left. It is bad enough I went against everything they ever taught me. I would spare them from having to know that both their sons turned out bad."

"Boone Scott, don't you dare. It was either kill or be killed. You are as fine a man as I ever met or I would not have given my heart to you. Your folks will understand. Eppley is the bad seed, not you."

Silence sat heavy on their shoulders until Sassy said, "You will do what you want no matter what I say. Is that how it goes?"

"They are *my* ma and pa."

"Then what will you do? Walk up to him and tell him to go for his gun and shoot him? Your own brother?"

"I suppose you would like for me to let him live."

"Do you want his death on your conscience the rest of your days? Do you really want that burden?"

"Brother or not, he tried to make worm food of me. It shows how much he cares." Boone shook his head. "Shooting him will not bother my conscience one bit. But I would like to do it without my folks finding out."

"How?"

"I am open to ideas."

A horse and rider suddenly loomed out of the dark, blocking their way. Sassy gasped in surprise and Boone's hand flashed to his Colt.

"It is only me," Drub Radler said.

"Consarn it, you gave me a start," Sassy complained. "You ought not to scare people like that."

"I am sorry. I just want to ride into Ranson with my pard. If you will let me."

"You are our friend, Drub. You are always welcome to ride with us."

Drub smiled and brought his big bay in alongside their animals. "I heard you talk as you were coming up the trail. Would you really kill your own brother, Lightning?"

"It is either that or let him kill me."

"I have wanted to shoot Vance a few times. Or chuck him off a cliff. He can be so mean."

"If you promise to keep a secret I will tell you all about mine."

Drub listened with the rapt fascination of a ten-year-old. "Gosh," he said when Boone was done. "Your brother *is* worse than Vance. I didn't think anyone could be that awful."

"Most of us never look past our own pasture," Sassy said.

Drub was gnawing on his lip. "And this Epp is the one my pa aims to sell the horses to?"

"I am afraid so."

"But if you kill him, how will we get our money? Can't you wait until after he pays my pa?"

"I can't promise anything," Boone said.

A cluster of lights sparkled in the distance. Half an hour later the three of them drew rein at the end of the main street. The babble of voices, tinny music, laughter and the clink of glass were a constant undercurrent.

"Look at those pretty ladies smiling and waving at me from that window!" Drub said.

"Do you want a woman, Drub?" Sassy teased.

"What for? I have Lightning. I would like to marry one day, though. A gal who is nice to me, like my ma was."

A hitch rail in front of the general store had rail left. The store itself was closed.

Boone dismounted and tied off the palomino's reins. He turned as a man staggered out of the dark, singing drunkenly. At the last instant the man veered to go around them.

"This is a fun place," Drub said.

"What now?" Sassy asked.

Hitching at his belt, Boone started down the street. "We mingle with the wolves and try not to get bit."

Revelations

The Acey-Deucey was a beehive of liquor, lust and larceny. Every square inch of floor space, every table, every chair, was filled by a bustling, buzzing swarm of humanity. Faces glistened with sweat. Eyes gleamed with envy, greed and desire.

Into the iniquity ambled Boone Scott. He had taken only a couple steps when half a dozen sharp glances were cast in his direction. Then he realized they weren't looking at him; they were looking *behind* him. He spun, gripped Sassy's arms and propelled her back out the batwings so fast and so unexpectedly that they nearly collided with Drub, who was just about to enter.

"What on earth?"

Boone pulled her to one side so they were clear of the doorway. "What in God's name do you think you're doing?"

"What are *you* doing?" Sassy tried to wriggle free, but he held on to her. "Let go."

"You need to wait outside."

"Like hell."

"A saloon is no fit place for a lady."

"I saw dresses in there."

"The women who fill them are not like you." Boone stepped back. "Wait here. If I do not find my brother I will come right out."

"Nothing doing. We are together now. Where you go, I go."

"Didn't you hear me? You are female."

"I am? My goodness." Sassy smoothed her shirt. "You did not seem to mind last night. Why are you making a fuss now?"

Boone glanced at Drub. "Tell her how it is so she will not think I am being unreasonable."

"How what is, pard?"

"About ladies and saloons. It's a rule, like never going to church drunk or spitting in the spittoon and not on the floor."

Drub peered over the batwings, his eyebrows nearly meeting over his nose. "You wouldn't want me to lie to Sassy, would you, pard?"

"It is not lying when you tell the truth."

"But she's right, pard. There are dresses in there. I can see them with my own eyes. And there are ladies in the dresses. Pretty ladies with their hair done up and everything."

"You are a big help," Boone said.

"Thank you."

"So much for that," Sassy said. "Lead the way."

"No."

"We are not hitched yet so you have no right." Sassy went to go by, but Boone snagged by her wrist.

"I mean it. My ma refuses to go in a saloon and no woman I care for will go in one either."

"I had no idea you were such a tyrant."

Boone snapped his fingers. "I'll tell you what. I have enough money on me for a room for the night. How about if I get one and you wait in it until I am done?"

"It is a wonder I can't see through you. You will have to do better than that to trick me."

"It's no trick, damn it. It is for your own good and my peace of mind." Boone tugged but she wouldn't budge. "If you're trying to rile me you are succeeding." Again he glanced up at Drub. "Aren't you going to help? Tell her you don't want her to go in."

"I don't?"

"No. There are men who will pat her on the backside and undress her with their eyes. Or try to get her to drink even if she doesn't want to. Or offer to take her into the private rooms at the back. Do you want that?"

"The saloon has private rooms?"

Boone sighed. "For a pard you make a fine lump of clay. Please, Drub. I need you to back me. Tell her a saloon is no fit placc for a lady."

"Should I tell the ladies who are already in there first? They look awful happy and I don't want them mad at me."

Just then two men in puncher garb separated from the flow of passersby. "Boone, is that you?" the taller of the two exclaimed. "Or are my eyes playing tricks on me?"

"If they are, my eyes are playing tricks too," said the second puncher.

Boone turned and a smile lit his features. "Jeffers! Pete! What are you doing in Ranson?" As they warmly shook, Boone said to Sassy and Drub, "These gents are friends of mine. They ride for the Circle V.

I have known Pete, here, pretty near half my life, and he is as good a leather pounder as you will find anywhere."

"I can't believe this," Pete said. "We heard you had drifted down Mexico way."

"I did but I am back." Boone clapped the rangy puncher on the shoulder. "I can't tell you how glad I am to run into you. I have missed the Circle V something awful."

"We don't work there anymore. Your brother up and fired me."

"What? Why?"

"For speaking my piece."

Jeffers nodded. "And when Pete was told to pack his war bag, I quit too. He is my pard and I will stick by him."

"Lightning is my pard," Drub said.

"Who?"

Boone shook his head in bewilderment. "Why did my pa let my brother cut you loose? Tell me about him and Ma. What have they been up to? I want all the news."

The two cowboys looked at each other. Pete cleared his throat and had to try twice to speak. "Then you haven't heard?"

"Heard what? Don't stand there looking as if you were just kicked by a wassup. Talk to me."

"God, Boone," Pete said. "I don't rightly know how to tell you this except to come right out with it."

"Maybe we should sit down somewhere," Jeffers suggested. "It will be hard enough on him as it is."

"I don't like the fork this trail has taken. Quit stalling, Pete. Say it now and say it plain."

Pain filled Pete's eyes. "Here goes, then. Your pa

is dead. He was thrown from his horse and his head was crushed."

Boone blanched.

"Your ma is dead too. She couldn't stand losing your pa and her heart gave out. Or that was what Doc Baker said."

"Ma? Dead?"

"Doc Baker died too," Jeffers said. "I am not sure of the particulars, but they found him in his office and stiff as a board."

"Your brother is running the Circle V," Pete related. "I was glad at first. He never impressed me much, but he is one of the family, and he had Dan Morgan to make sure things ran as they should. Then Dan was butchered by Apaches and—" Pete stopped. "Are you all right?"

Boone was quaking like an aspen leaf in a chinook. Clenching his fists, he pressed them to his sides as if he were in pain. "God in heaven," he breathed.

"As I was saying, Apaches got Dan. No sooner did we bury him than your brother hired a new foreman by the name of Blin Hanks and Hanks hired on a bunch of hands who don't know the hind end of a cow from the hind end of a horse. When I mentioned that some of us were unhappy with how the ranch was being run, your brother sent me packing."

"Ma and Pa and Dan Morgan too?" Eyes wide, Boone swayed as if he were drunk, then leaned against the wall for support. "What have I done?"

"You?" Sassy said. "You haven't been home in months. How can you blame yourself?"

"I should have caught on sooner. If I had, Ma and Pa would still be alive."

Pete did not hide his confusion. "I don't savvy. Even if you had been there the day your pa died, he would still have gone out to tally the cattle. He wanted to be sure none were being rustled."

"The Circle V is missing cows?"

"Your pa thought so, but he never got to prove it one way or the other. But most of the hands think that a few here and there have been driven off."

"And my ma? You say her heart gave out?"

"She died in her sleep. Went real peaceful, your brother said. I never would have thought it, as healthy as she was."

A wild look came into Boone's eyes, but it faded and a new look came over him. His face hardened, his jaw muscles tightened. "Where is my brother now?"

"We haven't seen him since he fired me. We've heard rumors, though."

"What kind of rumors?"

It was Jeffers who answered. "Some of the Circle V hands heard the new hands talking when they thought no one was around. Just snatches here and there. Enough to give them the notion that your brother is a big man here in Ranson."

"We came to find out for ourselves," Pete said. "We've been asking around, and while most won't talk to us, one jasper claimed your brother runs the whole blamed town."

Boone slowly straightened. He pulled his hat brim down and squared his shoulders, and when he was done, he was not the man he had been moments ago. "Drub?"

"Yes, pard?"

"Take Sassy back to camp. If she won't go, pick her up and carry her. Do I have your word?"

"You have it, pard."

Sassy took a step back. "Don't you dare lay a hand on me, Drub Radler. I will not be treated like a sack of flour, thank you very much."

Grabbing her wrist, Boone pulled her away from the saloon.

Sassy stamped a foot and poked him in the ribs, but he held on. "I am getting mad. We made a promise to each other, remember? To always be there when the other one has need of us. And you need me now more than you ever will." Sassy clutched at his shirt. "Dear God. Both your folks, and those others. If you want to cry we can go off alone and I will lend you my shoulder."

"Cry?" Boone uttered a sound that was the growl of a wolf and the snarl of a mountain lion rolled into one.

"I would if it was me."

"I can't afford tears." Boone gazed up and down the street. "They say my brother runs this town. I wonder how he will feel when there is nothing left to run."

"That is hate talking. You are one man. You can only do so much."

Boone patted his ivory-handled Colt. "I have a friend. Now promise me you will go with Drub and not give him trouble. I can't do what I have to do if you are here. I would be too worried."

Sassy flung herself against him. "You are scaring me. You don't want to worry? What about me, out at our camp? What do you reckon I will be doing? It won't be boiling tea."

"Aren't you always saying we must be open and true with each other?"

"So?"

Boone took her hands in his. He kissed her right hand and then he kissed her left. "This won't be easy. I am not used to airing my feelings. But I will try, for you." He paused. "You heard my friends. While I have been off feeling sorry for myself, my brother has been busy."

"So what if he stole some Circle V cattle? And so what if he is a big man here in Ranson?"

"You have ears but you don't hear." Boone closed his eyes and shuddered, then opened them again. "My brother did more than that. All those people who died? He is to blame."

"Pete said your pa was killed in a fall and your mother's heart could not take the loss."

"I will say it plain." Boone took a deep breath. "My brother is to blame. Don't ask me how I can be sure, but I am. He killed our pa and he killed our ma, and for whatever reason he killed our foreman and Doc Baker and God knows who else."

"You don't have any proof of that."

Boone squeezed her hands so hard, he had to stop himself before he hurt her. "I feel it, Sassy. In my bones. In my gut. In whatever you want to call the deepest part of me. My brother was never what I took him to be. He is a killer, and worse. I could never live with myself if I don't force a reckoning."

"But what about *me*? What am I to do if you get yourself killed?"

Boone kissed her on the cheek. "You will go on

with your life. You will find another man. In time you will forget me."

"Damn you to hell."

"There you go again."

"Forget you? A woman never forgets the first man to claim her heart. If she is lucky, the first is also the last. You go and die on me, Boone Scott, and I will be in misery the rest of my days."

"I am sorry, then."

"There is no changing your mind? What if I beg? What if I get down on my knees?"

Sassy started to bend her legs, but Boone jerked her back up. "Drub! Get over here."

"Here I am, pard."

"Take her. Do as I told you." Boone walked toward the saloon. He moved stiffly for three or four steps and then another quiver ran through him. By the time he reached the batwings he was his normal self except that his face resembled the keen edge of a saber.

"Lct thc bloodspilling commence," Boone said. And with that hc strodc on in.

Liquor into Smoke

Sounds slammed the ear like physical blows: the laughter, the swearing, the piano over in the corner, the bellows of customers trying to get the attention of the bartenders, the loud voices of those too drunk to talk quietly.

The Acey-Deucey was alive with vice. Greed lit many a face. Low-cut dresses revealed many a bosom. Cold eyes glinted with the perpetual threat of violence.

Into this liquor-seeped storm of lust and noise walked Boone Scott. He made for the far end of the bar. Some of the cardplayers and some of those standing about noticed his face—and when they did, they gave a start.

Boone was oblivious. When a winsome young woman in a green dress caught his arm and pressed her warm body against his, he fixed her with a glare that caught her breath in her throat. "Go away."

The woman went.

Boone reached the bar and shouldered two men aside. It angered them and one opened his mouth to say something but apparently thought better of it. Boone thumped the top of the bar. "Barkeep!"

The nearest bartender approached. "What will it be, mister?" he asked with the smile of a man who was just doing his job.

"Who owns this place?"

"Pardon?"

"You heard me. Who owns the Acey-Deucey?"

"If you want a drink I will pour you one."

"I want an answer." Boone placed his right hand on his ivory-handled Colt.

The bartender's eyes grew round with sudden concern. "There is no call for threats."

"There is if you don't answer me. A man named Condit owned this saloon a while back, didn't he?"

"No."

"Don't lie to me. I met him."

"Condit ran the Acey-Deucey but he was not the owner. He ran it for someone else."

"The name of this someone would be?"

"I am not supposed to say. The boss told us we are never to tell who—" The bartender stopped. "Wait a second. Haven't I seen you somewhere?"

"His name," Boone said.

"Something about you is familiar. Who are you?"

"I am asking the questions. And I will not ask this one again." Boone leaned toward him and his voice cracked like a bullwhip. *"Who owns this saloon, damn you?"*

The bartender stiffened. His gaze dropped to Boone's Colt, and then fixed on Boone's face, and all the color drained from his own. "Oh God. I remember you now."

"Do you?"

"You're him. The one who went berserk. The one

who killed Condit and all those others. I am right, aren't I?"

"You are right. And you will be as dead as Condit if you do not loosen your tongue. I will count to five." Boone paused. "One."

"Epp Scott owns the Acey-Deucey. He owns a part interest in some of the other saloons and businesses too."

"My own brother."

"Your what? Listen, all I do is serve drinks. I am not told much and I do not pry."

"I am obliged." Boone turned.

"Wait. That's it? You aren't fixing to cause trouble? That is all you wanted?"

"Does Ranson have a fire brigade?"

"A what? No. We aren't Tucson. Folks don't give much thought to fire." The bartender blinked. "Hold on. That's a damned peculiar thing to ask. What are you up to?"

"I would make myself scarce were I you." Boone threaded through the throng to the narrow hallway. He went past several closed doors and came to a door that was ajar.

The bed had seen recent use; the blanket was thrown back and rumpled. A plump woman sat on the edge, doing her dress up. She was so intent on the buttons that she did not realize he was there. She kept trying to get a tiny button through a tiny hole, but it would not stay.

"Ma'am?"

Jumping, the dove glanced up. "Damn it, mister. Don't you know better than to sneak up on someone like that?"

"You need to leave."

The dove tried the tiny button one more time and gave up in frustration. "I would like to shoot whoever made this dress. I bought it off the rack and have regretted it ever since. It is not made for a full-bodied woman like me." She wriggled a fleshy thigh and showed slightly yellow teeth. "How about it? I am easy to ride, if I do say so my own self."

Boone walked to the small table and picked up the lamp. The kerosene in the globe swished when he shook it. "Off you go."

"What are you on about?" The woman heaved up off the bed. "This is my room. Why should I go anywhere?"

Drawing back his arm, Boone said, "It will be awful hot in here in a few minutes."

"Dear Lord!" The dove backpedaled. "Don't do that! It will set the place on fire."

"That it will." Boone threw the lamp with all his might. The globe smashed to bits and kerosene splattered the wall. Instantly, flames erupted. Small flames at first, they grew rapidly.

Shrieking, the dove lumbered from the room. She began bawling at the top of her powerful lungs. "Maniac! Maniac! There is a maniac on the loose!"

Boone walked down the hall until he came to another open door. The room was empty. He never hesitated. The lamp suffered the same fate as the other. When he came back out, smoke was spewing from the first room. Shouts and pounding feet filled the front of the saloon.

Boone moved toward the rear. A bloodstain marked the spot where Jarrott had died. Boone stopped and opened the door to Lucy's room. It too was empty, but the lamp was lit. He smashed it on the floor.

Panic had gripped the Acey-Deucey. There were frantic shouts and screams and cries of "Water! Fetch water!"

Boone went out the back door. He left it open so the breeze would fan the spreading flames, and strolled around to the front.

A crowd was gathering. People raced from every direction as yells spread up and down the street.

No one paid attention to Boone. He leaned against a post in front of a restaurant to watch.

The Acey-Deucey was emptying just as fast as those inside could move their legs. Many coughed and streamed tears. Through the front window men could be seen dashing water on the flames or trying to smother the flames with blankets. The dry wood had caught like tinder, and before long the saloon was abandoned to its fiery fate.

The crowd quieted as it became apparent there was nothing anyone could do. Many were dumbfounded by the catastrophe. Then one among them woke up to the greater danger the fire posed and began bellowing that something must be done to save the rest of Ranson.

A stampede started. Some fled in blind flight. Others sought to stem the spread. Finally one man assumed command by virtue of his ability to shout louder than the rest. He reminded them that Ranson had been built over a spring, that the spring could save them if they formed a bucket brigade and surrounded the saloon.

Men rushed to the general store and anywhere else

that might have buckets. They filled the buckets and lines were formed. A lot of the water was wasted, sloshing over the sides as the men hurried to take positions.

The idea was a good one, but it had flaws. More men formed a line in front of the saloon than along either side, and fewer yet ran all the way around to the back. They did not think to space themselves and there were gaps here and there.

Then there was their fear.

A fire can be frightening. A large fire, with ten-foot flames roaring out of control, can chill the blood and stop the heart. By the time the hastily organized firefighters assembled, the saloon was nearly engulfed. Flames had climbed up the walls and shot from holes in the roof. A cacophony of sound exploded from the belly of the blazing beast. Wood snapped, crackled and popped. Glass shattered and tinkled. Bottles burst. Some of the shotgun shells behind the bar went off, and the people outside jumped and ducked.

The man in command bellowed for the fire brigade to close in and use their buckets. But by now the flames were so big and the heat so intense that few could get close enough. The fire changed the water that was thrown into steam. Hardly any of the flames were extinguished.

A new fear set in. When the wall facing the restaurant buckled and writhing flames poured out, the men on that side ran.

Boone reclaimed his palomino and walked over to join onlookers farther away.

The restaurant's owner pleaded to have his establishment saved, but few were willing to rally to its defense. Those who did had no chance of stopping the spread. They dashed water and produced a lot of sizzle and flash, but that was all.

From the restaurant the inferno spread to another saloon. Shock spread as the full gravity of the disaster became apparent.

Barring a miracle, Ranson was doomed.

There was nothing for the crowd to do but to watch in helpless dismay as structure after structure was consumed. Some ran to save personal effects. Some ran for their mounts or wagons and fled into the night.

Varied emotions seized the watchers. Excitement in a few, sadness in many, fascination in nearly all. The conflagration was spectacular.

Frontier towns suffered fires much too often. Some burned to the ground and were rebuilt. Several had burned down two or three times, only to rise, phoenixlike, from the ashes. Whether the same would happen to Ranson was anyone's guess.

Boone did not share in the general bedlam. The only time he showed any emotion was when a woman wailed that she had lost everything she owned.

Men railed and cursed and wondered how the fire started. Someone said that he had heard a drunk knocked over a lamp. Another said that, no, he had been in the Acey-Deucey when it broke out, and the fire had been deliberately set. When others asked who was to blame, he replied that he had not seen the culprit, himself.

The news spread. There was talk of a lynching, if only they could find the guilty party. When a man near Boone hollered that hanging was too good for the son of a bitch and they should feed him to the fire, Boone grinned and shouted his agreement. His grin was fleeting, though. By the time a tenth building was afire, he had seen enough.

Forking leather, Boone departed. The cool breeze was a welcome relief after the blistering heat. He looked back only once from half a mile away. Flames, scores of feet high, leaped from the tops of buildings. All of Ranson was awash in light as bright as day. People scurried about like ants.

"Serves them right," Boone said to the palomino. He rode on. He was in no hurry. He had a long ride ahead of him come morning, and he wanted the palomino to be well rested.

Boone had not seen any sign of Old Man Radler or Skelman or any of the other rustlers. He assumed they were back in Ranson, watching the fire. It was where he would be if he did not have to do what he had to do.

At length Boone came within sight of their camp. He was puzzled when he did not see a campfire or any sign of life. Bringing the palomino to a trot, he covered the last hundred yards and drew rein next to smoking embers.

Everyone and everything was gone. The rustlers, their mounts, the stolen horses, all had vanished.

Bewildered, Boone swung down. "Sassy?" he called, and did not receive an answer. Worry knifed through him and he roved frantically about. "Sassy? Where are you?"

A muffled sound stopped Boone in his tracks. He drew his Colt and advanced in the direction the sound came from. It was repeated, along with a series of thumps. But he could not, for the life of him, guess what was making them. Not until he nearly stumbled over a sprawled form at his feet.

Boone jumped back, then sprang forward again when he recognized the gagged face that reared up off the ground to gurgle and grunt at him.

"Drub!"

Boone knelt and pried at the gag. The knots in the bandana were tight and it took some doing to loosen them.

Drub kept on gurgling and grunting with great urgency.

Finally Boone got the gag off. "There you go. Tell me quick. Where is Sassy?"

Drub spat and coughed and sat up, offering his bound wrists. "Cut me loose, pard. My ankles too."

"Tell me what happened."

"It was my pa. My own pa turned on me. I never thought he would do that. He can be mean, but this time he went too far."

Boone gripped him by the shoulders. "Damn it, Drub. Answer me. Where's Sassy?"

"They took her."

"They what?"

Drub nodded, and a great dry sob escaped him. "They took her with them and it is all my fault."

"Took her where?"

"Please don't be mad."

Nearly losing his temper, Boone shook him. "*Where*, Drub? Where did they take her?"

Drub bowed his head. "To your brother."

Threads

Boone Scott whirled toward his palomino. He took two quick steps, then drew up short.

"You're not fixing to leave me here all tied up, are you, pard?" Drub smiled an uncertain smile.

Boone swore. He spun, took a folding knife from his pocket and quickly cut Drub free. "Where is your horse?" he asked as he helped Drub to rise.

"Pa took him."

"He stranded you afoot in Apache country?"

Drub nodded while rubbing his wrists and stomping his feet to restore circulation. "Pa was awful mad. He said that if I ever got loose, I could walk back to Ranson. And if I made it to Ranson, I better stay away from him until he simmered down enough not to shoot me. He said that would take about five or six months."

"What did you do to get him so riled?"

"I tried to stop them from taking Sassy."

Boone turned to the palomino, gripped the saddle horn and swung up. He raised the reins and went to jab his spurs.

"Ride like the wind, pard. If the Apaches don't get me, maybe I will see you again someday."

"Hell." Boone frowned, and lowered the reins. Bending, he offered his arm. "Climb on behind me."

Eagerly obeying, Drub added his considerable bulk to the palomino's burden. "I am sorry to slow you up. I know you want to go after them. But they won't hurt her. Pa won't let them. He said she is worth money."

Boone hesitated. North would take them toward the Circle V. East would take them toward Ranson, or what was left of it. He reined to the east and jabbed his heels. "Tell me everything from the moment I saw you last."

"That is a lot. And my head always hurts if I try to remember too much at once."

"Try anyway. For me."

"For you I would do anything, pard. For you and Sassy." Drub paused. "Well, let's see. You told me to take Sassy to camp. So we got our horses and started back. She was mighty upset, let me tell you. Blistered my ears something awful. And the more she talked, the madder she got. Finally she said she was turning back, and I could go to hell."

"What did you do?"

"The only thing I could. I grabbed her reins out of her hand and led her horse back here."

"You did what I asked. For that I thank you."

"Maybe it would have been better for her if I didn't."

"Keep going," Boone coaxed.

"Well, I asked her why you had acted the way you did and she told me all about you and your brother. How he killed your ma and your pa. How she was worried you would go after him and kill a lot of people yourself, and maybe get killed."

"It is him or me. But don't stop."

"We made it to camp and sat down to have coffee. But we weren't hardly there five minutes and Pa and the rest came back. They had someone new with them, a man I never met before."

Boone glanced over his shoulder. "This man had to have a name."

"Let's see. Pa told me what it was." Drub fell quiet, his forehead furrowed. Suddenly he snapped his fingers. "Now I remember! It was Hanks. Blin Hanks. He works for your brother."

"Go on."

"Your brother sent Hanks to talk to my pa about those horses we stole down to Mexico. Pa is to take them somewhere and wait, and your brother will come and pay him."

"Where, Drub? It is important you remember."

"It was a funny-sounding place. One I never heard of. Let me think on it awhile and it will come to me. I am slow but I remember things if I think on them long enough."

"While you are thinking tell me about Sassy."

"Oh."

"I am waiting."

"It was my fault, pard. When Pa mentioned how that man Hanks was sent by your brother to buy our horses, I told Pa what your brother had done to your folks. I figured Pa would want to know how mean your brother is. But then that man, Hanks, he said how your brother will be real interested to learn you are back in his neck of the woods. And how your brother would pay good money for bait he could use to lure you in." Drub smiled proudly. "I am using his very own words, pard."

"What was that about bait?"

"He meant Sassy. This Blin Hanks said he couldn't make any promises but it wouldn't surprise him if your brother paid my pa five hundred dollars or more to get his hands on her."

"And your pa agreed?"

"You know how he is about money. Hanks said they should leave before you showed up, so they threw on their saddles and lit a shuck, taking the rustled horses and Sassy with them."

"You missed the part about them tying you up."

"Oh. I told Pa it wasn't right. I told him you are my friend and Sassy is my friend and I wouldn't let them take her. Pa told me to let it be, that he knew best. But when a couple of them grabbed her, I hit them so hard I knocked them right off their feet."

"I bet your pa didn't like that."

"Not one bit, no. He yelled at me, called me all sorts of names, and while he was yelling my brother snuck up behind me and hit me over the head with a rock. The next I knew, I was tied and gagged and they were about to leave. Vance was standing over me, grinning, and crowed about what he'd done. Then he patted me on the head and said he hoped the Apaches found me and spared him the bother of having to kill me one day." Drub shook his head. "My own brother said that to me."

Boone rode grimly on.

"Why can't people be nice, pard? Why do they have to be so mean all the time?"

"It is just the way the world is."

"A stupid way, if you ask me. All I ever wanted was for folks to stop teasing me and calling me dumb."

"Did they hurt Sassy?"

"No. Oh, they roughed her up some because she fought like a wildcat. But they got her on her horse and settled her down. Pa said if she didn't behave, he would whip me with his rope."

"God," Boone said.

"What?"

"Nothing. Don't stop."

"There isn't much more. She told them she would do what they wanted, but they tied her on her horse anyway so she couldn't scratch or kick. Otherwise, she was fine."

"Damn them to hell."

"I don't think Skelman liked what they were doing. He didn't help, and Pa mentioned as how he never thought he would live to see the day that Skelman got soft on someone. What did Pa mean?"

Boone admitted he didn't know.

Drub lapsed into silence until the eastern horizon lit with an artificial sun.

"Look yonder, pard! Ranson is on fire!"

They were over a mile away, yet it looked as if most of the town was burning. Thick columns of coiling smoke, pierced by tongues of red and orange, rose to the benighted sky.

"How could that happen?" Drub wondered. "When Sassy and I left, it was fine."

The remark prompted Boone to draw rein. "Climb down. We are close enough that you can make it on foot without having to worry too much about Apaches.

Get a horse and head north for the Circle V Ranch. That is where you will find me if I am still alive."

"Why wouldn't you be?" Drub asked, and when Boone did not answer, he said, "Your brother will try to kill you again, won't he?"

"This time he will have cause. I will be out to kill him."

"Will you kill my pa too?"

"Not if I don't have to. He has treated me decent. But now he has taken the woman I care for, and if anything happens to her, there will be a reckoning." Boone wheeled the palomino and applied his spurs.

"Sorry about my pa taking Sassy!" Drub shouted after him. "Good luck, pard!"

Boone concentrated on riding. At night it was always a tricky proposition except on the open prairie, and even there, prairie dog burrows and any other hole or rain-worn rut might bring a horse down. Most people tended to forget that stepping into the stirrups was not the same as stepping onto a wagon. The perils on horseback were greater than on a buckboard.

After a while Boone slowed to a walk. He was letting his worry get the better of him. It would not do to ride the palomino into the ground.

The night was exceptionally still. Not so much as a coyote broke the quiet. Boone told himself it was normal, but it didn't help his frayed nerves any. He couldn't stop thinking about Sassy, couldn't stop worrying about her. He reminded himself it would take the rustlers days to reach the Circle V. By then he was bound to catch up.

"They are as good as caught," he told the palomino.

* * *

Epp Scott was sitting down to supper when the maid informed him that a rider was at the front door and anxious to see him.

"He has ridden far and is covered with dust, senor. I told him you are about to eat and he should come back later, but he insists he must see you right this minute."

Epp sat back and placed his fork on his plate. "I would have Hanks take care of it, but I sent him on an errand. Very well. Show this rider in."

The stout man she admitted had a balding pate and wore store-bought clothes with drink stains. He wrung a bowler in his hands. "Remember me, Mr. Scott? I worked for you. I was a bartender at the Acey-Deucey. Jackson is my name."

"Of course I remember. But I do not recollect firing you, or hearing that you quit."

"Then you haven't heard? It is good I came straight here. I figured you would want to know."

"Don't keep me in suspense, Jackson. I am a busy man. What brought you all the way from Ranson?"

"There isn't one anymore."

"Isn't what?"

"A Ranson. The town burned to the ground."

Epp shot out of his chair and came around the table. "You must mean a building or two. The whole damn town can't have burned."

"Most of it. There is one house and the stable left, but they are half black from the flames."

"The Acey-Deucey is gone? Tell me you are drunk and making this up."

"I wish I could. But the Acey-Deucey is where the fire started. I reckon he broke a few lamps to get it going. That is all it would have taken, as dry as everything was."

"You are getting ahead of yourself. Who is this 'he'? And why would he burn down my saloon?"

"It was that loco bastard who killed Mr. Condit and Jarrott. I was working when he came in. He asked me if you owned the Acey-Deucey and I wouldn't answer him."

Epp went as rigid as a board. "Wait. It was *Boone*?"

"He didn't say his name. But he did claim he was your brother."

"And he wanted to know if the Acey-Deucey was mine?"

"Yes, sir. And then he asked if Ranson had a fire brigade. I didn't know what to make of him. He went into the back, and the next thing, smoke and flames were everywhere. I was lucky to make it out alive."

Epp put a hand to his forehead. "The whole damn town, you say?"

"We couldn't put the fire out, Mr. Scott. We tried but there just wasn't enough water. The best we could do was save a few things and skedaddle before we were burned with the buildings. I never saw the like."

"Boone," Epp said. "But if he did that, then he must—" Epp put a hand on the table and bowed his head.

"Are you all right, Mr. Scott?"

"I'm fine." With a visible effort Epp regained control and forced a grateful smile. "You did right in coming to me as fast as you did. I might not have heard about the fire for another week and by then he will be here." He reached into an inner jacket pocket and produced a roll of bills. "I won't forget what you've done. After I rebuild Ranson—and I will rebuild it—I'll need someone to run the new Acey-Deucey. You are now at the top of the list."

Jackson nearly split his face grinning. "I only did what I thought you would want me to do."

Epp peeled off bills without counting them and held them out. "Here. Since it is almost sundown, you might as well stay the night. Have the maid turn down the bed in the guest bedroom."

Jackson could not take his eyes off the money. "I don't want to put you to any bother."

"The maid, Theresa, does the work. Not me." Epp ushered him out, closed the door and took his seat at the head of the table. But he didn't eat. He stared at his steak and potatoes. He stared and stared. Then there came another knock. "Who is it?"

"Theresa, senor. It is Mr. Hanks."

"What are you waiting for? Show him in."

Blin Hanks had the same tired, dirty look as Jackson. "You might want to sit down. I have news and some of it is not good."

"Would that be the part about Ranson burning to the ground?"

"You know already? But you still might want to sit. I have news you haven't heard."

"That my brother is back?"

"Damn. You plumb amaze me." Hanks grinned. "But they say the third time is the charm. Did you also know your brother is fond of a certain girl?"

"You don't say."

"Her name is Sassy Drecker. How would you like to meet her?"

"She's here?" Epp glanced at the doorway. "Why didn't you bring her in?"

"Sassy is with Old Man Radler. He wants to sell her and the horses, both. Him and his rustlers should reach the barrens in two days."

Epp rubbed his palms together in wolfish anticipation. "I can hardly wait. This Sassy is just what I need to lure my brother into an early grave."

Arrows and Lead

A speck moved in the vast emptiness. It was the only sign of life in the heat-blistered terrain. Northward, the speck traveled, the relentless sun overhead, the dry ground under his mount's heavy hooves.

Boone and the palomino were weary to their marrow. Both drooped with fatigue, but they forged gamely on, the palomino in response to Boone's urging, Boone refusing to stop for fear that it would cost him the precious life he held more dear than his own.

Boone knew he had to stop soon whether he wanted to or not. A horse could take only so much, and he had already pushed the palomino harder than he had ever pushed any mount. Guilt pricked him, but lost the inner tug of war to love. He could not stop thinking about Sassy; about her hair, about her eyes, about her lips, about her laugh.

"I am coming for you," Boone croaked, and was startled by the rattle that passed for his voice.

The sun burned him as it burned the land. An Arizona summer was hell on earth. Hot, hot, always hot, with scant relief in the shade, when there was shade.

Boone shut out all thought of the sun from his

mind. It was the only way to endure the oven. He shut out thoughts of anything save Sassy. His brother, the rustlers, the chaparral he was passing through, they were of no moment. Only Sassy mattered. Sweet, wonderful Sassy.

Then, as it often did, reality intruded. Boone was given something else to think about: a footprint in the dust. A clear track made by a moccasin-clad foot, the toes pointing in the same direction Boone was riding.

Boone drew rein. His numb brain stirred, his sluggish blood quickened. The track had been made by an Indian, and the only Indians in that region were Apaches.

Newspapers called them the scourge of the territory. Some whites called them heathens; a few referred to them as demons. The truth was, they were fierce fighters defending land they called their own. They were as much a part of that land as the rocks and the dirt and the dust.

All whites feared them. Even whites who boasted they didn't fear them, feared them. No one wanted to be captured by them. Whites who were that unlucky died in hideous pain. Most would rather shoot themselves than let that happen.

A drop of sweat trickled down Boone's spine. He spotted a few more tracks and surmised that a small band of Apaches was somewhere ahead of him. Not all that far ahead either. He could not tell exactly how many. It might be four, it might be six. But even one Apache was too many.

Rimming his dry, cracked lips with his tongue, Boone blinked up at the sun and then pulled his hat down. He freed his Colt in its holster, then clucked to the palomino. "Let's find a spot to lie low for a while."

Boone could not let the Apaches get their hands on him. If they did, if he fell, who would save Sassy? The thought of her in Epp's clutches terrified him. Surely, he told himself, he could not have met her only to lose her so soon after? Fate could not be so cruel.

Or could it?

Once, Boone would have said no. Back when life was good, when he lived in a fine house on a fine ranch and had all a man could want. Back when it seemed that fate had singled him out as special, as deserving of a happy life, free of want.

But now Boone knew better. There were two sides to life, the comfortable and the cruel. It did not take much to send a man slipping over the edge from one side to the other. From comfort to need. From safety to peril. From light to dark.

Six months ago, if someone had told Boone he would one day roam the Arizona wasteland homeless and friendless and as alone as a man could be, he would have branded the notion as silly. But the silliness was in his own head. Life should never be taken lightly. He was living proof it did not allow for mistakes.

A stretch of tall grass appeared. Beyond were hills, and the shade Boone and his horse needed. "Soon," he croaked, patting its neck. "A little while more and you can rest." Until the cool of night, when they would push on again.

The soft sound of the grass swishing against the palomino's legs soon had Boone's chin dipping to his chest. He fought the impulse to doze. He kept the tracks in mind, and what the makers of those tracks would do if they got their hands on him.

Manzanita broke the monotony of the grassland. Barely six feet high, their bark was cherry red. They did not provide much shade, so Boone passed on through. In the bare dirt near the last of them was another track, this one so fresh it was made minutes ago.

Boone drew rein. His sweat turned cold. His hand on his Colt, he searched the tall grass, but nothing moved. Not a bird, not an animal, nothing. He swallowed, or tried to, and realized he had made a mistake. He should have stopped hours ago. He was exhausted. Worse, the palomino was exhausted.

Apaches were never exhausted. Their iron sinews were capable of enduring heat that would wither a white. And they were also adept at conserving their strength and their energy for when they would need them the most. Such as when attacking a white man foolish enough to brave their territory alone.

Boone blinked sweat from his eyes, ignoring the sting. He was sure the Apaches were close. They might even be watching him. In which case, he must stop thinking about Sassy and his brother, and think about saving his own hide.

Apaches were smart. Apaches were crafty. They favored the element of surprise. Kill without being killed was always foremost on their minds.

Boone glanced at the track again. Army scouts could tell the size and weight of a warrior by the warrior's footprint. Some could even tell which tribe the warrior belonged to. Boone could not do any of that. To him a track was a track, and that was all.

It really didn't matter. *All* Apaches killed whites, and he was white.

Suddenly the palomino raised its head and pricked its ears.

Boone stiffened. Something was out there, or someone. He palmed his Colt and thumbed back the hammer. He had a Winchester in the saddle scabbard, but a Winchester was for distance. When the Apaches jumped him, they would be close up. Much too close for his liking, but there it was.

The distant hills and welcome shade, and maybe water, beckoned. All he had to do was reach them.

Boone moved into the open. He held to a walk and constantly turned his head from side to side, scanning, always scanning, looking for anything out of the ordinary, any sign of a dark bulk in the grass, any hint of movement, anything at all.

Boone was well aware that Apaches were masters at blending into the terrain. They were so skilled at it that some folks claimed they were ghosts in human guise.

The dull thud of the palomino's hooves, the swish of the grass and always the burning heat. Boone yearned for the hills, and relief. More than that, he yearned to see the Circle V. Not once since he took to the high-lines had he been homesick, but he was homesick now. It hit him like a physical blow. He missed the ranch where he had been raised, missed the great white house and the punchers and the cattle. Most of all, he missed his ma and pa. To think of them gone, to know he would never see the love in their eyes or hold them again, was almost more than he could bear. He felt his eyes moisten and his vision blurred.

The palomino nickered.

Boone shook himself. He had let himself drift, the very worst thing he could do. He scanned the tall grass again, and realized he was in dire trouble.

He was not alone.

Off to his left the grass rustled as if to the breeze—only there was no breeze, absolutely no wind at all.

Off to his right more stems moved, ever so slightly.

The Apaches were on either side.

Panic swelled, and Boone almost lashed his reins to get out of there. Every nerve, every instinct, screamed at him to ride, ride, *ride*. But he mustn't let on that he knew. The instant he did, they would be on him.

Boone had the Colt low against his leg, hoping they wouldn't notice. His hand grew so sweaty he wanted to wipe his palm, but he dared not raise the revolver.

Now more grass moved, ahead and to the right.

Boone reckoned at least three, possibly more. He tried to remember if he had five beans in the wheel, or six. Usually he kept the chamber under the hammer empty, but he seemed to recollect that the last time he reloaded he had filled every chamber.

More sweat trickled into Boone's eyes. He started to raise his arm to mop it, and stopped. That was all it would take. Him, with a sleeve over his eyes. The Apaches would be on him before he lowered it.

Boone wondered what they were waiting for. He almost wished they would get it over with. Or else that they would leave him be. But that was too much to expect. He was their enemy. He must die.

A shadow flitted across him. Startled, Boone glanced up, but it was only a hawk, circling in search of prey.

Icy fingers clutched at Boone's chest as he realized

what he had done. He had taken his eyes off the grass. He remedied that just as the ground in front of the palomino erupted and out of it reared an Apache. Boone glimpsed a stocky, swarthy body clothed in a long-sleeved brown shirt and a breechclout and leggings. He saw steel flash, and he fired from the hip, two swift shots that slammed the Apache back and down.

Boone used his spurs. To his right and left more figures reared, and they had rifles. He fired at a warrior on the left, swiveled and fired at a warrior on the right just as the warrior's rifle banged. Pain seared his side but he didn't stop.

Ahead rose two more, with bows this time. Strings twanged and arrows took flight. Boone fanned a shot, but the Apaches went to the ground. He reined to the left just as a feathered shaft whizzed past his neck. He was not as lucky with the second. It sheared into his left shoulder, and the shock nearly unhorsed him.

The palomino was at a gallop. Soon the Apaches fell behind; they never kept coming once it was pointless. They would follow, they would track him at their own pace, and if his wounds brought him down, they would finish what they had started.

Boone gritted his teeth and rode. Waves of pain rippled through him. But in a way the pain was good. It kept him alert.

He nearly wept for joy when the grass ended. Clattering up a slope, he paused to look back. There was grass and only grass. Not an Apache to be seen.

Boone put another hill behind him, and then three, and still he didn't stop. He had to be sure they wouldn't come on him in his sleep.

Another hill, this one covered with boulders. Boone reined in among them and went around one twice as big as the palomino, and stopped.

Whimsical fate had decided to be nice.

A tank lay in deep shade. A small oval that held no more than a few gallons.

Boone let the palomino drink while he gingerly lifted his shirt. The slug had dug a furrow a quarter inch deep. It could have been worse. Unless the wound became infected, it wouldn't kill him.

The arrow was another thing. Boone craned his neck to confirm it had gone clean through. The barbed tip and several inches of shaft jutted out the other side of him. He used his knife to cut his shirt, and gave thanks a second time. The arrow had caught him in the fleshy part of his shoulder, missing the bone. It would hurt like hell for a week or so, but already the bleeding had stopped, and as with the other one, unless it became infected he should be all right.

Boone was getting ahead of himself. He reversed his grip on his knife and clamped his teeth down on the blunt side of the blade. Reaching over his shoulder, he gripped the shaft, and with a sharp wrench, snapped the tip off. The easy part was pulling the arrow out. Easy, but it left him feeling queasy and weak.

Stripping to the waist, Boone splashed water on both wounds. He debated cutting up his shirt for bandages, but he had only one spare in his saddlebags and he wanted to keep it clean for when he saw Sassy again.

Boone lay on his belly and drank his fill, but not so much that it would make him sick. He refilled his canteen, then stretched out on his back in the shade, his Colt in his hand. He figured it would take the Apaches an hour or more to get there. He could afford to rest. He closed his eyes.

A whinny woke him.

Boone sat up. The sky had gone from the blue of afternoon to the gray of twilight. He had slept much too long.

The palomino was staring back the way they had come.

"No," Boone said. Scrambling to his feet, he donned his torn, bloody shirt. He jammed on his hat and forked leather. The rest had not refreshed him. He was stiff and sore and slow.

Boone climbed to the top of the hill. A check of his back trail showed he had gotten out just in time. Two-legged wolves were on his scent, and closing fast. They had their eyes to the ground and hadn't seen him.

Boone hurried over the crest and brought the palomino to a trot. He didn't trot long. Only far enough to be confident he had left the Apaches behind. Thank God they were on foot.

Night descended, and brought with it relief from the heat. Boone breathed deep, glad to be alive. He had survived a clash with Apaches. Not many whites could say that. Not many would want to.

A coyote yipped. A bird screeched. Reassuring sounds, in that if the Apaches were near, the wild creatures would be silent.

Boone thought of Epp, and a burning rage filled him. Epp, who lured him to Ranson. Epp, who hired Jarrott to gun him. Epp, who advised him to flee for the good of their parents. Epp, who killed his mother and father so he could lay claim to the Circle V.

Epp, as evil as a man could be.

Boone wondered how it was they had turned out so different. What made one man good and another bad? Their parents loved them both and never favored one over the other, that he could remember. Whatever turned Epp bad was inside him. It was as if he had a great empty hole where his heart should be. A hole that couldn't be filled this side of the grave.

"I am coming for you, brother."

Barrens Affray

The horses in the basin were weary from the long drive from Mexico. They were content to graze the sweet grass and drink from the cool spring. They didn't spook or snort when Boone Scott crept up on them. By his reckoning it was almost midnight.

The flickering firelight revealed sleepers bundled in blankcts and one man nursing a cup of coffee. That man was Wagner. He had a rifle across his legs and could not stop yawning.

Boone did not see Sassy. He figured she was one of the sleepers. He was tempted to march over and demand they give her up. But they might resort to their hardware, and in the dark Sassy could be hit by stray lead. Better, Boone reasoned, to be patient, as hard as it was to do, and wait until first light.

Boone was god-awful tired. Sleep had proven elusive since Sassy was taken. She was practically all he thought about. Whenever he closed his eyes, her face seemed to hang in the air before him. It got so, a couple of times he reached out to touch her and felt foolish when there was nothing there.

A rare gust of wind reminded Boone where he was

and what he was doing. He studied the sleepers, hoping Sassy would roll over or move so he could tell which one she was. When, in due course, someone did roll over, it was Galeno.

Only then did Boone think to count the bundled forms. He counted them once. He counted them twice. He probed the darkness past the ring of firelight for more, but either they had hid themselves or they were not there. Alarmed, he rose and moved toward the fire. He did not try to conceal his approach. He walked right up to it, his thumbs hooked in his gun belt.

Wagner had frozen with the tin cup halfway to his mouth. "Well," he said.

"Well," Boone echoed.

"This is a surprise." Wagner lowered the cup, careful to keep his hands where Boone could see them.

"You knew I would come. I would track you to the ends of the earth to get her back."

"I just did not expect you this soon. Old Man Radler thought it would be another two or three days."

"You shouldn't have done it."

"It wasn't my doing, Lightning. Or should I call you Boone now?"

"Where is she?"

"I tried to talk Old Man Radler out of it. I told him you would not rest until we were six feet under, but he wouldn't listen. All he could think of was the money your brother will pay for her."

"His mistake."

Wagner gazed past him. "By the way, where is Drub? Covering me with a rifle?"

"The last I saw of him he was heading for Ranson. Or what was left after the fire."

"Strange, it breaking out the night you rode in. There is talk you might have had something to do with it."

"Is there?"

"Tell me it's not true. Tell me you didn't burn down an entire town to spite your brother."

"Sometimes things get out of control. But whether I did or I didn't is not important here and now. You're stalling, and I don't like it."

"Am I?"

"No more beating around the bush. I will ask you once more and only once more." Boone tensed. "Where is she?"

"She's not here."

"I figured that out for myself. Some of you are missing. Old Man Radler, for one. Who else?"

"Vance and Skelman."

"Where did they get to?"

"Your brother invited them to spend the night with him at the ranch house. I wanted to go. I liked the notion of a hot meal and sleeping in a bed. But Old Man Radler left me in charge. I am to make sure the horses don't stray off."

"So that is where she is. I should have guessed." Boone sighed and started to turn.

"Don't be so hasty," Wagner quickly said. "I am afraid I can't let you leave."

"You can't stop me."

Wagner smiled and shifted so his hands were closer to his rifle. "That remains to be seen. But before you go and throw lead, hear me out. I would rather do this without swapping slugs. You are worth more alive than you are worth dead."

"Make sense."

"You haven't heard? Your brother is offering five hundred dollars for your body or a thousand for you alive."

Boone whistled. "Why so much more if I am breathing?"

"The way I understand it, alive he gets to do things to you he can't do if you are dead. Things Apaches would do."

"And you aim to collect?"

"I will have to share. Which is why I'd rather you were alive. More money to go around that way."

Several of the blanket-shrouded figures had sat up, among them Galeno. As yet none had drawn a pistol or produced a rifle. Or if they had, the guns were under their blankets.

"You can see how it is," Wagner said with a nod toward the others. "I saw Galeno wake up and he nudged the others. Why make it hard on yourself? Hand over that fancy Colt of yours and we will take you to the house come first light."

"That won't happen this side of the grave."

"Be reasonable," Wagner said. "Would you rather we shoot it out when we don't have to? You are not bulletproof. Then where would Sassy be?"

"You shouldn't have reminded me of her."

"Why not?"

Boone's hand was a blur. He drew and fanned the Colt's hammer and a hole appeared between Wagner's eyes. Even as it did, Boone was spinning. Galeno's arms were rising from under the blanket; he had a rifle. It went off a split second before Boone triggered the Colt, but in his haste Galeno missed.

Boone didn't.

The rest tried but they were rustlers, not gun sharks. Of the two who cleared leather, only one got off a shot.

In the silence that followed, Boone's ears rang. He immediately reloaded, but his hours of practice had paid off. None were breathing.

Boone sat and poured himself a cup of coffee. The tantalizing aroma of food made his stomach growl. He was famished. He had not had a meal in days. A cast-iron pot was the source of the aroma. In it was leftover rabbit stew. Boone stirred the stew a few times with a large wooden spoon that was in the pot; then he dug in. He ate as any half-starved man would, wolfing the morsels. It was too salty for his taste, but he didn't care. He felt guilty eating when he should be lighting a shuck to go to Sassy, but a full belly would give him the stamina he needed to carry out his vengeance.

Boone bit into a thick chunk of rabbit meat and juice dribbled down his chin. He wiped it off with his sleeve and sat back. In doing so he bumped Wagner's body. "Sorry," he said, and chuckled.

"It is not so damn funny to me," said a voice out of the dark, and a gun hammer clicked.

Boone turned to stone.

Vance Radler advanced on the fire, a Winchester wedged to his shoulder. "I wanted you to know it was me who killed you," he said, and stroked the trigger.

At the head of the table sat Eppley Scott, puffing contentedly on a cigar. At the other end sat Old Man

Radler. Skelman was to Epp's right, Sassy Drecker to his left. He addressed her with mock sincerity, saying, "It is a shame you let that food go to waste."

"Go to hell."

"I am beginning to see what my brother likes about you. You are well named."

"And you are a murdering bastard. I know about your ma and pa. I know you hired an assassin to do in Boone."

"That boy is harder to kill than a bedbug." Epp puffed and blew a smoke ring at the ceiling. "He must care for you an awful lot to have told you so much."

"He will come after me."

"I am counting on it," Epp informed her. "Blin Hanks and nine gunnies are outside my house right this moment, waiting for him to show."

"*Your* house? If it belongs to anyone it belongs to Boone. You do not deserve it."

"What the hell does deserve have to do with anything? In this world we take what we want when we want, and keep it however we can."

"You have an answer for everything."

"That I do," Epp crowed. "It is why I am sitting in this chair, comfortable as can be, while your lover is off in the wilds somewhere, riding to your rescue and his death."

"I hate you."

"You don't even know me."

Old Man Radler drained his glass of whiskey and set it down on his plate with a loud *chink*. "Enough of this silliness. We have business to discuss."

"I suppose we should get to it," Epp agreed.

"You owe us money and it is time you paid. First

for the horses I sent my oldest to fetch. Then for this girl that Hanks said you wanted so bad. Five hundred dollars was the amount he mentioned."

"I must have a talk with him. He is too generous with my money." Epp tapped ash from his cigar into an ashtray. "Two hundred is the most you will get for her."

"I brought her to you for five hundred and I expect five hundred."

"Expect as much as you want. But you only get two hundred."

Old Man Radler drummed his fingers on the table. "I should have expected this from you. Our deal is off. I will take her with me when I go."

"But she is already here," Epp said. "It is an easy two hundred, if you ask me."

"I knew her pa. I have known her since she came to my knees. Handing her over to you is harder than you think. It is five hundred or you do not get her."

"Oh?"

Old Man Radler nodded toward Skelman. "Any objections, take them up with my right-hand man, here."

"You would like that, wouldn't you?" Epp faced the scarecrow in the black slicker. "I have heard of you. They say you are hell on wheels. As fast as Holliday or Ringo or any of that crowd."

Skelman did not say anything.

"You deserve better than to rustle for a living. What do you earn? A thousand on a good month? How would you like a thousand each and every month without fail? And for a lot less work?"

"What are you up to?" Old Man Radler demanded.

"I am talking to Mr. Skelman, not to you." Epp

calmly blew another smoke ring. "Think about it. No more riding day and night in the worst of weather. No more dodging the bullets of vaqueros and lawmen. You would have a roof over your head at night and three meals a day."

Old Man Radler laughed, but it was a nervous laugh. "You are wasting your time. Skelman and me are partners. He always gets as much as I do. I treat him right and he appreciates that."

"There is cold and hot and hungry right, and there is soft and easy and a bed at night right," Epp said.

"You talk like a fool."

"Do I?" Epp gestured at Skelman. "Tell me. Your partner here. Does he ever let you give the orders? Does he ever let you lead? Or is it him in charge, and only him, and you have to do as he says?"

"Damn you," Old Man Radler said.

"I am only looking at both sides of the coin so Mr. Skelman can decide on his own. Where is the harm? If you and him are true partners, what I say will wash off his back like water off a duck."

"You are glib with words."

"We are all good at something," Epp said. "But tell me. How many men has Mr. Skelman had to kill for you? Does he get extra for that? Or do you take his pistol skills for granted?"

"Rot in hell."

Epp shifted toward Skelman again. "I will pay you extra for every set of toes you curl."

"He is not interested," Old Man Radler said.

"A thousand a month and, say, three hundred each kill is more than generous."

"Do you know what I think?" Old Man Radler

snapped. "I think you are trying to get out of paying us for the horses and the girl, but it won't work. We will have our money and we will have it now or you will find out the hard way that Skelman is no bluff."

"I never said he was." Epp placed his cigar on the ashtray. "What do you say, Mr. Skelman? Blin Hanks is good but he is not your caliber. With you working for me, no one will be able to stop me. You can start by shooting your former partner. I will still pay you for the horses, and for bringing Boone's girl to me, plus a thousand in advancc, and all that money will be yours and yours alone."

Old Man Radler shoved to his feet. "That is enough. We refuse to sit here and listen to more of your prattle." He turned to go. "Come on, Skelman. We will sell our horses somewhere else."

Skelman stood. As his hands rose above the table, they filled with his mother-of-pearl Colts. Each Colt boomed. Then Skelman moved to the end of the table and shot Old Man Radler once more, in the head. "To be sure," he said.

Epp Scoot grinned. "I like a man who gets a job done right."

Hell Bound

"I wanted you to know it was me who killed you."

Even as Vance Radler boasted of what he was about to do, Boone Scott dived. The Winchester went off, but Boone did not feel the jolt of impact. He hit on his wounded shoulder and pain spiked through him, pain he ignored as he rolled up into a crouch and his hand lived up to the nickname the rustlers knew him by. Lightning, they called him, and lightning he was. His short-barreled, nickel-plated, ivory-handled reaper thundered, and Vance Radler, impaled, staggered back, a look of astonishment crawling over his face.

Radler swore and tried to work the Winchester's lever, but his movements were sluggish and disjointed.

Boone had not gone for the head or the heart, for a reason. Now he gave voice to it. "Is Sassy all right?"

Vance Radler still stood, confusion replacing his disbelief. "What?" he said.

"Sassy. Has she been harmed?"

"She was fine when I left them at your house." Vance swayed, and groaned. A red ribbon seeped from a corner of his mouth and trickled down over his chin. He let go of the Winchester and pressed a hand to his chest. "What have you done to me?"

"What you were about to do to me." Boone slowly unfurled. He kept his Colt level.

"I . . . I . . ." Vance stammered. "I didn't know what I was doing. It was the idea of all that money."

"The bounty my brother put on me."

"You know about that?" Vance coughed and the red ribbon grew wider. He took a shuffling step toward the fire and abruptly pitched to his knees. "Oh God. I think you have killed me."

Boone kept the Colt trained on him.

"I don't want to die."

"Most folks don't."

Vance sank back and braced himself with his hands. He looked down at a spreading scarlet stain on his shirt. Mewing like a kitten, he trembled. "No, no, no, no, no, no. Please no."

"Is there anything you would like me to tell Drub when I see him?" Boone asked.

"Drub?"

"Your brother. The one you treat like dirt. The one you always poke fun at. The one who is a better man than you ever were. He will show up at the Circle V eventually."

"What do I care about that moron? He has no more brains than a tree stump. I was embarrassed to be his kin."

"I will say you wanted me to tell him that you loved him."

"You go to hell."

Boone gestured at his chest. "You first."

Vance coughed and more blood appeared. He

swiped a sleeve across his mouth, then gaped in horror at the sleeve. "Not like this. I don't want it to be like this."

"We do not always get to choose."

Vance's eyes narrowed. "At least I die knowing you will die soon too. Your brother is ready for you. He has Blin Hanks and a lot of killers surrounding the house. When you show, you are as good as dead."

"I am dead when I stop breathing. Not before."

Vance sagged but thrust himself up again. "I feel so damn weak." He gazed at the sprawled forms ringing the fire. "You got all of them? Galeno and Wagner and all the rest?"

"Every last mother's son."

More coughing delayed Vance's response. "I didn't like you that day we met you at Porter's and I like you less now. We should have killed you that day. If I had it to do over again, I would."

"You would try."

"You cocky bastard. But you will get yours. And I will be waiting in hell to laugh in your face."

"We can drink a cup of brimstone to old times."

Vance mewed and sank onto his back. His fingers clenched and unclenched. His face twitched. "I have no strength at all. But there isn't much pain. Isn't that strange?"

"I hear it happens."

"Why am I talking to you? You killed me."

"There is no one else."

"God help me," Vance said, and then added, "If there even is one."

"You will find out for sure soon enough. Write me and let me know."

Vance swore. "You are worse than my brother and that takes some doing."

"Drub has one thing you never did."

"And what would that be?"

"A heart."

Vance snorted and scarlet drops sprayed from his nose. "That is a hell of a thing to say about a man. Even a man as worthless as my stupid excuse for a brother."

"A man without a heart is no man at all. Look at *my* brother. He murdered my ma and my pa and God knows how many others."

"He is a ruthless son of a bitch, but I respect him. Which is more than I can say about you." Vance gasped. "It is taking longer than I thought it would. Maybe I won't die after all. Maybe I will lie here a spell and my strength will come back and I will get up and bandage myself and in a couple of weeks I will be good as new. And then I will come after you and do it right."

Boone stood over him. "That is not going to happen."

Vance grinned. "You never know."

"Yes, I do," Boone said, and shot him twice more. He reloaded, slid the Colt into his holster and walked back to the fire. Hunkering, he refilled the tin cup and drank as if trying to wash a bitter taste down his throat.

The drum of hooves snapped Boone out of his crouch. He cast the cup down, drew his Colt and retreated out of the firelight so he would not be an easy target. The hooves came closer. Out of the night materialized a plodding sorrel and a hulking rider. The sorrel was close to collapse. The rider brought it close to the fire and stared down at the ring of bodies.

"Can any of you tell me where I am? I am lost and in a hurry."

Boone stepped into the firelight. "Drub?"

The hulking figure squealed in delight and ponderously dismounted. "Lightning! I have done it! I found you!" In a rush he flung both huge arms around Boone and lifted him off his feet. "I am so happy I could dance!"

"Don't," Boone said. "Put me down." But he smiled with genuine delight. "We were just talking about you."

"Who was?"

Boone nodded at Vance. "Your brother and me."

"What is the matter with him? Why is he just lying there?"

"Don't you see the holes in his head?"

Drub bent down. "Oh. Now I do. Why, he is dead. The rest too. What happened, pard? Were they mean to you?"

"First things first." Boone put his left hand on Drub's arm. "I am plumb amazed to see you so soon. I figured it would take you a month of Sundays."

"I am proud of myself, pard. I remembered you saying your ranch was north, so after I got me a horse I headed north as fast as I could. That horse died and I had to get another. Then it died and I had to get a third."

"Where did you get all these horses?"

"One I bought from some folks with a wagon train and the sorrel here I took out of a corral."

"That is stealing, Drub. You could be hung for that."

"I don't care. I was worried sick about you and Sassy and I wasn't letting anything stop me."

"You came quick," Boone marveled.

"I know where north is. I know where south and east and west are too. It is the one thing I have learned that I have never forgot. My pa taught me when I was little so I could always find my way back to him." Drub stopped and looked across the benighted basin. "But I didn't know how far I had to come. Or that I was this close. Then I heard shots. And I figured where there were shots, there were people, and I could ask them how to find the Circle V." His gaze shifted to the crumpled forms. "Thank goodness you were still here. They wouldn't have been able to tell me."

"Would you like some coffee?"

"Gosh, would I! I have not had a bite to eat or anything to drink since you left me."

"That was days ago."

"No wonder my belly won't stop growling. Sometimes when it growls it tickles my belly button."

"I have missed you, pard."

Drub swelled with happiness. "And I have missed you. And Sassy. Where is she anyhow?"

"My brother has her. At first light I am going to pay him a visit and get her back."

"I'll go with you."

Boone opened his mouth, then closed it again. "How about that coffee?" He filled a cup and gave it to Drub, who gulped it down.

"That was good. Can I have more?"

"Help yourself." Boone squatted with his forearms across his knees. "We will rest until daybreak."

"You are the best pard anyone ever had." Drub poured and drank and poured some more. "You didn't say what Vance did that you had to put those holes in him."

"He tried to kill me."

"Vance never did have much manners." Drub tilted the tin cup. "I have not been this thirsty since that time Pa took me across a desert. I was so hot I thought I would melt."

"We need to talk, pard."

"Go right ahead. I am so glad to see you, you can talk my ears right off my head and I won't mind." Drub put down the cup and picked up the pot. "Say, there is food in this. Can I have some?"

"Finish it."

"For real?" Drug laughed and scooped some out with his hand. He slurped and chewed noisily. "This is the best stew I ever ate. Did you make it?"

"I don't know who did."

"What do you want to talk about?" Drub asked while dipping his big hand in the pot. "If it is that horse I stole, I am sorry."

"It is about tomorrow. I am going to the ranch house alone."

Drub's head jerked up. "You don't want me to come? But we're pards, aren't we?"

"That we are."

"Then I go with you. A pard always sticks by his pard, no matter what. That is the other thing I learned good." Drub scooped out more stew, but stopped.

"How come you don't want me to go? Is it you don't like me anymore?"

"There will be shooting, Drub. A lot of shooting and a lot of killing."

"I know how to shoot. Remember those Mexicans? I point my gun and I thumb back the hammer and I squeeze the trigger. I never hit much but the shooting is easy."

"Drub, these will not be vaqueros or rustlers. My brother has likely hired men who are as good with guns as they are at blotting brands."

"So? If they try to hurt you, I will hurt them."

"I don't want you hurt, Drub."

Drub cocked his head. "That is why you don't want me to go? You are afraid I will be shot?"

"That is why."

"Why, that is the nicest thing anyone ever said to me." Drub grinned a huge grin. "You are a good pard."

"Thank you."

"And I want to be a good pard too. It is why I killed those two horses getting here. It is why I am going with you in the morning."

"Damn it, Drub."

"Be mad if you want, but the only way to stop me is to shoot me and you would never do that." Drub slurped and licked his fingers. "I never ate stew with my fingers before. It's a lot more fun than with a spoon." He gave the pot a playful shake, then pursed his lips. "Why have you stopped talking? Are you mad at me? That is what Pa does when he gets mad. He stops talkling."

"I am not happy with you, no."

"Because I want to go so much?"

"Do you care for your pa, Drub?"

"What kind of question is that? He is my pa. I reckon I care for him more than I do anybody."

"He might try to kill me tomorrow, Drub. He might try to shoot me like Vance did and I will have to shoot him."

"Oh."

"I would spare you that, pard. No man should have a part in the killing of his own pa. It would make you no better than my brother. You don't want that, do you?"

"I guess not."

"Do not take it personal. I am doing this for your own good. You will thank me when this is over."

"If you say so."

"Give me your word. Promise me here and now that you will wait here for Sassy and me."

"All right. If it is what you want." Drub smiled his boyish smile. "You can count on me."

Reckoning

The sun had been up an hour when Blin Hanks rose from the rocking chair on the front porch of the ranch house. He switched the Winchester he was holding from his right hand to his left, and stretched. Moving to the steps, he nodded at the pair of gun sharks he had posted at the stable, and raised his hand to the rifleman in the door of the hay loft.

The rosebushes to the right of the porch rustled and a man's head popped out.

"What do you think you're doing, Carns?" Hanks demanded.

"You got up so I figured we were done waiting."

"You figured wrong. Sit back down. I will tell you when we are done."

"Damn it. We have been out here all night and I am hungry."

"Do you want me to let Mr. Scott know? I can ask him to bring you a hot breakfast."

"God, no," Carns said. "Are you loco? He might get mad and there is no telling what he will do when he is mad."

Boone Scott heard every word. He was on his stomach at the front corner of the house. It had taken him hours to crawl there from the wash where he left his horse, hat and spurs. Now he carefully peered out.

"Smart man." Hanks turned and stepped to the front door. He knocked, waited and knocked again.

Boone couldn't see who opened it.

"Sorry to bother you but he hasn't shown. Do you want me to let the men get some rest?"

"When I do I will say so."

At the sound of Eppley's voice, a flood of fury coursed through Boone.

He felt his face redden and he dug his fingers into the dirt until the knuckles hurt.

"Are all the punchers out on the range?"

"Yes, sir. I sent everyone away like you wanted. When your brother gets here, it will just be us and the gunnies and that new one you hired last night."

"I expect Vance Radler with the horses sometime before noon. Keep him at the stable until I come out. It is best he not suspect about his pa. He and his men might cause trouble."

"They are bound to wonder when Old Man Radler does not come out talk to them."

"I will say the old man is resting. Then I will look at you and rub my eyebrow. That will be your signal. You and the others shoot the rustlers dead. Not one is to be left alive."

"Not one. Got it."

The front door closed and Blin Hanks returned to the rocking chair.

Boone backed from the corner. Twisting, he crawled toward the rear of the house. He was on the west side, in shadow, and near invisible. He passed under a window and came to another. Stopping, he scanned a nearby shed and other outbuildings.

No one was in sight.

Slowly rising, Boone tried the window. It wasn't latched. He opened it high enough for him to swing a leg over the sill and ease inside. He was in the parlor. It was empty, but sounds came from the direction of the kitchen. Filling his hand, he crept to the hall.

Again, no one.

Boone sidled out. He did not go toward the kitchen, but to the stairs instead. Climbing them two at a stride, he reached the landing. The bedroom doors were shut. He crept to the first and quietly opened it. The bed his parents had slept in all those years was unmade. A jacket flung over a chair told him who was using it now. He scowled and moved to the next room.

Boone put his ear to the door. From within came faint sounds. Rustling, and the soft tread of someone pacing. He was reaching for the latch when a gruff bark of annoyance saved him from making a mistake.

"Stop that, girl. It is getting on my nerves."

"I can't help it," Sassy said. "I get restless when I am cooped up. If it bothers you so much, go out in the hall."

"Mr. Scott says I am to stay in here with you and that is exactly what I will do. You do not cross Mr. Scott."

Boone scratched at the door with a fingernail.

"What the hell was that?"

Scratching again, Boone did the best imitation he could of Mabel, their mouser. "*Meow.*"

"Sounds like a cat," Sassy said. "Can I let it in and pet it?"

"And have you throw the thing in my face and run out while it is clawing me to ribbons? Hell, no. You sit there on that bed. I will shoo it off."

Boots clomped. Boone moved past the door. When it opened, he was ready. The gunny who stepped out was short and cleft jawed and had his left hand on a Smith & Wesson revolver in a brown leather holster. Boone smashed his Colt against the cleft.

Squawking in surprise, the gunny stumbled back, flailing his arms to keep from falling. Boone was on him before he could regain his balance, slashing the Colt's barrel across the man's throat. The man gagged and sagged, and Boone punched him twice in the side of the neck.

With a groan the gunny sank to the floor. He feebly sought to draw his Smith & Wesson.

"No, you don't." Boone brought his boot heel down hard on the man's neck and there was a *crunch*.

The gunny stopped moving.

Sassy had tears in her eyes. "Boone!" she breathed, and threw herself into his arms. "Oh, Boone, Boone, Boone."

"Hush. They will hear us," Boone cautioned despite a lump in his throat. He stroked her hair, her back. He cupped her chin. "Did they hurt you?"

"Not yet. But your brother said that after he was done with you he would start in on me, and he promised I would be a long time dying."

"He did, did he?" Boone embraced her, his cheek on her head. "Don't you fret. I won't let anyone hurt you. Not ever." He moved to the door and checked the hall. "No sign of anyone. Let's go. With any luck we can sneak out as I snuck in."

Sassy was bent over the dead man.

"What are you doing?"

"What do you think?" Sassy held up the Smith & Wesson. "It's not my rifle but it will do."

"This is my fight. You are to keep out of it and keep low. Once we are outside, head northeast until you come to a wash, and my buttermilk. Don't wait for me if I am not right behind you. Light a shuck for Tucson."

Sassy came over and took his hand in hers. "You forget who I am."

"You are the girl who means everything to me."

"That is nice but I am more. Remember when you found me? I was raised in the wild places and I am half wild myself. I never went anywhere without my rifle and I was not afraid to use it." Sassy's eyes glistened with something other than tears. "You are my man now. I am your woman. And I am not timid. We will fight your brother and his cutthroats together."

"I would rather you didn't. I am too worried about you making it out alive as it is."

"And I am less worried about you?" Sassy shook her head. "No, Boone Scott. If we are together, then we are together in everything, good or bad. This is bad, but two guns have a better chance than one."

"Sassy, please—" Boone began, and stopped.

Shadows flitted on the stair wall. Whispering broke out. A face rose above the top step and sank down again.

"Wasn't that Hanks?" Sassy asked.

Boone thought it was. He extended his Colt, but the face did not reappear. "They have us trapped."

As if it were an echo, from down the stairs came

"We have you trapped! Give up without spilling blood and we will go easy on you."

"I wasn't born yesterday, lunkhead." Careful not to show himself, Boone edged forward.

"It was me who saw you," Blin Hanks said. "I was out in the rocking chair and I looked in the window and you were climbing the stairs."

"Good for you."

There was a commotion, and movement, and a new voice hollered, "You shouldn't have come back, brother."

"Eppley," Boone said, and stopped. His chest hammered and his mouth went dry.

"What was that? I didn't quite hear you."

"Ma and Pa—" Boone could not bring himself to say the rest.

"What about them? I reckon you heard they are dead. Pa died in a fall and Ma's heart gave out and—"

"Don't!" Boone exploded, his whole body quaking. Sassy clutched at his arm, but he shook her off.

"Why, little brother, is it me or are you about to cry?"

"I know the truth, Epp."

"What is the truth? Is yours the same as mine?" Epp laughed. "Can you guess where I got that from? Remember all the reading Ma did to us when we were kids? God, how I hated that."

"I didn't." Boone started toward the landing again, placing each boot with care.

"That was always the difference between you and me. You listened and did whatever Ma or Pa wanted. You cleaned up after yourself. You did your chores without having to be told. All they had to do was snap a finger and you jumped."

Boone stopped when Epp stopped talking and resumed his silent advance when Epp went on again.

"I only did what I had to do in order to keep them off my back. To me it was a game. To see how much I could get away with without being punished. And I got away with a lot." Epp chuckled. "The truth is, I am nothing like you thought I was. I pulled the wool over all of your eyes. And now I have the Circle V to myself, and you are about to be turned into worm food. Strange how life works out, isn't it?"

By then Boone was crouched low near the landing. He took a deep breath, held his Cold at hip height with his left hand palm-down over the hammer and sprang. He caught them flat-footed.

Half a dozen steps below crouched Blin Hanks, one hand on the railing. Hanks was looking down, not up, at Epp and several gun sharks. Epp saw Boone, and his eyes widened in consternation.

"Look out!"

Blin Hanks spun, the revolver in his hand rising. "No, you don't!" he bellowed.

Boone fanned a shot into Hanks' chest. In the close confines it was like the boom of a cannon. Hanks was punched back. A low, animal snarl burst from his throat as he tried to take aim. Boone fanned a second shot and a new hole appeared in the center of Hanks' brow.

Eppley was bounding down the stairs. He said something to the gun sharks as he flew past them, and whatever he said, suddenly they came charging up the stairs shrieking like Comanches and shooting just as fast as they could.

Boone fanned three shots in the blink of an eye and two of the gunnies went down thrashing and gurgling. The third took lead but stayed on his feet and gamely sought to fire, but his arm would not rise high enough.

"Damn you to hell."

Boone cored his eye and vaulted over the body while it was falling. He only went a few more steps, then stopped and quickly reloaded. From outside came shouts. Other killers were converging.

Boone raced to the bottom. He glanced at the front window. The man who had been in the rosebushes, Carns, was about to shoot. Swift as thought, Boone fired and Carns dropped.

The front door burst open and two more spilled in, spraying lead. Boone felled the first and sent the second spinning. Through the open door Boone saw yet another gun shark leap onto the porch. Suddenly a gun blasted *behind* the man and he sprawled in a dead heap. More shots pealed.

Boone moved toward the front door, reloading as he went. He was not quite there when thunder cracked behind *him* and he was slammed to his knees. He swiveled, plenty of fight still in him. "You."

"Me," Epp said, and banged off another shot.

Boone fired at the same instant. He fired as Epp swayed, fired as Epp teetered, fired as Epp pitched onto his side, fired as Epp roared like a maddened beast and fired his final shot smack between Epp's eyebrows.

The acrid odor of gun smoke filled the hall. Boone tried to stand, but he was suddenly weak. He had been hit again, in the leg. He propped his back against the wall and heard more shots outside. Then a shadow fell across him and he looked up into the twin muzzles of mother-of-pearl Colts. "Not you too."

Skelman was a statue. He didn't shoot. He didn't say anything.

"Don't you dare!"

At the outcry, Skelman spun.

Sassy was on the stairs, pointing the Smith & Wesson at him. "Please," she pleaded. "For me."

For a span of heartbeats no one moved.

"I still have the flower you gave me," Sassy said softly. "That day on the trail."

Skelman slowly straightened. He glanced down at Boone and the corners of his thin mouth quirked. "I reckon not. But just so you know." And the mother-of-pearl Colts were in their holsters. It happened so fast, Boone did not see Skelman's hands move.

"Damn," Boone said.

Skelman touched his hat brim to Sassy. "You are the only one who is immune." He smiled and strolled out, his spurs jangling.

With a squeal of joy, Sassy flew down the stairs and over to Boone. "Where are you hit? How bad is it?"

"In the other shoulder and in the leg. But I think I will live."

"You better." Sassy pressed a wet cheek to his.

A large form filled the doorway and darkened the hall. Both of them turned, tense with dread, only to beam in relief at who it was.

"I found you, pard!" Drub happily exclaimed, entering and squatting. "I was afraid you would be dead."

"That was you out there?"

"I had to shoot some men who tried to stop me. One got me in the side." Drub showed a crimson circle on his shirt.

"Oh, Drub!" Sassy said.

"I'm all right. The bullet hit a rib and went somewhere else. It hurts, but I will be around a good long while yet."

"I hope so, pard," Boone told him.

"How about me?" Sassy asked, her face aglow with her feelings for him. "Once we clean you up and bandage you, do I get to stick around a good long while?"

"For as long as you want," Boone Scott said.